Haunting Melody

by

M. Flagg

*The Haunting of Pinedale High
Series*

Copyright Notice
This is a work of fiction. Names, characters, places, and incidents are either the product of the author's imagination or are used fictitiously, and any resemblance to actual persons living or dead, business establishments, events, or locales, is entirely coincidental.

Haunting Melody

COPYRIGHT © 2024 by M. Flagg

All rights reserved. No part of this book may be used or reproduced in any manner whatsoever without written permission of the author or The Wild Rose Press, Inc. except in the case of brief quotations embodied in critical articles or reviews.
Contact Information: info@thewildrosepress.com

Cover Art by *The Wild Rose Press, Inc.*

The Wild Rose Press, Inc.
PO Box 708
Adams Basin, NY 14410-0708
Visit us at www.thewildrosepress.com

Publishing History
First Edition, 2025
Trade Paperback ISBN 978-1-5092-6003-4
Digital ISBN 978-1-5092-6004-1

The Haunting of Pinedale High Series
Published in the United States of America

Dedication

This book is dedicated to family and friends who encouraged me to step outside my comfort zone and try something new. For all of us whose talents emerged in high school but took years to blossom, this book is dedicated to you as well.

Chapter 1

Aggressive Anxiety

Why don't you put that out on social media and get ten thousand hits this time! You bitch! You deserved more than a punch in the face for destroying something so sacred to me. Frickin' clueless bullies, all of you. I sit in the principal's office, grinding my molars with my arms crossed and my hands balled into fists. My face is unreadable because this isn't the first time I am here. I let my mother do the talking. She's exceptional with her words. And whether or not I want to believe it, I'm just along for the ride.

"Then suspend her again, Marina," my mother huffs with her hands in the air.

The principal matches my mother's move. "I can't, Zoey!"

"We work in the same school district, for Christ's sake. I'm just down the road at the middle school!"

"So you should know that the board policy on bullying is clear. And with your daughter's IEP being put in place, she qualifies for the Crossroads School to finish out her senior year. They'll take her now."

"My daughter is not a special education student and that Instructional Education Plan is crap. She's smart. And she wasn't the person doing the bullying. She was bullied. And she defended herself. Listen.

They've called her names, taken books right out of her arms. Check out their social media pages. I've seen it all and nothing, *nothing* was done here."

"Zoey." The principal I really don't like shakes her head. "You know the rules. You know the policy. That girl ended up with stitches, probably traumatized for life. It's another lawsuit waiting to happen if we don't act according to school policy."

"So what you're saying is that because they didn't put hands on my daughter, they're some kind of well-raised angels? Words hurt, Marina. Sometimes more than a shove."

"Your daughter leaves Willow Valley High now and enters the program at the Crossroads School tomorrow morning. All the paperwork is ready with the Child Study Team, waiting for your signature. She'll have personalized attention—"

"No. I swear to God, Marina. Put her into in-school suspension for a week. For the rest of the school year or put her on home instruction. I'll agree to anything." Okay. So now Mom's groveling. And she doesn't do that well.

The principal I really don't like sits back in her expensive lumbar chair and shakes her head again. "I can't. Give her the rest of the week at home, if you prefer. But it's the Crossroads School on Monday. She'll be marked absent until then. We'll have someone clean out her locker and bring everything over to the house."

My mother stands up, ready for war. "You do that, Marina. But get it there quick because I'm calling in and taking my sick days until I sell the house and get the hell out of this miserable town."

That gets my mother a wince. "Oh come on, Zoey. Don't overreact like this. We've known each other for years. We've been through too many sad things together."

"Let's go, Melody Marie," my mother orders. "As for board policy and IEPs, I told you I wouldn't sign it. I told you exactly what I'm going to do. I'm through here. My daughter is too."

The principal I really don't like keeps calling out my mother's name, but I pick up my dad's old guitar case that holds the pieces of something that can never be replaced, and we just keep walking out of the huge office. We pass all the high school ghosts standing against the walls like some reverse reception line. I won't miss them, either, because I have Jonathan at home and I hate when they try to talk to me, seeing no reason to listen to their sob stories. We turn the corner and come to the wall of trophy cases, pass the art display, courtesy of all the talented drawers, and out the glass doors of Willow Valley High School in Willow Valley, New Jersey.

"Get in the car," my mother bites out like she has lock jaw. The engine starts, but she pulls out her cell phone, scrolls through her contacts, and waits for that person to answer. I don't recognize the voice. "Hey, Donna. It's Zoey. Remember what we talked about when I saw you at the supermarket?" There is a pause. "How quick do you think my house will sell? As is. I'm not fixing a damned thing." There is another pause. "Can you come over tonight and bring the listing papers with you?" A briefer pause. "Great. I'll see you around seven?…Great! Thanks, Donna, I appreciate it. See you later." She clicks off the call and throws her phone on the console between us.

"Mom...I'm—"

"Don't say it. I don't want to hear another I'm sorry from you right now." We pull off the curb and into heavy traffic on the main road. "Talking to yourself. Telling kids off before they even say a word to you. And now you physically attack someone you've known since kindergarten? What the hell was going through your head when you punched her in the mouth? No. I don't want to hear it."

I really want her to slow down, and the term road rage suddenly means something.

"I'm listing the house. This is over because I can't take any more of it."

I know she is talking to herself and not to me.

"It's time. It's more than time. My little brother needs me. I miss him more than ever lately. I should have done this right after he died. Your father. That's who I'm talking about, not my brother. It will be a fresh start with all this crap behind us. I can't take it anymore. I can't worry every day if I'm going to be called down to the office, wait for class coverage, just to drive here and explain my own daughter's strange behavior."

I close my eyes and let my head loll back against the headrest. I don't hear her talking anymore. The only sound is the rhythmic clickety-click of the blinker as we turn onto another main street that leads to home. Our home. Just my mother and me. Oh. And Jonathan. He's a ghost.

Chapter 2

Leaving What You Know

There are no such things as ghosts, or so my mother says, but I know differently. It's like a gift, reading her reaction…as if she hesitates a second to see if I'll challenge her belief that ghosts don't exist. That gift is only one of the reasons I'm strapped into a seatbelt in the only vehicle I call an old blue box-on-wheels that still has an ashtray and cassette player on Route 71 watching the scenery change from New Jersey to the Blue Ridge Mountains. Yeah. My mother thinks the move to Pinedale, North Carolina, is going to wash what she calls bad karma all away. All the things that go bump in the night, the endless sessions with the school psychologist and private therapists, and all the demerits and suspensions because, hell, Willow Valley High is just full of mean girls and meaner teachers who like to target me.

And I'm an easy target. That's what they think. But I'm not. And I'm not weird or crazy or unable to cope with teenage life, my oversized, fleshy, I'll-never-wear-a-bikini body complete with racing hormones, *or* pressure to "do good" in school.

Even though I went from kindergarten to my junior year in high school with most of those mean girls, they don't know me. Not the real me, at least. They see an overweight, oh-please-mess-with-me average student who enjoys chorus more than football rallies and shouting cheerleaders. I could care less about their perfect hairstyles and their more-perfect bodies. I see inside them. Every single one of them. Their fears, their insecurities, even their darkest well-kept secrets. I mean, what is it with all the envy of a skinny plastic doll they made a movie about... like some weirdo wannabes of a bubblegum-pink world full of dream houses? Just put the masks aside and show a bit of humanity once in a while, instead of armoring up like some medieval knight getting ready for a joust. Would it hurt? Yeah. Maybe. But at least it would give all us sensitive sixteen-year-olds a break once in a while. And to be honest, I just don't like what I sense about them. Period.

Hell, yeah, they taunted me. Plastered their antics on multiple social media sites time after time and waited for the thousand likes or thumbs up or red hearts. I sidestepped their cruelties a lot, and when I'd go ballistic—using my words instead of putting my hands on them—I'm the one who ended up suspended, like every time, for "aggressive language inappropriate for a student in Willow Valley." What a bunch of horse crap. I just said it out and in the open, not behind their mean-girl faces and their skinny backs.

Now, *I'm* the one who had to pack away my life in cardboard boxes and label each one, getting more anxious that somehow all my important stuff will end up in Oklahoma instead of Pinedale, North Carolina. All that organizing and packing took soooo many lonely hours. And Jonathan was angry. No. I mean really, really angry. I even detected like a blood-red aura all around him. Plus, all that negative energy rattled the bed the boxes were on. I sensed him wallowing in some kind of teenage snit, all furious but not saying a word.

Last night, I had just fixed the flaps on the fifth box and set this one down on the floor of my bedroom without labeling it when Jonathan appeared over by my bedroom window. "I'm sorry the house sold so fast and that my mother got a job in a school in another state because she went to college with some school administrator who has pull you know in the hiring category," came out in one breath with no punctuation, not even a slight pause, or a comma, or something.

"*This can't be happening! Who will I talk to, Melody Marie?*"

He had used both my names. I was surprised he didn't add the Warkowski, too. "I know, you waited until Dad died to show yourself to me. It's been a good six-year run."

"*It's not fair*," he continued with a frown and a finger pointed at my heart that was already breaking, "*You couldn't have let the mean things, the cruel words just slide off your back? You had to get suspended again? Is that why you're leaving me?*"

I didn't want him to know about the alternative high school plan. Some things you keep to yourself. But I had to give him something. My eyes narrowed to capture his. "Those stupid girls took my chorus folder and ripped every song to shreds and then sprinkled them not only in front of my locker, but right down the north corridor while chanting 'Melody shmelody come sing us a song' and I…I just lost it! I guess this video will get them five thousand likes before it disappears on social media." I took a step closer to him. "They're hoping it gets more likes than their last video of me in lunch, when they tipped my tray over and taco sauce drenched my jeans to make it look like...ugh! You don't understand! They posted these things, Jonathan, and waited for the shares and likes. What happened yesterday, well, it just took me too far over the top! It was the last straw!"

His iridescent baby-blues went wider. "*Kid stuff! Mean stuff! You know they're all worthless pieces of shit and—*"

"No. They go too far beyond just mean." I had to tell him the truth, even though it hurt to say it out loud. "Yesterday, I got to chorus, and I opened my guitar case...my father's guitar had been stomped to pieces, Jonathan! It's chunks of garbage now...ruined. Something like that can't be replaced. It's just another memory now. I'll never get it back. Never!" More scenes with Dad played inside me, dressed as his purple princess, sitting close enough to cuddle, flooded back. He was gone six years already.

Then, tears lit my eyes. My lips quivered. Saying another word wasn't happening as my shoulders sagged and supper soured in my stomach. I swiped the salty drips away, wanting to grab the scissors from my desk and shred the box I had just put down.

"*Oh, jeez, Mel,*" he whispered in that soft voice. "*I'm so sorry. I didn't know.*"

I had sniffled and steadied my growing anxiety about leaving the home I grew up in, leaving the only person...the only ghost...I could confide in without judgement, someone who never gave me useless advice. Jonathan heard me. He got the *real* me. "No.

You couldn't know. And you couldn't have done anything about it because you're bound to this house, this room."

If he had been able to walk the halls of Willow Valley, would anything have been different? Would he have been able to protect me or manifest his anger at those mean girls? I'd never know. I sank to the edge of the bed that didn't have a box on it and I grabbed the bedpost.

"Doesn't reality suck?" I whispered while swiping my eyes and staring at the tears on my hand.

Jonathan knelt in front of me, trying to make me look at him. Was his sorrow as deep as mine? I knew he had feelings. I also knew he was kind and gentle. We've talked to each other since the day my father died. *"I'm still sorry it happened and I don't want you to go away."*

My shoulders had shrugged. I mean, he couldn't help the fact that no matter what the circumstance, he was bound to the place where he died at the age of eighteen from a heart condition his parents and doctors had no knowledge about. In this very room. On a hot August night. No warning. Just one breath after another in sleep and then nothing at all.

"Where did you go, Mel?" he asked as I sobbed and sniffled and swiped.

I felt his hand on mine and stood up as he stepped away to give me the space I needed. Then he came close again and hugged me. His energy, ethereal and still powerful, shimmered around me. I rested my head on a chest that no one but me could see or feel. It had been a place of comfort and safety since the loss of my father.

Mom and Dad bought this little house, the last one on a dead-end street in Willow Valley, right before I was born. Beige with burgundy shutters, the Cape Cod had a huge fenced-in yard right next to a forest. After my father died, Mom took on a second job tutoring and left me in the care of neighbors I had known all my life.

My parents had a dream back then, to buy a bigger house in the swanky lake section of town. It would have an in-ground heated pool and a living room big enough for a baby grand piano.

Instead of moving up, we were now moving on. All the way to North Carolina, where my mother had a brother, where we would both have a fresh start. I really didn't want to leave Jonathan. But my feelings didn't matter. Yeah. Reality really sucked.

I still had not answered him. Jonathan had his own set of memories, most of which he had shared over the years that I slept in his room. I often wondered if it had been missing my dad so much that allowed him to take form and show himself to me. "I'm sorry this is happening, too. I'm so gonna miss you," I whispered.

"*How long do we have?*" he asked in a gentle voice. But I could sense the new loss of a friend and confidant had grown wide as an ocean, as deep as the valley we both existed in.

"The movers are coming tomorrow," I had answered. "Mom and I will drive down as soon as the truck leaves." I knew what he would say, and I bit down on my lips and told myself to stop crying.

"*It's too soon. I'm really going to miss you. I'll never find another you.*"

Was it possible to hold me any tighter, you may ask. After all, he's a ghost and I'm just an overweight girl who guards my secret power like a pit bull. Yeah. He held me tighter. He was warmth and comfort, just as he had been when he held a ten-year-old who missed her father and found herself lost in a world of hurt and anxiety. That he was ageless, timeless, made no difference to me.

Tomorrow would be a final good-bye. Both of us sensed it. Once I left this house, both of us would be alone again. I couldn't tell Mom about the best friend I was leaving behind. I couldn't tell anyone about the boy ghost who had my heart. I wouldn't share with a new therapist that I had the ability to see someone long gone or that I could read other people's feelings.

I thought of the old choral piece our vocal ensemble performed at last year's spring concert. "Make new friends and don't forget the old…" As I started to hum the melody, we began a slow rock. I had tucked tighter to his chest, and just let myself feel…

No. Tomorrow had come and we are travelling on the road to somewhere new. In my brain, I am still in Jonathan's embrace when we hit a patch of grooved pavement, and I jerk back to the here and now. An eighteen-wheeler's horn blares so loud that I feel the window rattle. My mother aims a few choice words at the truck driver. "How about we stop at one of those restaurants I see on the billboards?"

Her question pulls me farther away from Jonathan than all these hundreds of miles we've traveled so far. We are like eight hours into an eleven-hour drive—to somewhere I know nothing about and don't want to be.

"Sure," I reply, because, *"No! No! No! Please turn around, Mom! I want to go back to Willow Valley. I swear it won't happen again,"* won't cut it. Something inside says I have to just accept the inevitable. Maybe there would be no mean girls, no delving school guidance counselor waiting to get me alone for a one-on-one to "discuss" my anxiety issues and my "abrupt switch to violent answers."

I scoff. Like moving to a different state will magically change everything about me.

Mom takes the next exit somewhere in West Virginia and follows signs identifying something new, which Jersey's Garden State Parkway doesn't have at like every exit. She slows down as she takes another unknown road. "How are you doing?" she asks with a great deal of motherly care in her tone.

Why make her life as miserable as mine? She's been through Hell on Earth, just like I have, maybe more of it having to bury my father, take on a second job, and now, get used to a new teaching position in some forgotten, lower Podunk town called Pinedale, with a population *way*, way less than Willow Valley and with no New York City skyline lighting the night just ten miles away.

"I'm okay," I answer, throwing in a soft, "And you?"

I glance at the tension on her face and sense that, like an iceberg, only a small amount shows on the surface. Yeah. I can feel it, too, as if it were mine.

I suppose it's on me, the fact that I don't connect with her like this too often. She acts like a general most days, with everything in its place and neatly organized. We fight about my preference for dessert over dinner, my so-so grades except in music and language arts, my desire for loose-fitting clothes to hide my weight issues, and even my desire for purple everything. She calls me overly dramatic, and I call her nosy. Maybe I take her concern for granted and feel forced to rebel. Maybe I'm just acting like a typical sixteen-year-old.

"We're gonna be okay," she says, with hope in her heart—as if she knows what I'm thinking. "I haven't been back to North Carolina since my college years. Uncle Tim's been looking for houses and says there's one right down the street from his that will suit us just fine. At least you'll be able to get to know your cousins now. His youngest, Liam, is a senior at Pinedale High, so he'll be able to show you around. Oh, I forgot to tell you, I didn't take the teaching position in the high school. My friend Jeffrey says it's only a maternity leave."

A twinge of panic sets in. "So you don't have a job? God, Mom."

"I didn't say that, Melody. He put me in touch with the county board of ed. There's a full-time position for a fourth-grade teacher in Pinedale Elementary. I'll be able to use some skills with the little ones that I've really missed. It's perfect for me. And with Jeffrey's recommendation, it's mine if I want it."

Well, I could thank my new vice principal for one thing. At least my mother wouldn't be in the same school as me. Showing interest is the right thing to do, so I ask, "Will you be happy teaching little kids again?"

Mom actually smiles. "I would. And I've already said yes. Even though it's early April, but late in the school year down south. I will have the in-person interview right away and then start next week. I can get a feel for the school district and the kids. Who knows? I might even have time to do an end-of-year play with my students."

Was that *joy* that entered her voice? Yeah. It fills a little piece of my heart as well. I smile easily, the first time in eight boring hours of trees and cars and trucks going well over the speed limit as they all pass us by.

The first thing that enters my mind is to tell Jonathan. I close my eyes and shake my head. Leaving behind what and who you know takes hold again.

"Are you getting car sick, Mel? I can—"

"You have reached your destination," the voice of the GPS states, cutting Mom off.

My mother makes a hard right turn into the restaurant's parking lot. She pulls into a spot close to the door, and I unlatch my seatbelt. Once I step out of the car, the humid, heavy April air slams into my north Jersey lungs. I take a shallow breath and meet my mother's brown eyes with a grin.

"It's only a couple more hours," she states as the car alarm beeps and she rolls her neck from side to side while standing at the front of the old vehicle she loves.

"No worries," I reply, because a snippy comment will only start another argument.

"You should try some cheesy grits," she says with a bit of excitement. "There's nothing like them up north."

Walking behind her and into my first-ever southern food-chain experience, I don't reply. This move is suddenly very real. All because of mean girls and nosy teachers who didn't care to try and understand me. I'd miss my chorus teacher. Maybe my English teacher, too. But not the rest of those small-minded individuals that called themselves educators. With any luck, Pinedale has a chorus. Maybe even a marching band. Maybe I'll even find a resident ghost like Jonathan, only this time, walking the halls of my new school, not standing in the corner of my bedroom.

An old blonde woman who looks as cranky as hell walks us to a table and slaps down two menus. *So much for southern hospitality,* I think, but I grin at Mom again, and tell myself to hold off on the judgy thing…at least until we get to my uncle's house in Pinedale, North Carolina.

Chapter 3

Family

After like *twelve hours* of bouncing around in the old blue box-on-wheels, I feel hesitant to take the mini-hug from an uncle I've only seen four times in my life. Uncle Tim and Aunt Sarah didn't make the trip to New Jersey too often. Except for my father's funeral, they had only come up north for three Christmases, but stayed at a local hotel with their two boys, David and Liam.

Mom and Uncle Tim go right into family catch-up like our long hours on the road never happened. Uncle Tim says that their oldest son David is away in law school in South Carolina. Liam, a senior at Pinedale High, has no prospects of going to a trade school or college—I learn within five minutes of sitting in their kitchen, nursing a "sweet tea" which is *way* too sweet and not cold enough, with two dweeby ice cubes bobbing about. And I sense that Aunt Sarah is even sweeter than this tea. Uncle Tim's easy nature is almost visible to me. I sense he puts up with a lot and has little or no control over Liam, who looks like a nightmare waiting to happen.

My cousin is skin and bones, with sunken cheeks and dull brown eyes—outlined in dull-black eyeliner. You wouldn't figure a small-town southern boy from a good Christian family for the Goth wannabe type, but then again, those thick silver chains hanging from his jeans, both ears pierced with metal cylinders, and the all-black everything on him belie the hot, humid night. I mean, what do Goths wear in the southern states, anyway? Black shorts to show off their boney knees?

I grin at Liam's sour expression and eyeliner eyes, hoping he'd at least crack a smile or lift a lip or anything! I let that glance go and look at calm Uncle Tim as he puts his hand over my mother's. "You and Mel can have David's room, Zoey."

My mother shakes her head. "We don't want to put you out, Tim. I don't know how long it will take to find a house and until we find a place of our own, maybe we should—"

"My sister is not staying in a hotel. Besides, Pinedale doesn't have one. Nope. You two are family and you'll stay right here in Dave's room. Besides, the house down the block is empty and, if you're liking it, well, you know how fast closings are these days."

"I have the promise of a job," Mom insists, "not a paycheck yet."

"And I'll guess the Jersey house sold at full market value," he counters.

"For cash and thirty thousand above asking price within two days," she proudly states.

He whistles with a "Gosh-golly wow! You won't have a problem because I'm gonna guess you don't need to apply for a mortgage. We'll see it first thing tomorrow, right after you get Mel registered at Pinedale High."

Mom looks at me. "No, Timmy. Mel sees the house with me. It's her decision, too."

I perk up. *Hey, I matter! I really matter!* And that last thought sinks like a water balloon, seeing the look on Uncle Tim's face. "You want to get settled in fast, right? There's a perfectly fine house at the end of the block and in this real estate market, it could be grabbed up by someone else, just like that." His finger snap is as impressive as his whistle.

"How long has it been on the market?" I ask out of nowhere, and his kind eyes actually narrow as he tilts his head and studies me.

"A while," he offers. "I still say get Mel enrolled at school first thing tomorrow. Besides, you have an in with Vice Principal Moore. He's been acting principal since the principal went out on medical leave. I heard she's not coming back until August when school starts up again. So it's settled, Zoey. Mel gets right into a school routine, and then I'll take you to the listing agent so you can see the house. If it fits your needs, grab it fast."

Mom sighs. "It's really late. Let me sleep on it."

Leaning on the kitchen door's threshold, Liam sneers, gives a tight "Night ya'll," and vanishes. His floppy work boots, the only thing not black on him, just a muddy brown, and the jingling of chains can be heard stomping their way upstairs before a door slams. I sense anger over having two unknown relatives invade his space and a moodiness I assume typical to him. It clings to him like all those black clothes. I smile at my uncle and aunt, their embarrassment visible, and file Liam Cooper away in the "Danger: Do Not Read" box in my brain.

****

Cousin David's bed is a trundle with a twin pull-out that is lower than Mom's mattress. Tired from the long day in the car, I take a shower and put on a pair of sweats to sleep. The air conditioning is cranked pretty high, but the room isn't an icebox. Yet I get the feeling that a sheet and one blanket won't be warm enough if I sleep in a shirt and shorts.

"I'm going to take my brother's suggestion and register you before I look at the house."

I feel my own version of anger and moodiness rise, replying, "Okay." If I say what I really think, we'll be in the middle of an argument that would go nowhere anyway. Once Mom makes up her mind, well, my feelings, as usual, are history. She is strategic that way, which earned her the title of General Warkowski given by her many friends.

"Don't be upset, Mel. We need our own place, and we need to jump into our new life in Pinedale. Besides, the sooner I find a house, the sooner I can get our things out of storage and settle in. And we don't want to put Uncle Timmy and Aunt Sarah out any more than we have to."

"I said okay," burst forth before I can tame my inner demon.

"There you go, from zero to sixty already. Honestly, Melody Marie, there's no talking to you sometimes."

"Sorry," I mumble, turning on my side and away from her.

Another long sigh sounds. "You'll see. We'll be settled in no time. Did you research Pinedale High already?"

"Just a little," I answer, which is a lie. I know it has a miniscule student population of four hundred forty, compared to fifteen hundred at Willow Valley in New Jersey. Their website has a memorial to a bunch of students, which I think totally creepy.

"I like their school colors," I add to smooth it out between us before I fall asleep, giving her a little more info with "Purple and teal. Two of my favorites. And their football team is called the Pinedale Pythons."

Yuck! Who uses a snake as a mascot? If they were going for the double P, how about Pinedale Pit Bulls or something a little less vicious, like Pinedale Ponies. Ponies are strong, just smaller than a horse.

When I did my research, I couldn't believe the pictures on the website. Their cheerleaders all look like southern belles, with only two darker-skinned girls and no boys at all. Their mascot, the purple snake, has teal eyes and scales! That has to be some sight to see at football games and pep rallies. Some fantabulous image there, right? A purple and teal snake standing on two legs instead of slithering in the grass. Willow Valley's mascot is a howling wolf. Now *that* made sense since they dominated in the league, year after year.

"Well, tomorrow, you'll be enrolled and get to meet my college buddy, Jeff Moore…uh… Principal Moore to you, though. Thank God we kept in touch all these years and then I friended him on my favorite social media site."

"Yeah," I reply. How cool is this? Thanks to good old Jeff, my mother has a job to go to and a good reason to finally leave New Jersey and all of my troublesome "aggressive anxiety" behind—because of mean girls and meaner teachers. I pull the covers almost all the way to the top of my head. "Night, Mom."

"Night, Mel. Sleep well," she replies with a yawn

in her voice.

I eye the corner of the dark room and my heart sinks. That's where Jonathan would be standing. When I said goodnight to him, he'd settle on the floor next to my bed—after I told him about my day. Of course, I had seen a few ghosts roaming the high school halls, but like I said, I didn't talk to any of them. Only Jonathan. But there is no one in the corner tonight. There never will be again. I close my eyes and stop my brain from racing into all the unknowns I will encounter tomorrow morning. I know it won't be painless. New things never are.

****

My sweet aunt must have gotten up at the crack of dawn to prepare a breakfast feast with two different brands of sugary cereals, grits, scrambled eggs, muffins, and toast with a variety of homemade jams. I like the peach jam the most.

Uncle Tim puts down his newspaper when we sit at the kitchen table, and more conversation about the vacant house down the road and Mom's in-person interview begins. I'm a nervous eater, so I taste-test everything except the cereals. I just listen and keep smiling at Aunt Sarah.

Liam doesn't join us at the table. At least he had lost the eyeliner. I guess he wants to look somewhat normal for school, dressed in a pair of baggy black jeans and a matching T-shirt. Maybe his chains were in the raggedy black backpack he had slung over a shoulder. He gulps down a cup of black coffee while standing at the kitchen counter and then shoves half a slice of dry toast in his mouth before mumbling a "See ya'll later," departing without looking at anyone. The mud-brown work boots really top off his leave-me-alone look. I have the strong sense that he'll avoid me at school, which is fine and dandy.

Aunt Sarah blushes as she smiles, and breakfast continues with Uncle Tim silent and Mom looking as nervous as she feels. Her head is filled with all kinds of worry: new job-related stuff, money issues, anxious to see this house, and getting us settled in our own place with the hopes that nothing in the new storage unit is smashed to smithereens, not to mention the same anxiousness as mine about making a happy life in small-town North Carolina, a town that we know very little about.

The ride to school in Uncle Tim's SUV isn't too long. I take in the flat, rural landscape, trying to see myself walking their streets and fitting in here. I wonder why Liam was in such a rush this morning—until we pull into the parking lot and I get a glimpse of him and three look-a-likes leaning against a green dumpster on the other side of the paved spaces to the side of the main entrance. Even at a distance I can see that Liam and two other Goth-boys wear eyeliner. One does not, but all four of them have chains hanging off their belts, and all are dressed in black. As Uncle Tim pulls away, it seems as though the entire student body is milling outside in groups or alone, waiting for the first bell to sound.

From the front, the red-brick building looks nothing like Willow Valley High, which has three wings sprouting off the main hub and with more than three times the number of students. I think for a brief minute that I have stepped back in time. I mean, right down to the windows that look ancient. It's a two-story structure with a brick, posted staircase leading up to the main entrance of the school. The only thing modern about it is the required steel security doors we walk through and the whoosh of cool air from vents in the ceiling. The principal's office has a sign sticking out in the hallway, not far from the entrance. Mom and I make a beeline right to it, but not before I note clean halls lined with beige lockers on either side.

Mom is suddenly shaking an African-American man's hand. He doesn't appear tall but has a frame like a boxer. Vice Principal Moore is not what I had expected, that's for sure. He eyes me in a kind way, and I sense genuine concern for a new student starting so close to the end of their school year. In Jersey, we sweat all the way through the end of June with less than half the classrooms air-conditioned. In North Carolina, school closes down before Memorial Day, apparently in cool country comfort. Then Vice Principal Moore shakes my hand as well. Warmth and kindness radiates through my skin. Nothing about him is an act or a deception. It eases my anxiety a bit.

"I'm pleased to meet you, Melody Marie. Your mom and I go way back. She has your eyes, Zoey," he adds with a laugh. "And I hear you're musical like your father."

Cue my answer, and I have to keep it real. "Yeah," I reply. "I like to sing." I leave out that I played Dad's guitar, which is now smashed and beyond repair, and that I play the piano.

"Well, we have an award-winning choir made up of juniors and seniors right here at Pinedale. I'll have one of the Student Council members take you around and give you a tour of our building while your mother and I go through this paperwork. You okay with that?" he asks.

Wow. The man's giving me a guided tour? More of that anxiety unknots. "Sure. Thanks." And what do you know, a pretty, average-looking girl with light-coffee-colored skin in a purple T-shirt with the name of the school written in teal letters stands at his office door and knocks.

"Hi, Shareese, this is Melody Warkowski. She'll be joining us as a junior here at Pinedale."

Shareese walks over with an engaging smile. "Hi, Melody. Ready for a tour?"

As I answer with a smile and a head bob, Principal Moore says, "Melody is particularly interested in our vocal music department. Make sure you stop there. If Mrs. Montgomery doesn't have a class, maybe take some time and introduce her?"

"Sure will, sir. You up for that, Melody?" Shareese asks me.

"Yeah. Thanks, but please call me Mel?"

"No worries, Mel," Shareese answers. *Another genuine soul. Go figure.*

As we leave the office, I don't look back at my mom. I am here. There is no going back. The sooner I accept it, the better. Besides, a quick read tells me Shareese isn't putting on an act or lying, either. There is a calmness about her, a sense of worth and wholesome goodness. I dare to hope that she is "the norm" and not Goth-boy Liam and his friends.

Halfway down the hall, I see the janitor mopping the floor. I slow my step, not wanting to face-plant in the first minutes in Pinedale High. He smiles at me and tips his baseball cap. I smile back and then look down to make sure I don't slip. Funny thing, though. He is definitely mopping, but the floor isn't wet.

Shareese rambles on about lockers or something, and as I look back, the smile leaves my face. I stop and bend down to retie my sneaker, which doesn't really need retying. My eyes rest on the janitor. The woman walking past him says, "Good morning, Hank." Why hadn't sweet Shareese?

He smiles my way and winks, humming along as he mops the floor. I make a really small wave. He stops mopping and waves back. "Do your janitors always mop the floors during the day while class is in session?" I ask Shareese.

She squints with a tilt of her head. "Nope. Just Hank. Can't figure out why."

That little prickly feeling creeps up my arms as I stand up straight and tug on the hem of my blouse. The janitor does the same head tilt and squint as Shareese before he shakes his head and chuckles.

"Oh. Good to know," I reply. Nothing shows on my face. I take a deep inhale through my nose, grin as my shoulders settle. "I'm sorry. What were you saying about lockers?"

"These are for freshmen. We'll take the stairs up to the junior-senior wing and start there. All of our classes are on the second floor, anyway."

I follow Shareese up the stairs and get the strangest feeling ever. There is something about Pinedale High that I do not know. And I am sure that whether or not Shareese greeted the janitor in the hall, he won't be the only one on another plane of existence.

Why? How could others see him? Why had he smiled at me like I knew his secret? Because the same feeling I had in the bedroom of my old house quivered in me…just before I saw Jonathan for the first time at the age of ten.

And just like Jonathan, I get the sense that the janitor is a ghost at Pinedale High. And he isn't the only one.

Chapter 4

Pinedale High

Okay. So I was wrong. Pinedale High is pretty big, not only a one-dimensional building block, but actually a three-sided square with a long, glass-enclosed walk-across on the second floor at the back of the school.

Shareese says Pinedale High is shared with three adjoining small towns, and that is how they are able to afford the sports teams, as well as multiple art programs like general chorus, a special motet choir (invitation only), band and jazz band, and life-drawing, along with a slew of other art classes, including ceramics. Pinedale has two kilns. And yeah. I am impressed. I figure if motet choir is by invitation only, I won't be stepping into the established program until my senior year. I'll have to wait until August to audition. Just my luck.

The two wings of the three-sided square had been added on twenty years ago when the consolidation took place. The junior-senior wing has bright, state-of-the-art classrooms with white boards and up-to-date technology. Since this is the south, air-conditioning hums from huge vents in all the halls and classroom ceilings. So that is definitely a step up from Willow Valley High, where you sweat like nobody's business through the last eight weeks of school even though schedules switch to early dismissal.

All my classes will be up here with special subjects across the enclosed second floor walk-across. And jeez, I am anxious to see the music rooms, but I tolerate the slow narration of this class or that room from my personal tour guide, Shareese. I think it's weird that music rooms are on the second floor with the auditorium on the first floor. But hey, who am I to complain or even comment? At least they *have* a music program.

I must get used to this. And I must find a way to fit in. Special chorus had been my comfort zone at Willow Valley. Without that connection to music *here*, fitting in will be pure agony, enough to sky-rocket my anxiety level into the danger zone. But Shareese says that years ago, the PTA insisted on an all-out, awesome arts program, so that's a plus, right? I mean, back in New Jersey, football rules like a greedy king. Then the extra funds, if any were left over, went to the arts. Here I am in North Carolina, where football still probably rules—but maybe *this* king is also into singing, trumpet solos, and something more than sports trophies.

When three beeps sound for change of classes, I step aside with my back to the wall and observe. Down the hall, Liam bursts out a classroom and slams someone shorter than him against a locker before he bolts like an outlaw. Other than that, this rush of students looks pretty normal, with a mix of skin tones and hair styles and colorings. Some students have teal or purple highlights in their hair. *Go team spirit, right?*

The hall fills with conversations and hoots—confirming the reality that I am *definitely* not in North Jersey anymore—but also quick chats and laughter and friendly glances. I avert my gaze, not yet willing to interact, but Shareese is all smiles with a truckload of "heys" and "hi ya'lls" and too many waves of her hand thrown in. Yeah. I observe it all and refuse to open up my sixth sense to the chaos of changing classes.

"We have a one-minute warning coming right about now," Shareese states. And what do you know…three shorter beeps that remind me of Morse Code sound over the PA system. Several students hurry their steps—another non-Jersey student attribute. As classroom doors close and it goes back to just her and me in the hall, I feel myself breathing easier.

Nervous much? You betchya. I tug at the dark purple blouse that I chose specifically because of Pinedale's school colors. Why? Because I want to make a statement that the new girl is not a threat or because I really want to fit in without any strange looks from the locals…whatever. No, my blue jeans don't have shredded rips in the knees or anyplace else. And you know what? Neither did any other student's blue jeans.

Shareese opens the security door to the walk-across and I look out the huge glass windows with interest. Students run freely about the open field in what I assume to be a gym class, followed by a teacher in purple sweats with Pinedale High written across the back. The football field is set to the side and behind the building, with another parking lot keeping it separate from the school. "Go Pythons," I whisper like some dork.

And there is that winning smile again. "We almost took State this year," Shareese informs.

"Oh, neat," I reply.

"And that field over there is for soccer and field hockey. We have gym class outside on it most of the time," she added, pointing to the right as we continue to the next set of security doors. When we walk through them, the sounds of instruments tuning up blends with vocal exercises like an eclectic cacophony of tone colors in my brain.

"Oh wow," I whisper.

Another winning smile accompanies, "Follow me," and we enter the vocal music room.

So this is what Heaven feels like, I think. Five, not three, tiered levels and wall-to-wall students doing vocal warm-ups in harmony!

"This is general chorus class, which is offered for any grade level to get credits," Shareese says, just loud enough for me to hear. "The motet choir and jazz band are also for-credit courses. Now don't they sound good? Some group, right?"

I spy Liam in the back row with the tenors, standing next to one of his flunkies, looking like an angel, which he isn't.

"It's great to see every row filled," I reply. With fifteen across and more boys than girls, the harmony sounds evenly matched. Funny. You'd think the vocal exercises would fill the room. It doesn't balance with the soft volume of the music teacher's piano accompaniment.

Shareese turns with a curious look on her face. "The chorus isn't as large as it used to be."

Wait a minute. Something's off. Liam's turn to the side with a sudden sneeze causes a creepy crawl up my spine. That my cousin's elbow goes right through the chest of the tenor next to him tells me why the sound and the number of singers doesn't match. Not to mention the shoulder-length hair on three boys who look like a throwback to a different time. In the alto section, long bangs and straight hair pulled back into high ponytails on, count 'em, three girls in the second row and four in the soprano section. Their white blouses with Peter Pan collars and neckerchiefs look out of place as well.

Mom likes to watch old movies, so let's talk about retro fashion tips. Bell-bottom blue jeans that hug the boy's hips? *Check.* Ohmygod…poodle skirts and white sneakers and socks on the girls? *Check.* The boy ghosts have on black leather jackets. I instantly know why *I* hear a fuller chorus than Shareese. Ten voices don't belong to living, breathing students!

"Melody," I hear my name repeated again.

"Oooh…sorry. I just got caught up in the harmony," I answer and follow her out of the chorus room door.

"You look a little off. Maybe we should hit the caf and get ya'll some water," Shareese says with a concerned look.

"Yeah…sounds good," I answer, still trying to accept what I saw. I mean. First the janitor. *Okay. That's freaky enough.* But like ten ghosts all in one classroom? *What the hell!* Apprehension sets in big time. What if there are more in the cafeteria? What if half the population of the school are spirits?

We take the first staircase down. The cafeteria is sub-ground level with high windows. The air comes from humongous overhead ducts that hum in the background and mixes with typical cafeteria conversations. The seating capacity chart at the entrance reads two hundred, so I assume, unlike in Willow Valley, two lunch periods accommodate the entire student body.

"Are we allowed to leave campus for lunch?" I ask as the aromas of fried chicken, burgers, and corn, *definitely* corn, come at me all at once. Not that I know of anywhere to go, anyway. There is no strip mall across the street where kids can grab lunch or a latte.

"Oh no. Pinedale doesn't allow it. Not even for seniors," she replies as we walk up to the service area. She hands me a bottle of water and explains to the cafeteria server that I am a new student. I get a weary, narrow-eyed look instead of a "Hi, how are ya," in spite of my dark purple blouse.

I take the bottle, and Shareese hands me a bunch of napkins to wipe off the condensation. I find the trash bin successfully on my own to deposit the wet paper napkins before we walk back to the entrance and take seats at the last long table. There is no way I'm going to say what I know to be true—while staring at a group of not-so-solid boys with strange hairstyles channeling their inner Elvis.

I concede a small grin with a truthful, "Thanks for the water," before twisting off the bottle top and taking a long draw of cool liquid to quench my thirst. I start counting ghosts in my head. Unlike Willow Valley with just a few non-corporeal entities walking the halls and sitting in classrooms trying to get my attention, Pinedale's score is already into double digits! I feel the hair on my arms start to prickle and duck my elbows under the table. *Holy crap! Am I really seeing this?* Snap out of it, I tell myself, and focus on Shareese.

Good vibes shimmer off of Shareese in a cascade of caring. "We'll stop by the gym and the auditorium, just so you can take a peek before I get you back to the main office."

"Sounds good. So… You like it at Pinedale High?" I ask after another swallow.

"It's a good school. The academics are solid, and I feel prepared for college," she offers.

"Are you a senior?"

"Yep. But there are two juniors on the Student Council board, you know, to take over in September for the graduating seniors."

Okay. Show some interest. "Are you really going to college?"

She smiles wide. "Oh yes. I was accepted to all three schools I applied to, but I'm doing North Carolina State near Raleigh. I can commute, and my older sister goes there. She's a sophomore."

Okay. Some more interest. "Do you have a major already?"

"Uh-huh… Early Childhood education. They have a great program and an internship track. The small towns around Raleigh are growing fast. Lots of young families moving in, which means more of a demand for pre-school teachers. I just love the little ones. The major fits perfectly with my life-plan."

"Wow. It must be great to know your future already."

Her head tilts to the side as I take another swallow. "How about you? Any ideas?"

I shrug a shoulder and give a sigh. "Not a one, but I'm pretty good at English."

"You looked thrilled to see the chorus room. You like to sing?'

More than anything in the world. "Yeah. It's okay, and, you know, music comes easy for me."

Shareese rolls her soft, brown eyes and laughs. "Not me. I can't carry a tune for anything. I just about whisper-sing at Sunday church service. But I guess with a name like Melody, you kinda are who you are, right? Ready to continue?" she asks.

"Yeah...all better," I answer, eyeing the poodle skirt group from general chorus, who had probably followed me, as their ponytails waggle and they eye me back.

"Great. Let's get on with our tour."

"Wait a minute," I quickly say. "You're, like, missing another class, aren't you?"

That friendly smile happens again, which I suppose is pertinent and perfect for a member of the Student Council. I mean, they wouldn't vote in a sourpuss, would they?

"Oh, no worries. I'll copy someone's notes, but honestly? With going into the last weeks of the last semester at Pinedale, the teachers know me pretty well. It's like all the seniors have one foot out the door already."

"Good to know," I reply.

No. I'm not an A-plus student. Maybe a low B in most classes except English and Music. Always a C in PE and Math. So forget about Student Council being in my future. But I want to go to college. Mom would kill me if I didn't, anyway.

As we head out to see the gym, I wonder if Liam is going to college. That cherubic look on his face in General Chorus had to be a joke. Nothing about him said angel. My best guess is that the eyeliner and chains were either in his locker or in his backpack, put on before school starts but not at home in front of his parents. From the shove in the hall to someone much shorter than Liam during change of classes, I get the impression that his idea of after school activities means menace instead of football practice. Should I ask Shareese if she knows him?

"Hey," I say as we approach the gym's multiple doors. "Do you know Liam Cooper?" *Yeah. I just had to know.*

Shareese stops mid-step. "Everyone knows Liam. Why?"

I take the plunge. "He's my cousin."

"Oh," is all she replies.

I get the feeling that maybe I should have kept that connection a secret. Just like me to ruin a good thing the first chance I get. How much do you want to bet that Shareese does the avoid-her-like-the-plague thing after she waves a sweet, "Bye now," in the main office and never talks to me again? *Guilt by association, here I come.*

****

Mom looks like she wants to get on with what she has to do today when I walk back into the principal's office. Their conversation ends quickly. Mr. Moore gives a kind smile and thanks Shareese. I do too, but a lot of good that will do me. This weird anger about Liam rumbles through me. *Already a cast-out on my first day once word gets out that I'm his cousin. Great going, Melody Marie.* I sink into the other chair facing my new school administrator.

"So. All the paperwork is in order and complete. Guidance has your records. Miss Marciano has your schedule. She'll give you a map of the school campus. We have a locker for you and the combination is in your school folder. After talking to Mom we signed you up for our exclusive Motet Choir. She says you have a super voice," he adds with another kind grin.

"Oh. Wow. Thanks," I reply. And that is my cue to leave. Mom stands and shakes his hand. I stand as well.

As we leave his office, Mom whispers, "Isn't that great that he was able to get you in without an audition? I told him you have a lovely voice and was always picked for solos back in Willow Valley High."

"Yeah. Thanks," I reply.

She takes my hand and I turn to her. "You're going to do fine here, Mel. Pinedale is much smaller than Willow Valley and you have your cousin right here in case you need anything."

That causes another anxious twinge. Liam doesn't come off the helpful type. And school size doesn't matter. Bullies like my cousin are everywhere. So are ghosts. Not wanting to drag this good-bye part out, I say, "You better get going and see that house."

She looks pretty nervous again, answering, "Yes. Uncle Tim's on his way back to pick me up. You'll see. This move is just what we need," she adds as I take the folder from the secretary's hand with another "Thanks."

"It's all self-explanatory," the secretary says. "If you have any questions, just find your way back to me, honey." Well, that felt condescending, but I smile as I leave the office with Mom at my side.

"Want me to look at it with you?" my mother asks in the hall, but I know her thoughts are somewhere else. House hunting and an in-person job interview have to weigh heavy on her mind.

I open the folder and pull out my schedule and the campus map. Her hand grips the edge of the paper.

Boy, am I grateful that Motet Choir will be the first class I attend at Pinedale! "No. It's pretty straight forward with English Lit, American History, and Bio Lab like it was in Willow Valley. The school's layout is simple and I already know where my first class is," I answer.

The last thing she needs is an Anxious Annie on her hands. There's just so much a mother can take.

"See? You're going to do just fine," she repeats. Her phone dings and she unlocks it, swipes the text, and turns to me. "Uncle Tim's coming in with something." Her palm comes to my cheek. Her eyes water. A shot of anxiety worms its way into my chest and I bite the inside of my cheek as we walk toward the main entrance.

Both of us watch my uncle enter the building. He comes over with a dark purple backpack and hands it to me. "Welcome to Pinedale High, Mel," he states. "There's a five-section notebook and a couple of blue gel pens inside. There's twenty dollars in the zipper part. And I put your cell phone in here as well. It's fully charged but turned off. You know. School rules," he says with a smile.

I hug him with a grateful, "Thanks, Uncle Tim. You're the best."

"Awww, it's the least I can do to help my niece settle in. Your mother said you like purple so…"

"It's perfect. I would have picked it out myself," I reply because that's what he needs to hear. That awful feeling telling me Uncle Tim doesn't get too many hugs or warm fuzzy feelings from Liam quivers through me. I make sure to hug him tighter.

I give a brave wave watching both of them leave. It

says everything's gonna be "fine," exactly what my mother and my uncle need to see. I take a deep breath and turn to the left, heading for the first set of stairs I see. And what do you know. The janitor is right there mopping in front of the steel door to the stairwell.

That sixth sense tingle has me in its grip again. I look at him. He looks at me. "You know I can see you, right?" I say with a squint.

"Sure do, little lady. So do the others. I'm Hank," he replies. With a face full of lines, he looks old in life-years, well, at least much older than my mom. I have to say, maybe somewhere in his early sixties? I sense he's been mopping this floor for many decades. Fully curious about how everyone could see this ghost, I wonder about the others. Is Pinedale High in some type of interdimensional loop or something?

Totally curious, I say, "I'm Mel. Melody Marie Warkowski."

"Pleased to meet you, Miss Melody."

"Everyone calls me Mel."

"You don't say… You have a very pretty name. Never met a Melody before. Not in all these years mopping the floor."

Or straddling two worlds, I guess. Okay. Time for snarky. "You're bound to two places… not like the others that are only bound to the school's campus. You're different."

His brown eyes widen, which makes his brow crinkle. "Ya caught that, huh?"

I nod with my eyebrows high. "I'm guessing there's a story."

"There always is, little lady." He leans on the wooden pole attached to the mop. "Welcome to

Pinedale High. How many did you see already?"

I shrug, holding onto my backpack's strap. "Enough to know it's unusual."

His eyes pop wider. "That many? Gosh golly, girl. Never had one with this special gift here before."

Not about to be conned, I reply, "Really? So how many others are bound here with you?"

"With me? That's an assumption." He clicks his tongue and focuses on mopping again. "We'll see when we see. You have a good first day at our school, Miss Melody. Jeepers. I like the sound of that name." He goes back to humming a tune, pretty much on key.

I look at my schedule and then the clock on the wall. Just then, the beeps signaling change of class sound. I open the safety door to the stairway—to a place where I hope I'll fit right in. I put the conversation with Hank the janitor out of mind. *First things first, Mom always says. Because I need to fit in somewhere.* With a little bit of luck, maybe Motet Choir is the place.

Chapter 5

My Space

Okay. NOW I'm in Heaven. Walking into the vocal music room again, I get to be the first student there. Well, the first alive one. The ghost singers are wandering around the room. All eight of them again. The five girls looked like they stepped out of *Grease* starring Olivia Newton John. Mom loves that movie. The same three boys from General Chorus, in their black leather bomber jackets and hip-hugger blue jeans, remind me of a different time period. Not Marlon Brando style, more like the *Easy Rider* type.

I'll admit to watching old movies with my mother, a weekly Saturday night ritual since like forever. So I know what I'm seeing. I avoid them, even though they know I see them, and focus instead on fixing my purple blouse before slinging my new backpack over one shoulder, not two.

The typical ghost tingle continues as anxiety starts to take over because the music teacher, Mrs. Montgomery, is nowhere in sight, and that worries me. Maybe she went home sick? Maybe she has an early lunch? Maybe a prep period? I stand off to the side far away from the ghosts and keep my eyes cast down.

Even though I had tucked my "Welcome to Pinedale High" folder in my backpack, I'm still clutching my schedule like it's my favorite novel. The paper it's on is warming up as that anxiety transfers from my shaking fingers to the printed schedule. Just to be sure, I check again to see if the time on the wall clock matches the time on the page. *Yep. 11:30 on the dot and, oh yippy, I have lunch after this.* Great. Just great.

Still avoiding eight sets of haunting eyes, I take a better look at the vocal music room while it's still empty of other living students. The tiers are wide enough for desks, which tells me that there has to be a music theory class somewhere in the course catalog. It's not on my schedule, but maybe I can talk to a guidance counselor and fit it in next year.

I feel the frown start and the frustrating tension return. Nope. I'm avoiding *that* person, for sure. Because the first question is going to be about the last incident that ended with the move to North Carolina. And I don't want to think about my father's smashed guitar or the social media buzz and that cruel scene in the hall or being called Melody-shmelody ever again. Had I had some self-control and just swallowed my anger, all this change wouldn't be happening. Had the teacher reported the incident, I wouldn't have gone off like I'd lost my mind in the classroom. And I wouldn't have punched that girl. No. I'd be coming home to Jonathan and telling him about my day and what they did. He'd sympathize and then help me with my math homework so I could pass math class with a decent grade again. Not anymore… *Okay, enough*, I tell myself, *because you can't change the past.*

So…back to the choral music classroom. Nice bulletin boards decorated with the ever popular eight-inch black music notes of different values. Clef signs, both treble and bass, are also visible around different pieces of sheet music used as a background, examples of both classical and contemporary compositions. Painted on the back wall in purple and teal cursive letters is a great saying: *Music is the heart, the soul, the rhythm of life.* I like it. Plus, I totally agree.

"*So who are you and how long are you going to avoid us?*" comes from over my right shoulder. I don't jump at the soft girly voice. Never do. "*It's right here on her schedule. Her name's Melody Marie War... Warkowski, ya'll.*"

That's my cue to turn and stare into a pretty face with brown bangs and one hell of a high ponytail. Unlike the other girls, she's in a light-purple blouse and what we now call capris. Black capris. With a side zipper. White socks and sneakers and red lipstick complete the outfit. "Love Me Tender" plays in my head as if Elvis is in the room.

In a noncommittal tone, I say, "I'm not avoiding you. Not avoiding the others, either."

My answer causes her eyes, the color of weak coffee to grow wide. Her pencil thin eyebrows arch as she turns away. "I knew it! I knew it when she came in with Shareese. Didn't I say she could see us?"

A chorus—pun intended—of "yeps" and "uh-huhs" come from the other *Grease* groupies as well as the 70s biker jacket wearers. One boy's voice is very deep, and I can't figure out why he was standing next to Liam in the tenor section before.

They form a circle around me, and we study each other with my eyes shifting from side to side. It is like a Throwback Thursday on Mom's favorite social media site, only in two different eras at the same time, that tells me these ghosts love to hang around the music room like some ethereal ensemble.

Now *that* gets my curiosity clanging while anxiety steps down a notch. I never engaged with ghost groups back at Willow Valley. Well, there weren't any, only solo actors.

The tall good-looking one, I'm assuming the one with the deep voice, suddenly stands nose to nose with me. "Well, aren't you going to freak out or something, Melody Marie?"

I tilt my head, and he mirrors my move. "No," I reply standing my ground, "are you?"

He is a real looker, even with all that long messy dark-brown hair and the greenest eyes I've ever seen. They just grab you and make you stare. His face hints a scruffy beard as if he hadn't shaved for a day or so. I remember seeing that look on one-too-many TV actors now, like it was a popular look way back when as well. His two ghost buddies aren't eye-candy like him. No. Just average looking boys with long hair. This one, however, has high cheekbones and thin lips that seem destined for a scowl. His wide shoulders drift back as his lips form a slight smile. "Well aren't you a fascinating one, Melody Marie."

"Just call me Mel, and I could say the same about you and your BFFs."

"Leave her alone, Hammer, even if someone *finally* talks to us," one ponytail quips.

Boldly I state, "Yeah, Hammer. Leave me alone and I won't tell anyone how all of you haunt the music room."

Yeah. Those dreamy green eyes go wide. "Holy

shit! Cool, man. You see *all* of us?"

"Why? Think you're special or something?" I answer back. "Uh-huh. And the ones in the cafeteria. And Hank, the janitor, too. Please tell me there aren't any more of you."

He doesn't answer because, just then, the door opens and the music teacher walks in. Her salt and pepper hair is done up in a loose bun, and she has on a purple golf shirt with Pinedale High embroidered in teal letters. Just like me, she has some extra pounds on her, so her shirt isn't tucked into her black denims. I wouldn't tuck a shirt in, either, so I sense some common ground here. I smile, push my anxiety aside and say, "Hi. I'm new…uh…I'm in Motet Choir."

"Melody, right?" she says with a smile.

"I, um, prefer Mel," I reply, suddenly feeling awkward.

"Well then Mel it is," she says. Walking over to the desk and now tapping the computer screen, she is probably taking attendance as the room fills. "I'm Mrs. Montgomery, choral director at Pinedale. Principal Moore told me you've been scheduled into our advanced choir. Welcome." As students enter in clumps of two or three and take their places on the tiers, she smiles again. "Soprano or alto?"

"Soprano," I answer.

"You're on the left, then."

Well, I already knew that.

"Merva, get a spare folder from the file cabinet for me?"

A tall African-American beanpole answers, "Sure, Missus M," and gets right on it.

"Merva is your section leader," Missus M says, and

just like that, a thick leather folder is in hand, placed there with a winning smile that matches the one on Shareese.

By now, all the singers are in place, including one of Liam's friends, the one without black eyeliner on. *Wow. A total of, count 'em quick, eighteen breathing students and eight ghosts hovering in the four sections.* Hammer is the only bass. His two leather jacket friends are in the tenor section. The black capris wearer is an alto, and the other ponytails are sopranos. Great. As the nineteenth solid human, I am the odd man out. Just my frickin' luck.

That familiar worm of anxiety starts its slither through my gut again. What I wouldn't give for a chocolate bar with a creamy, nutty center to chew, always my first go-to when I feel like this. I don't automatically follow Merva up to the second tier, and not knowing what to do next without looking like a total dork, I just stand there.

"Everyone, this is Mel. She's new to Pinedale, but I understand, not new to small ensemble singing."

Again, no pun intended, a chorus of "Hi, Mel," and "Hey, Mel," hits me square in the chest. *Could this be acceptance? On my very first day? In my very first class at Pinedale?* Nah…I am the amoeba under a microscope, not a pleasant feeling as that familiar anxiety elevates.

"Stand between Bev and Merva." Missus M doesn't say it like a question. But that's okay. Just from the few minutes in General Chorus, I can tell she's a pro at the piano. Probably sings like a professional, too.

Clutching the leather folder, I smile and say, "Thanks."

"No problem," she replies in a kind way before sitting at the piano.

I'm extra careful getting to the second tier, making sure I don't trip in front of everyone I want to like me. Merva moves aside so I can fit my bulky self between her and Bev. Bev side-eyes me. I have the strong feeling that being wedged between them isn't to Bev's liking.

Three chords sound, one right after the other. The group-inhale through the nose is audible. Three tones are hummed, each a different note of a major chord. The vocalese begin, and like it's second nature, I grab my tone and join in after the second "ma-may-mi-moe-moo." Two chords indicate a key change and I easily sync with the other singers.

As the chords climb up the chromatic scale, Merva glances over. Her eyes smile. So do Bev's on the other side of me. Slowly, *very* slowly, that anxiety, which is my oldest and dearest friend, slides down from ten to eight, and by the end of warm-ups, down to a comfortable three.

But I don't want to open the folder, not overly confident I can sight-read the soprano line of the first octavo. I follow just a half a beat behind as everyone sits, positioned on the edge of their chairs, putting down the writing panels so that they rest at the side. I tuck my backpack beneath the chair. Missus M strikes another chord and everyone goes quiet. I know the "all eyes on me" routine. I think choir directors use it as a common signal.

"Okay," Missus M states. "Let's start with *Hallelujah Chorus* before we work our way through the concert program."

I think she did that for my benefit. Whoa, boy, do I breathe a sigh of relief. I mean, what serious singer doesn't know that piece, right? It is a General Chorus nightmare, but a slice of silky cheesecake for a seasoned vocal ensemble member. I can sing it with my eyes closed.

Miss brown-eyed ponytail walks right through Merva and leans in to me. "You've got a nice voice."

I bite my lower lip and give a small grin, not about to ruin being accepted by answering a ghost and looking like I talk to myself. Nope. Not a chance.

As the familiar introduction begins, I straighten my back and open my mouth to sing the first note. I let familiar harmonies lead me to that safe space where I know I belong and as a decent soprano, hands-down accepted.

From time to time, I glance around and take in the eight kindred-musical spirits. Funny how they perfectly fill up the spaces between sections. I sense that what sounds like twenty-seven voices to me, only sounds more like nineteen to everyone else who is breathing. Probably to Missus M as well.

I can't tune them out, I mean, no way. You hear what you hear and you see what you see. That makes me think about the janitor for a split-second. I have never been in a room, let alone a chorus, with so many of the unbreathing variety. *Welcome to Pinedale*, I think as I sing.

I turn my head to catch Hammer singing along with the other basses. Assuming he, like many ghosts, is bound to the place where he has died, and by the look of his jeans and leather jacket, this means he had to be singing the bass part to this famous piece for…fifty years. *Okay. Some things never get old, but fifty years?*

Back at Willow Valley High, there had been two ghosts that hung around the chorus room, but I never talked to them. They saw me and I saw them. As for ghosts on the street or anywhere I went, I didn't bother with them. I didn't want to hear their stories or know how they died.

Willow Valley High is on a very busy street. Ghosts of all ages had met the afterlife there. They roamed it night and day, and I had learned to tune them out and turn off the gift of sight. I didn't want to end up being one of them—instead of *safely* crossing that busy street.

No. I had only talked to Jonathan for the past six years back in my old home town. So this music room choral experience is my first multiple encounter. What a perfect place for it to happen, right? In the one place where I *have* to fit in and be accepted. The one place where I would be comfortable enough to be myself. But if they hadn't died together, then why were these two groups of ghosts here? Had they all belonged to choir when they lived? Were they all gifted music students? Is this music room cursed or something?

Okay. Maybe they had all belonged to choir, but during different time periods. Maybe they had died in different places on campus and just somehow came together through a love of music.

I get that tingly feeling again. Had they all been juniors or seniors? Had something happened at Pinedale where whole groups of students died at one time?

I jerk out of my thoughts as the last, brilliant "*halleluiah*" sounds. I look at the classroom clock. Oh wow! That had been the most enjoyable ten minutes of my life so far in North Carolina. I take a chance and leaf through the other octavos in the leather folder.

My heart skips beat after beat! Randall Thompson's *Alleluia*, a choral version of *The Battle Hymn of the Republic*, and two other compositions I already know! *Ohmygod…*

I am *so* ready to drop down on my knees and praise the Lord.

Chapter 6

Tagged

I know I am walking, but I am actually like three feet off the floor on a choral high. I mean, it feels like I totally belong already, like I have stepped into my version of glory days in the music room. Bev and Merva keep complimenting me, and so do three other sopranos who stand in front of us on the first tier.

Checking the schedule on the QT, lunch is next. On the way down to the cafeteria with Bev and Merva, I have a rumbling empty stomach. But forget about eating alone. They say I can sit with them!

Just as my hand grabs hold of the security door from them, I hear Shareese say, "Wow. Now look at this. Here I thought I'd have to comb through the lunch line to find you. How was your first class at Pinedale?"

"Great," I reply, clutching the strap to my backpack like a security blanket.

"They need you in Photo Lab for an ID. Sorry. My bad that I didn't take you there first before the school tour. It just plum slipped my mind." The southern drawl, which seems to accentuate the differences between us, sounds breathy but easy at the same time.

Shareese's smile still looks friendly, so keeping fingers crossed that being related to Liam doesn't matter and that my first connection to another living person hasn't already fizzled into oblivion, I grin back, meeting her at the side of the cafeteria entrance. Bev and Merva wave goodbye, and I wave back.

I follow Shareese through hall traffic, all going the other way toward food. Like Willow Valley High, the noise level is up there, with a few hoots and "ya'lls" smattered about. But in the sea of purple and teal T-shirts and school polos, I guess my purple blouse fits in, right?

We take the next stairwell back up to the main office. The crowd has thinned in the old-fashioned cavern of a corridor with no windows, the decibel level much lower. The Photo Lab is located below ground level in the *other* wing of the school. Two students, one male and one female, are sipping soda from cans with their lunch trays pretty much empty. They both look up at Shareese and me. They have me sign a release form for a school-issued laptop. Thankfully, one is fully charged and ready for me to create my school login. I shove it into my backpack.

Introduced as Alvin and Cathy with a C, I give a soft "hey" when Shareese confirms my name. Cathy with a C smiles so wide that her gums show. "Ooooh…I've never met a Melody Marie before. What a joyous name."

Thanks, Mom, for the stand out name with no chance of them forgetting it now, I think. "Most everybody calls me Mel," I state.

"Let's get you standing over here, Mel," Cathy with a C says while indicating a background screen with hues of light purple and teal and a huge lamp with an umbrella putting me in the spotlight. Two of the ponytail girl ghosts keep picture-framing me with their hands. I ignore them as she centers me and says, "Smile for the camera." Alvin snaps away, totally unaware of the two entities peering over his shoulder, commenting with "Ooohs" and "She doesn't show her teeth when she smiles. Why is that? I'd take another picture."

I throw them a "really" look. They disappear through the walls of the Photo Lab.

Not even a minute later, Alvin indicates a choice of headshots on the computer screen. Oh jeesh, another decision looms in front of me. At least my eyes are open and I have not smiled like a horse. I choose the second one, although it doesn't much matter. As far as school IDs go, any of them will do.

After Alvin points to my name to confirm it's spelled correctly, which it is, another machine spits out my very own personal identification card. It doesn't take too many brain cells to recognize the next step.

All Pinedale students wear lanyards, just like at Willow Valley High. I get to choose between a teal or a purple one. I'm sure you can guess my choice. Alvin shoves the photo into a clear plastic holder and hands the finished product to me.

It isn't a struggle getting the purple lanyard over my head. My hair, which I call dark caramel-brown, has no curls and even less body. Not one soft wave, but just thin and bone-straight. I wear it shaggy with lots of mousse to at least give it a tinge of bounce.

As the purple lanyard settles on my neck, my stomach grumbles loud enough to be heard. We wave a duet of good-byes and Shareese walks me back to the cafeteria. "I've got to hoof it over to physics after I get you there," Shareese informs as we climb the same set of stairs we took before.

"Oh. No worries," I offer in a semi-friendly voice.

I grin before my face takes on that bland look I have perfected, especially in awkward situations. Lunch is only forty minutes and we have just used up half that amount of time. But maybe it is a blessing—because what if there hadn't been an extra seat at Merva's table? Ohmygod…I would have died! Thank God the cafeteria crowd has thinned. I am saved from stares and whispers about the new girl.

"What class do you have after lunch?" Shareese asks.

"English Lit, double period," I answer after sneaking a peek at my withering paper with the schedule because I always like to know what happens next. Adding a genuine, "Thanks for today, Shareese," I glance at the emptying cafeteria and give a friendly wave back to my tour guide.

Terrific. Just a few stragglers left in the expanse with my choice of tables. And no Merva or Bev. That leaves my next awkward steps up to me…all alone! I walk up to the counter before choosing where to sit. This being the tail-end of last lunch, there are fewer food selections: no more fried chicken and corn, but mac and cheese, chicken wraps, or a scoop of tuna salad on a bed of lettuce.

I steer away from anything with gobs of mayonnaise, so I take a chicken wrap. No way I could even look at the array of desserts because that is my real craving. Something so full of sugar that I'd pink-cloud it like a druggie and take the high it promised.

I fish through my backpack and dig out the twenty Uncle Tim gave me. Then my eyes bug out when the register reads $2.00! A chicken wrap would easily have been a five or six-dollar lunch back in Jersey. And who ever heard of free, ice-cold water in a bottle just ripe for the picking?

I leave the change on my tray and accept a warm smile from the lunch lady handing back my cash, and then turn to the right and take a table far away from the stragglers.

Reaching into my backpack now on the table, I shuffle the bills back into the zipper part, throw the four quarters into the bottom like some magical wishing well, hoping that my next class will also be a breeze, and then zip up the backpack.

Oh. Wow. That tingly sensation starts. The look up had my eyes resting on Hammer and his two ghost BFFs staring down at me. His pals sit across the table from me, but Hammer stands behind them with a hand on each one's shoulder. One of Mom's favorite oldies, "Leader of the Pack," plays in my head—complete with the *vroom-vroom* of a gunning motorcycle.

At least I was smart enough to sit with my back to the lunch ladies cleaning up at the end of the last lunch of the day, just in case my ventriloquist lips don't work. I snap the top of the water bottle and take a long, smooth draw before putting it down. Picking up the chicken wrap, I venture a big bite and chew before saying, like I'm so with it and tough, "Give me a clue."

The one with an uncombed mop of blond hair rests his hands on the table with his pointer finger inching closer to my tray. "I'm Terry. This here's Andy," Terry says in a grumble. His curls hide most of his eyes. Andy's red hair also touches the collar of his leather jacket.

I take a swig of water, really wanting another bite

of the chicken wrap. Walking through the empty cafeteria tables to get to us are three ponytails from choir, back together again. Since they all have purple on them, I'll call them the purple ladies.

"This here's Suzette, Betty Ann, and Carmen. Karen and Maria don't come into the cafeteria too often," Hammer says in that deep voice I could listen to for days.

"Damn. She really sees all of us," Carmen says with a hand flying through Betty Ann.

"Myohmyohmy," Betty Ann replies and adds a click of her tongue.

"Ooh…I like the picture she chose," Suzette says.

Really? Before hangry sets in, I break down and take another bite, curious about my table mates but saying nothing. I mean, why seek me out? They have a whole school to roam and hundreds of students to haunt. I keep my mind closed and my distance as well. Then they all speak at once.

"Put a lid on it, ya'll," Hammer says. I guess leaders always show their truth first. Confidence could be his middle name. "It's your turn to talk, Melody Marie, that is, if you really can see and hear everything we say."

I need another hit of cold water and take my time. "Yeah. I see all of you and I hear you, too."

Suzette zeroes in on my lanyard, like she hadn't been in the photo lab with Carmen. "Melody Marie Warkowski."

"You can just call me Mel, Suzette," I reply.

Terry and Andy stand up as the purple ladies take their seats. "Can't say this isn't spooky," Carmen mutters.

"It's been like twenty years since anyone saw us, right, Carmen?" Betty Ann, taking the award for most talkative ghost, beams with awe.

"Yeah, and that one left like a tornado after only one week like we were scary or something," Carmen interjects with a snicker and a scoff.

"Maybe she couldn't handle it," I suggest, barely moving my lips, just in case anyone sees my mouth moving in conversation with nothing but air.

With a bob and weave of her head that I thought only happened in the New York area, Carmen shoots back, "Like you think you can, girly?"

"Hey, Carmen," Hammer said, "The last thing we need is drama with a Latin spin."

Carmen clicks her tongue, and with a one ghost-finger push, the rest of the water in the bottle forms a gushing stream on the table—aimed at my lap.

All sorts of worries zoom through my head as I shoot up fast. The mini waterfall drenches me from the right knee down. All the ghosts are guffawing like hyenas. Betty Ann's hand covers her mouth with a look of surprise. Hammer's expression turns angry as he says, "What the hell is *he* doing here?"

"Drink much," I hear with a chuckle, and it doesn't come from a ghost. Nope. Not at all. "Hey. You're the new girl, right? I saw you walk into General Chorus and then again in Motet Choir this morning."

Well, damned straight you did, didn't you? So I guess word gets around real fast at Pinedale. I look over at the fully human, deep voiced person—dressed in all black with some thick silver chains hanging from his belt, just like my cousin had last night, only this Goth boy doesn't have on black eyeliner or black nail polish—standing right next to me. My neck has to crane back because, yikes! He is tall. Not hard on the eyes, either. His long brown hair looks messy but those dark-blue eyes have my full attention. He is wearing silver earrings and has a shiny black ring pierced through the side of his nose. I can't reel in the gawk, not to mention the embarrassment of a sopping-wet leg. I could deal with what is caught by my socks and sneakers, but thank God I had moved fast. It doesn't look like I'd peed myself.

I reach for the wad of paper napkins that I had been smart enough to take—along with a fork and knife. Dabbing at the dark stain down my jeans, I reply, "Wow. You're in both?"

"Nope. I didn't do study hall this morning just because I can."

"Yeah, right. Wait. You were standing next to my cousin." *And this Hammer ghost had leaned right through you!*

He chuckles. "No shit. Liam Cooper's your cousin?"

"Uh-huh," I reply, then think better of it. "Why? Do you know him?"

"Yeah. We hang out some."

Just my luck. A talkative Goth boy. I glance up to see the ghosts walking away, still laughing. Well, all except Hammer, who looks intense, too serious, giving Liam's friend a once-over from the nose-piercing right down to his work boots. Honestly, the black-on-black says that he and Liam are in some kind of me-monotone-macho-man club.

"Don't talk to him, Melody Marie. Get away. He's bad news," Hammer says and my head moves to where

I see him, but good-looking Goth boy right next to me does not.

"You okay?" He ducks his head and holds my plastic-coated ID with two fingers before adding, "Melody Marie War...war..."

"Warkowski," I give him. "Just call me Mel."

"Got it, but no way I'm saying it. Anyway, Liam said some relatives were coming to stay with him awhile. You must be one of them."

"That would be me and my mother," I say turning to face the dreamboat, completely forgetting about my wet knee and all.

I just about come up to his chin. He has wide shoulders like Hammer, a strong jaw and full lips. Those dark-blues have little flecks of lighter streaks thrown in for good measure. His messy mop of brown hair falls into his eyes, which has me mesmerized by what I can't fully see. As the bell rings, I all but jump, grabbing my backpack, slinging it over one shoulder.

"Gotta run. I definitely don't need another detention," he says. "See ya around?"

"Sure." Okay, so the walk-away with confident strides is a sight to behold! He bursts out the steel doors like he owns the school and disappears. I quickly pull out my schedule to grab the next class's room number again.

Hammer walks through the table and stands behind me, looking over my shoulder. "Let's go. Follow me," he says. Now that stride isn't too bad to look at either. But then he slows down, grabs my arm, and hustles me up to the first-floor corridor to the junior-senior wing on the other side of the school, walking through the solid students I have to dodge. "Oooh...sorry," comes out my mouth like some kind of repetitive mantra. We rush up the next staircase, this time going with the foot traffic instead of against it.

I feel Hammer's tight hold, the way I could feel Jonathan's. This is no tingle, more like a physical feeling like what I experienced every time Jonathan held me in his arms. "Room 212 is the next door on the left. And stay away from Justin, okay? He's bad business."

"Justin," I whisper with a quick glance at Hammer's green eyes as the corridor empties and doors start to close.

"Justin Hammersmith. He's my brother's grandson. And he's nothing but trouble," Hammer answers.

Just like that, I make the connection to the nickname. My feet take me into Room 212 and, as I come eye-to-eye with Liam, my mouth drops open. "Don't sit by us," he mumbles before walking away. I take an empty desk in the back—on the other side of the room, as far away from my cousin and Justin as possible.

The only adult in the room comes over to me, and I hide my wet knee under the desk. "You're Melody, I presume?" Her voice is liquid and soft, her smile a nice one.

"That's me, Miss, uh—" I pull out the schedule to read her name.

"Miss Woodson," she replies.

"Oh. Sorry. Miss Woodson, and I go by Mel," comes out oozing with embarrassment.

"Welcome to Pinedale, Mel." She presses something on her little laptop and then looks around the room, probably taking attendance as she walks up and down the rows. "Harold, please pass out the scripts. We begin Act Two in a few minutes. Justin takes over for Randy, who is absent today."

Liam snorts loud enough for everyone to hear. He punches Justin's arm with a "Go for it, dude."

Why is my senior cousin sitting in a junior English Lit class? Had he failed it last year? Wouldn't be a shocker, that's for sure.

My anxiety shoots up like a rocket, not only because my cousin is an idiot, but because I *hate* out-loud play readings. The drama queen in me is so very hard to repress. This new girl at Pinedale High doesn't want to sound like a total weirdo to classmates I don't yet know. I scrunch down in my chair, praying that Miss Woodson won't pick me today. Or maybe she will, just to see if this Jersey girl can read.

When a script hits my desk, I breathe a sigh of relief. Just before Christmas break, we had read and analyzed every single sentence of *Romeo and Juliet.* Act Two included Romeo's declaration of love.

"Everyone else take the same roles as yesterday. Oh. Except Bev. You're our new Juliet opposite Justin's Romeo," Miss Woodson announces.

I know this play inside and out. My anxiety hits a comfortable low. Once again, I give thanks that I wouldn't be lost like a stray kitten in English Lit, either. Between choir and this class, some you-go-girl, you-got-this inner-confidence replaces my usual level of anxiety.

Chapter 7

Another Nosy One

Halfway through one of the best parts of Act Two, not to mention one of the best readings of Romeo that I'd ever heard, my euphoria comes to a screeching halt. Miss Woodson puts down the phone on the wall and says the words I do not care to hear. "You're wanted in the guidance office, Mel. Harold will walk you down." She smiles. "Wouldn't want you to get lost, would we?"

Why me? Why now? I bite my lips, look aside with a soft "thanks," and close the script.

"Take it with you and finish the next two acts so you'll be up to speed tomorrow," she says.

Of course, I wouldn't say that I knew this play inside and out. It's one of my go-to reads when I'm in the mood. Jonathan would read Romeo and I would read Juliet. We'd pick and choose the juicy scenes.

After stuffing the script into my backpack, I follow Harold out the door. His blond hair is cropped shorter on the sides and he is only an inch or so taller than me. Not like Hammer or Justin. We pass the janitor by the security door that opens to the first floor. He gives a nod, and Harold responds with a cheerful, "Hey, how are ya, Hank."

"Not bad, kid. Be careful on the wet spots," Hank

answers.

My eyes slide to the side. "Is he always mopping the floor on the main level?"

"Funny," Harold says with a chuckle. "I mean, that's always where I see him."

We pass the main office and then two more closed doors. I thank Harold before I knock. The sign on the door reads: "Mrs. Eugenia Babcock, Guidance Counselor."

I plaster a friendly smile on my face, take a deep breath before settling my backpack square on my spine, and walk in when I hear the sing-song "Come in" command.

The first thing I notice are the gray roots on her dyed red hair. The second thing I notice is her fire engine red lips on a long oval face. Her blue eyes are mere slits sizing me up. "Well, I'm just pleased as punch to meet you, Melody Marie Warkowski," she says indicating a chair across from her neat-as-a-pin desk, except for my school record's file—obviously thick and open already.

For the eighth or ninth time today, I reply, "You can call me Mel."

"Why ever would I do that," she says with even more narrow eyes. "Melody is such a unique name. Add Marie and it just roles off your tongue like a buttered biscuit." The pause and the point to my records are painful. "I see that you are an average student who has had several run-ins with classmates, which resulted in sessions with the school psychologist in Willow Valley."

At least she shoots straight from the hip, as Mom often says. "Doctor Jim," I offer.

"Yes. Multiple detentions and so very many suspensions for unacceptable behavior. I've read his notes. He labels your reactions as exhibiting aggressive anxiety. I've not had any students at Pinedale categorized with that type of tag before. I've heard of anxiety disorders and aggressive disorders, but never the two of them put together. There's oppositional defiance, too. I guess you didn't fit into any of those. And it says here that you like to talk to yourself," she adds.

As if I didn't know that she just hit bingo with a capital B, I shrug. I grin. But I do not get all cranky and roll my eyes.

"It must make you feel very anxious to change schools, not to mention moving all the way from New Jersey to North Carolina with your mother. Acting Principal Moore says you're staying with the Cooper family. Your cousin is Liam Cooper?"

I bob my head with a no-word affirmative answer.

"Yes, well, I know all about Liam. So. How are you finding your classes?"

Now that makes me bite my tongue, but I give her a crumb. "I love the motet choir class. I already know the choral selections and I feel like I fit right in, Mrs. Babcock." Was it said in a friendly enough tone? Her next question would tell.

"It was by special request from Acting Principal Moore. He's a friend of your mother?"

"Yes. They went to college together."

"Oh," she says with more-open eyes. *Finally.* "I hear she's a teacher."

"Uh-huh. I think she's taking a job in the elementary school."

Again we have wide eyes under those pencil-thin brown eyebrows. "What a wonderful coincidence that there was an opening right when you moved to Pinedale. I always say the Lord works in mysterious ways. So. Tell me how you're feeling today."

Keep it nice and positive, Mel. "Okay. I guess. Everyone seems really nice."

"Have you already made any friends?"

"Uh-huh. Two girls from chorus asked me to sit with them at lunch." *And several ghosts introduced themselves to me.* Yep. I swallowed that one.

"Which girls?" she asks.

Damn. She is taking notes? "Uh…Bev and Merva?" *And she's writing again.*

"I see you have a class with your cousin Liam…English Lit, which he failed last year."

Would it be guilt by association? "Yes, ma'am."

"Liam has…a certain reputation around campus. But I'm sure you'll want to distance yourself from him and make more wholesome friends as the days fly by until the end of the school year in May."

"Yes, ma'am," I answer again.

"Now down to the business at hand. Pinedale High's guidelines have our school district's very own version of a placement test. We also require a career goals quiz for all juniors and new students as well. Why don't I show you to a quiet place so that we can get the placement test out of the way today?"

Anxiety rears its gnarly head. "But I already have a schedule."

Those red lips grow a condescending smile. "Rules are rules. Your schedule is only temporary until these tests are completed, Melody Marie. I suppose our *acting* principal failed to mention that." She picks up the desk phone and holds up one finger. "Hi, Coreen. Do you have room for one more today?… Great. I'm sending Melody Marie Warkowski down the hall to you. Meet her outside the door?… Oh. Perfect." She puts the phone down and says, "In-School Suspension is two doors down on your left. Miss Cutter will meet you outside."

That is my cue to stand. *In-School Suspension? Really?* I fix my backpack and take the manila envelope Miss Nosy Red Lips hands over. I don't give a sweet good-bye or thank you.

So this is the *real* Pinedale High. All nice on the outside with rot at its core. I get the impression that *Acting* Principal Moore's favor to me and my mother is not acceptable to her.

Oh God! What if I bomb on the placement test? What if I'm pulled out of Motet Choir? I quickly blink, telling myself not to tear up as I leave the guidance office.

Hammer is leaning against the door where this Miss Cutter stands. His arms are crossed against his black leather-clad chest and his jaw is locked. I sense that his molars are grinding. He frowns as if he can read the look of despair on my face.

As Miss Cutter checks her phone and types with one finger in response to what had to be a text, Hammer pulls off the wall and touches my arm. "Babcock's a bitch. Cutlets is, too," he says in that deep voice.

"You know what? I think I agree," I whisper.

Miss Cutter suddenly looks up and scrunches her fleshy face, scanning down the hall first left and right. "Agree with what? I didn't say anything, young lady."

All the saliva has left my mouth. Anger rumbles up as my nostrils flare and my lips slam shut. *Crap! You did it again!* "Oh… Sorry, Miss Cutter. I was just thinking that…that I agree with my mother about something."

"And what might that be?" she asks as I walk into the room for wayward students.

"Pinedale is a really nice school. I'm sure I'm going to like it here," I lie.

The "*humph*" says it all as she turns her wide body. Her shoes clip-clap against the wooden floorboards until she reaches the old-fashioned teacher desk in front of the blackboard. This is the original part of the school, I imagine. The cork bulletin board has no fancy paper covering it, only a list of rules in bold black letters:

No talking.
No eating or drinking.
Do not leave your assigned seat.
No cell phones.
Escorted bathroom trips, only for emergencies.

Okay. No purple or teal positive school spirit in here, either. Just bland off-white walls with student desks at least two feet apart. I take the empty seat right in front of Miss Cutter's desk and barely look at any of the fifteen students with open books on their desks. Naturally, a front row seat has probably been waiting just for little old me.

Hammer walks through the closed door and takes up the same stance he had in the hall, only this time right against the blackboard behind Miss Cutter. She opens the envelope, walks over, and hands me a printed booklet. "It's all self-explanatory. You can use pencil or pen. Do you have a calculator on your phone?"

"Yes," I whisper.

"You may use it for the math section only. If I see any texting or use of the Internet, it will be confiscated and you'll have to do all the mental math without assistance. Calculator app only," she repeats with a glance up to the clock on the wall. "You have an hour and ten minutes until dismissal. I will take the booklet from you when the bell rings."

"Sure. Thanks," I say as I pull out my phone, placing it on the desk.

Hammer moves to the edge of the teacher desk, and, when Miss Cutter turns to go back to it, he sticks out his foot. She shrieks with an odd sort of jelly-jerk and reel before both her hands slam like brakes on the desk. Muffled snickers and snorts come from behind and on both sides of me, but I keep my head down, bite down on my lips to hide the gotcha-grin, and open the booklet.

I quickly fill out the information on the first page with my new blue gel pen. I have to look at my photo ID for my student number to complete it, and then turn to the next page. Thankfully, it is the language arts section first, you know, where you read the paragraphs and pick out the correct multiple-choice answers below it.

Being an ace at comprehension and a fast reader, it is not a challenge. Neither is writing the essay from a prompt on page six. Seven pages down and forty-five minutes later, I stare at the first mathematical sentence and swallow. The next five pages consist of simple mathematical functions. Not a problem. But I don't like math, and I blow out a long, noisy breath.

Hammer leans over my shoulder. "I know all the

answers. If you get stuck, just tap the word problem twice. And don't, I repeat, *do not* say a word. She'll run right over to Babcock and say she saw you talking to yourself. We wouldn't want that to happen, would we?"

I slightly shake my head, watching Miss Cutter grade papers with a red sharpie. She looks mad as hell. Willow Valley teachers aren't allowed to use red *anything* when grading papers or making comments. The color is considered too much of a negative connotation of a student's self-worth. I guess Pinedale doesn't buy into low self-esteem and self-worth issues. After all, this is the south, not a trendy suburb in the progressive north where sensitivity to a student's feelings and selective pronouns of he/her/they comes first. Personally, I don't have an opinion one way or the other.

I promise myself to get through this without Hammer's help, but halfway down the fourth page of the section, I slump back and blow out another breath, refusing to tap the problem twice. I hate geometry!

PT is a tangent to a circle, center O. PT = 18.5 cm and PO = 19.5 cm

Yeah. I did the math and I keep staring at the multiple-choice answer by the letter A: 5.8 cm. Minutes drag on. I push my phone's calculator aside. Then Hammer's lips come close to my right ear to whisper, "It's B. 6.2 cm. Fill that circle in."

I hesitate. So much for doing this on my own. I have another ten questions and only twenty minutes left. His hand comes over mine, reaching across the page since I'm a lefty. The tight grip has me aim the gel pen at the correct answer and he moves my hand to fill in the little circle by the letter B.

My eyes tear. I bite my lips together. I am not a cheater. Just the idea of doing this bothers me. No way would I start cheating now. I jerk my hand away, very aware of his groan. "Oh, man, you just don't get it, do you?"

The rest of the questions blur, but I grit my teeth and read each one again and again. Miss Cutter opens her laptop, and I feel relief that she focuses on entering grades instead of watching me flounder.

The minutes are ticking by. I have too many questions left to answer. Students all around me shuffle as they wait for the bell to signal freedom. Books slam shut. Grunts begin, and shoes scuffing on the wooden floor are like firecrackers going off all helter-skelter. So I do the *eeny-meeny-miney-moe* thing with the remaining math problems.

Right in front of me, Hammer stands shaking his head. "Right on, man. You just blew it. So be like that and fail the math section."

I want to blurt out, *"I can't ace this! Everyone will know I'm a cheater!"* But then, I'd end up back in Mrs. Nosy Red Lips' office being accused of talking to myself! And every student in the room, as well as Miss Cutter, would be witness to the new girl's weirdness.

Hammer watches me pick out random answers in silence. Then my eyes flip up to his. "You just landed your grade somewhere around a C-minus on the math section, Melody Marie."

I look aside as I close the booklet and push it far away from me. I swipe my eyes.

Miss Cutter looks over the laptop. "Finished?" she asks.

"Yes, ma'am," I answer.

"Well don't that beat all. And you've got one minute until the bell rings," she states. She pushes her wide body off the chair and comes around to take the booklet from me. She walks right through Hammer who appears to scrunch and cringe before jumping to the side. I note the teacher's unconscious shiver as her shoulders rise. She walks back to the desk with my future in her hands.

Like restless, raging bulls just before charging, the sounds in the classroom ramp up. Putting my pen and phone back in my backpack, I glance at Hammer walking through the wall without looking back at me. I suddenly feel lost and alone.

Miss Cutter closes her laptop and looks just as ready as the students to run out of the room. Three beeps sound and the whooping and laughing herd of angry bulls charge the door with Miss Cutter at the rear. I stand, sling my backpack over a shoulder, and lag behind in a slow shuffle.

The hall is full of lockers slamming, loud conversations, and happy freshmen and sophomores as I make my way to the opposite staircase that leads to the junior-senior wing on the second floor. Once again, I am moving in the wrong direction as a tsunami of students head down and out of the building, not up to the wing. I hug the wall to let them pass.

When I see an opening, I trudge up the rest of the stairs and enter a semi-quiet hall searching for locker J-68 down a corridor of look-alike, matte-beige, tall boxes with combination locks dangling. Mine is far down and midway between two classrooms.

I keep glancing at the combination on the front label of my welcome folder. It takes three tries before I get the lock to spring open. The empty metal box smells of antiseptics and not sweaty gym clothes. There is no graffiti on the inside of it, either. I push the combo ring back up and unlock it again, just to make sure I won't look totally stupid tomorrow morning when I need to work it easily and get to my first class. I had packed a magnetic mirror and two of my favorite little stuffed animals in my suitcase with this in mind. I also had a picture of me with my Dad to stick up inside. I had no picture of Jonathan, of course.

With that task accomplished, I find the other classrooms where I'd be the new girl tomorrow morning. Biology Lab, American History, Algebra II, and World Languages are all on the same side of the wing. *Not too bad, Mel, you've got this*, I think as I head to the same stairwell I came up just minutes before.

With any luck, my mom's blue box-on-wheels would be waiting out front.

Chapter 8

Hammer

Sitting on a wooden bench outside the front of the school, I watch Liam, Justin, and two other black clad misfits-in-my-book strut off campus with the rest of the students. There isn't a purple or teal Pinedale High golf-shirt or tee among the four of them. Liam pushes a puny boy and takes his backpack, throwing it across the street. It lands on a car's roof. They all seem right at home harassing another group of kids, who look like underclassmen, before Liam shouts the F-bomb a couple of times, adding afterward a he-man hoot—while dodging cars to cross the street and head away from the school. Of course, my cousin is in the lead with Justin pulling up the rear.

I wonder if my aunt and uncle know Liam has a reputation. There would be no way they *couldn't* know. Bad vibes shimmy off my cousin like rain drops on a wet dog, or maybe tear drops if I think in terms of my kind Uncle Tim and gentle Aunt Sarah. Liam gives me the creeps.

I open my phone to see two text messages, one from my friend Hailey back home and one from my mother. My finger does a little dance between the two before I click on Mom's. She'll pick me up in like ten minutes from now.

Before I can swipe to read Hailey's message, Hammer walks through a tall tree and heads my way. I angle myself aside from the main entrance, sitting with my face turned, just in case anyone is looking.

Right in front of me, Hammer sits cross-legged on the ground and squints up with a scowl. Good move, I realize, because with my elbows on my knees, no one can easily see my mouth move if I talk.

"Wanna tell me why you didn't take my help on the last ten math questions, Melody Marie?"

He seems irritated, maybe too much so. "Look. I'm a C student in math. If I aced that placement thing, I'd be way over my head in an AP class I'd surely fail."

"You did great in the language arts part."

I grin. "Thanks. Reading is my thing."

"Babcock might place you in AP ELA. Then you won't be able to be in choir anymore. And you belong there."

Blush much? I shrug. "Thanks. I'll have my mom write a letter or something so I can keep the schedule as it is."

"I saw you eyeing Justin in class," he answers.

"I didn't see *you*," I reply. *So now he's watching me in class?*

"I stood against the wall at the back, right behind your desk," he admits.

Funny. In class, I hadn't felt that tingling sensation I usually get when a ghost is near. "Really? Worried I might talk to him again?"

"He's trouble. I mean it. Man, the kid has no common sense, and he runs with a bunch of...I hear students call them wannabe Goths, following Liam Cooper around like he's some flunky." The shake of his head with locks of long brown hair fascinates me. So do his green eyes that a girl could get lost in.

"Liam's my cousin," I confess as I roll my eyes. "Mom and I are staying with him and his parents until she buys a house."

"No way, man," he replies. "Just keep your distance from him and his crew. Justin, too. They're bad news around campus, and beyond it, I'm sure."

Now I had to know more. Hammer didn't come off as an angel, either. "How so?"

He straightens his shoulders with his hands locked to his knees. "Most of the graffiti on the rocks behind the school is their handiwork. Sometimes, things go missing and they get away with it. They act real tough with the teachers, especially the nice ones, the good ones, too. They like to push younger kids around."

"I think I just saw them do that," I say.

"I'm surprised none of them were in the ISS room with you today." He chuckles. "Old lady Cutlets gets all hot and bothered by them. The principal, she's out on medical leave, removes them sometimes and sends them down to the football coach. He sets them straight, but it doesn't last too long."

"Really? They're that incorrigible?"

His lips slide into a half-grin. "Now isn't that a fifty-cent word. Maybe a whole buck. I can see how you aced the reading comprehension section."

"Thanks. Answer my question." I need to know more about my cousin. Justin, too.

He scoffs. "Yeah. They aren't about peace and love or anything sweet."

I eye his leather jacket. "You don't look like you're about peace and love, either, for that matter."

He stands and looks down at me, straight through my eyes, it seems. "Looks can be deceiving. Don't let the outer package fool you. I aced all my classes at Pinedale. I was accepted to some cool colleges. But I never got there."

My mother's gun-metal blue box-on-wheels pulls up, and when she beeps the horn, he turns to the sound. "Wow. Way cool, man. Haven't seen one of those around in like, ten years. Nice."

"That's my ride," I say as I stand, fixing my backpack over a shoulder and then tugging down my purple blouse.

"I'll walk with you," he says.

Definitely curious, I have to know. "How far can you go?"

"You know about the ghost being bound thing?"

I give a soft, slightly open-mouthed, "Uh-huh," that wouldn't be noticeable in the event my mother is looking, which she probably is.

"The curb's my limit, but I roam the entire campus. Hank does, too."

I don't chance another question, whispering, "See you tomorrow," with my hand over my mouth while appearing to scratch the side of my nose.

"Yeah. Peace out." He has his left hand over his heart and his right giving me that 70s iconic two-fingered "V."

I twist my torso like I'm repositioning my backpack and whisper, "Bye, Hammer."

His long strides back to the main front door completely captivate me again. His legs are long, his hips narrow, and those are definitely football shoulders, for sure. His long brown hair brushes the back of his leather jacket. I'm taking a mental snapshot. And he never looks over his shoulder and back at me.

"Hey," I say to my mother as I throw my backpack on the floor and fasten my seatbelt.

"Hi, honey." She puts the car in drive and we pull away from the curb. "So. Tell me all about it. How was your first day?"

"It was okay." My eyes stay on Pinedale High even after Hammer walks through the closed main door.

I cannot get him off my mind as if he has some kind of special power over me. I mean, I'm not anything special to look at, that's for sure. And Hammer didn't seem the type to take newcomers under his wing like an angel of protection. But he had, hadn't he? First in the cafeteria and then again in In-School Suspension with Miss Cutter. I start to goofy grin, recalling her "trip" over to the teacher desk.

"Well, at least you're smiling," my mother says, which pulls me back to traveling down a road I don't know. "Did you already make a friend?"

"Yeah. Two girls from chorus asked me to sit with them at lunch."

"Oooh. Tell me all about it," she says with a hint of excitement. After all, nobody wants their daughter to be left out and miserable in a new school.

"It was nothing special. Besides, I couldn't take them up on their offer because I had to get my school photo ID," I reply fingering the purple lanyard around my neck.

"Maybe they'll ask you to sit with them tomorrow," she offers.

I hear the hope in her voice. "Maybe," I reply.

My head rests against the headrest and I close my

eyes. How could I tell her about the best parts of my day that included a good-looking hippy ghost?

Hammer isn't like Jonathan in temperament. There wouldn't be hours alone in my room with him. There would have to be minutes grabbed from the school day, somewhere that is hidden from everyone. I have so many questions. I have so many feelings that range from curious to full-blown crush—for someone who died years ago by the way he looks and talks. That southern drawl is charming. Almost musical to hear. And he isn't hard to look at, either.

"So what else happened today," my mother asks. I tell her about Mrs. Babcock and the placement test and my fear about being taken out of motet choir. Her lips purse and her nostrils flare like this is a call to war. "I'll text Jeff when we get to Uncle Tim's. But there's someplace I want to show you first."

"Mom. Don't get involved just yet, okay? Maybe nothing will change," I say with hope in my heart.

"Nonsense, Mel. The principal himself set your schedule."

"He's only the acting principal."

"It's the same thing. He's been appointed by the school board until the current principal returns. So drop the word acting, okay? Anyway, this Mrs. Babcock isn't going to change your schedule. Not if I have anything to say about it."

I know my mother. She'd get involved, no matter how hard I fight to let it be. So I change the subject. "What do you have to show me?"

"You will love it. Such old-fashioned southern charm. Not like Uncle Tim's house."

"What? You already found a house?" My skin

tingles. "The one down the block from Uncle Tim's?" *Please say it isn't so. Liam and his weirdness will be too close for comfort.*

"Oh, Mel. It's perfect. And the price was better than I thought it would be because it's been on the market for months."

That skin tingling now had alarm bells clanging in harmony with it. "Mom. What's wrong with it?"

"Nothing. Nothing at all. I think it was waiting for us," she replies with a smile. "You know that feeling when you walk in and, you know, you feel something?"

"Uh-huh," I answer, but *her* tingling and *my* tingling are two very different things.

And that difference was something we would *never* talk about. What would she do if she knew that I see and talk to ghosts? What if she *really* knows why the last school psychologist said I have aggressive anxiety and that I talk to myself? Would she take me to a doctor and put me on some kind of mind-altering meds or something? Would she shrink away from me and put me in some type of therapy on a daily basis?

I reel it all in and swallow it. I go to my happy place that calms me and I say nothing, closing my eyes like I need a nap. I feel the car accelerate. I rock through the left and right turns. I feel every stop sign and yield. I sense it all. And when the old blue box-on-wheels slows and she shifts into park, I open my eyes.

"Welcome home, Mel. They accepted my offer, and the bank who has the property agreed to let us move in any time, even before we close, because I can pay cash for it." She turns off the engine and gets out.

I unlatch my seatbelt and, after I get out, I slam the door. *Why wouldn't you let me see it first before you bought it? Why didn't you ask me if I wanted to live here? Don't you even care about me?*

She stops and turns back to face me. Her inner-dragon surfaces, just like that, and I brace myself, still holding onto the car door. "Don't be like that, Melody Marie. I don't want to impose on my brother and sister-in-law any more than I have to. He's already had a heart attack and he isn't even fifty yet! And I don't want you around Liam. My nephew has issues. Sheesh! Black clothes and chains! Black eyeliner and nail polish! He'll send my brother to an early grave!"

"So why buy a house right down the block from him?" I blurt out.

She draws in a breath as her eyes grow wide. Did that inner-dragon go back to sleep or would it fire back? "I'm sorry. I didn't mean to… If anything happens to him, I'll be close to help Aunt Sarah get everything settled."

"Why now all of a sudden? Why North Carolina instead of south Jersey or someplace else?"

"It's what family does, move closer to each other in a time of need, and God knows, I've handled things alone and kept my distance long enough. Your father wanted us to move down south years ago. Maybe he wouldn't have…had so much stress if we had come down here instead of staying in that rat-race up north."

"What does stress have to do with him dying? Cancer is cancer; it doesn't care about age or stress or who you leave behind or…or anything."

Tears blur my mother's eyes and change her facial expression, knitted eyebrows and all. *Now you did it. This stupid outburst really hurt her.* I blink my own tears into the wells of my eyes.

"That's not fair, Melody. I know he worked long hours and maybe you remember very little of him. He was a good man and a wonderful father. A great provider. On the weekends, he always put family first, you especially."

She reaches out and I shrug away. I do remember him! I remember everything about him! I see ten-year-old me, clutching my dad's hand at the Jersey shore and running into the waves as they crash. Fun times galore that include trips to New York state and our favorite dude ranch where I could ride a horse in the corral until my chubby little legs ached. Then, as cancer weakened him, we crammed every kind of happiness a little girl could wish for into one last summer before my world came crashing down like a split-open pinata. All that was left was quiet sadness as that special dad-strength slipped away. Now I have old pictures. Big deal.

But that last summer, the color purple worn in support of pancreatic cancer took on more than one meaning for me. I felt closer to a father I missed because that ugly disease took him faster than my mother could manage. Faster than I could understand as a ten-year-old.

Right after he died, I began to see Jonathan standing in the corner of my bedroom. I think I always sensed him there, but now I could see and talk to him. We talked about Dad, and Jonathan helped ease the hole in my heart. And now I miss him, too.

The permanence of this move is becoming clearer by the minute. Mom takes my hand as reality rushes back. Pulling my hand away would hurt her far too much and I'm not prepared for her tears, or another run-in with her inner-dragon, because she's stressed to the limit. I let her lead me up the walk to a set of brick steps that leads to a white house with colonial-blue shutters.

She keys a code into a lockbox on the door handle. She puts the key in the lock. The blue door that matches the shutters swings wide open. I stare into the eyes of an old man in worn blue jeans and a red plaid shirt, standing off to the side that opens into the living room with a white marble mantel. His hair is gray and his eyes are green. Just like Hammer's. I don't tell my mother.

Chapter 9

Touche, Mrs. Babcock

Within twenty-four hours of my new life in Pinedale I have a new address and a new schedule that doesn't include motet choir! The injustice roils me and rustles up not only my anxiety issues, but also that hidden aggressive streak that I feel when being bullied into something I cannot rationalize.

As soon as I enter Pinedale High, so happy and looking forward to that incredible choir class right before lunch period, and the possibility of being asked to share a table with Merva and Bev, good old Mrs. Babcock motions me aside and walks me into the guidance office. I take a seat across from her desk.

"I'm so sorry, Melody Marie, but after reviewing your placement test, there needs to be an adjustment to your schedule." Papers shuffle on her messy desk before she hands over my newly assigned classes.

My eyes bug out as I chew my lower lip. That heavenly breakfast waffle made the old-fashioned way by Aunt Sarah is like a brick in my stomach. I swallow as I blink. *No way! Basic skills English and math? Two, not one, study halls with an instructional aide assigned? Earth science instead of biology and lab…and no chorus!*

"There has to be a mistake," I whisper.

I swear I see a glow of gotcha on Mrs. Nosy Red Lips. "Willow Valley's Child Study Team was just about to classify you due to your diagnosis. Pinedale's team will comply with their initial findings. As a special needs student, you're entitled to an instructional aide to assist you. And even though your ELA score was much higher than expected, I thought it best to place you in classes you could handle easier, so as not to add to your aggressive anxiety."

Still in some high-level of shock, I reply, "But choir class…I can sing! I love music!"

"Yes, however the stress of preparing for a concert when you are so new to the Pinedale environment might cause you more anxiety, which might lead to an aggressive outburst and—"

"I'm not going to go postal on anyone! I need to be in that class, and English Lit, too! Just give me a chance!"

"Melody Marie, it's a state mandate that we help each and every student who has a special need," she says in a sympathetic tone, more condescending than yesterday. "Miss Cutter heard you talking to yourself, even before you entered the ISS room. The mathematical portion of the placement test clearly shows that you reached a high stress level toward the end and filled in any circle on the remaining multiple-choice questions—which supports my point… that you were stressed."

"It was the end of the school day and I wanted to finish," I say in defense of my actions.

She shakes her head and leans forward with her hands clasped on the messy desk. "Nevertheless…I agree with Miss Cutter that it was a sign with possible aggressive tendencies. You'll have enough credits to go on to senior year, and as a graduate with a classification, we can find a community college program for you to attend with in-class support."

Fury sizzles inside like a frying egg. "I don't need in-class support! I don't need basic skills classes, and I sure as hell don't need an instructional *anything* following me around and holding my hand like some labeled asshole! This frickin' sucks!"

As she scribbles some type of note-to-myself in my folder, I won't just let it go.

"Look, lady, I don't know what that stupid file from Willow Valley says, and I don't care, either. Instead of fitting in, you're casting me out, just like that! You're putting me into a square hole when I'm a...a circle! My mother knows the principal."

"Acting principal," she corrects.

"He's the principal!" I screech.

"You're getting worked up for no reason at all, Melody Marie," she offers in an eerily calm voice.

"People call me Mel," I fire back, ready to turn her desk into a clean top and the floor into a mess of papers.

"Miss Warkowski," she exclaims as she stands.

I fold my arms across my chest and give her a narrow-eyed glare. "This frickin' sucks," I repeat while gritting my teeth. I bolt out of the chair and run out of the office as fast as I can.

In the hall, that disgusting excuse of a junior's new schedule flutters to the floor as I run past the janitor. All of a sudden, a loud buzzer sound begins. Classroom doors spring open. The hall fills with students and teachers I don't know. I use the disruptive commotion as a cover, running down the corridor toward the back of the school.

Mrs. Nosy Red Lips still screams my name like I'm an escaped convict. I couldn't care less, heading with a whole swarm of students out the back door of the building.

I sneak off to the left, run toward some gym class on the back field. Huffing and puffing, because I'd never make the track team, not in my current state of *not* physically fit like a skinny cheerleader. I eyeball the graffiti-filled rock formation behind the open field. I zig-zag through clumps of students toward the football field house, leaving them walking to the end of the campus. I stand behind the cement structure to catch a breath. Then I take another chance and run for the shadows under the bleachers. My heart pounds. So does my head with the fire alarm still buzzing.

In the dark, with slats of sun lighting the dirt under my sneakers, the humid air seems cooler. But I'm not far enough away from the madness of a guidance counselor with a mean streak.

I find an opening in the bushes and slip through into a patch of tall pine trees, keeping the rocks with graffiti in sight. Unless someone at the school has binoculars, this is pretty much out of anyone's view. So I slow my pace. The closer I come to the rocks, the more I smell cigarettes. White and orange butts are all over the place, and what do you know, the ripe scent ends at puffs of smoke coming from Liam, Justin, and two other black-clad boys sitting with their backs against their ugly art work.

My cousin's black eyeliner eyes narrow as he sneers like a Billy Idol wannabe. "Shit. How the hell did you find us?"

I could lie and say I followed the smelly scent of tobacco, but all that comes to mind is, "I hate your school."

Justin says, "Yeah. Join the club," and takes a deep drag on his cigarette.

The other two raccoon-eyed boys guffaw, but Liam says, "Plant your ass before someone sees you."

Survival instinct kicks in with a quick duck down before sitting with my back against a tree trunk, just staring at them. "So this is where you end up instead of a classroom?"

"We usually skip first period. Gym doesn't cut it for me." Liam blows perfect rings of smoke as he eyes me. "Why are you here?"

"You don't look like the class-cutting type," Justin says.

Deflecting any more questions I ask, "So who are your friends?"

"That's Cam and Blaze," Justin answers, not Liam.

They both bob their heads with no evidence of who is who and continue their leisurely smokes. But both of them look as though they don't shower daily. Scruffy, and I'm sure if I get close enough, smelly as well.

"You didn't answer my question, cuz," Liam says.

I shrug. Does it really matter? I feel like a loser. Maybe taking up smoking and cutting classes is the way to go. "I hate Mrs. Babcock. I hate this school, and I hate living here," I mutter.

"You looked pretty happy in class yesterday," Justin offers.

"Shut up, J," Liam says.

"But she did," he answers with a chuckle. "I think

she's smart."

"Yeah. Just like you," either Cam or Blaze say. I still don't know who is who.

"You too, Cam," Liam growls.

Okay. Now I know. "Are you always so rude with your friends?" I ask with a smirk. Eye-candy Justin chuckles again.

"You shouldn't be here with us. You'll get a reputation," Liam states. "Wouldn't want that to happen. Ya'll be labeled like us. And you don't fit in."

"Why? Is it a boys only club?"

"We ain't a club," Blaze says. "We're a teacher's worst nightmare."

"Funny. I didn't see any of you in ISS yesterday."

All four of them snicker and suddenly act as if *I* were a ghost, simply not there.

Hammer appears next to Justin and my eyes snap up. "I told you to stay away from him," he angrily states. He kicks Justin's side. The solid one of the two starts coughing like he can't catch a breath. I know enough not to say anything, watching Justin slap his chest and continue to hack as he snuffs his cigarette out on the bottom of his work boot.

"All right, boys, get to class," I hear and look toward a familiar voice. "You too, Miss Melody." Hank the janitor crosses his arms and eyeballs my cousin. "The way you're going, Liam Cooper, I'll be seeing you again next year. Now scram. All of you. Before I tell the principal where you boys like to hide. All four of you will be suspended this time, not just Liam."

They all get to their feet mumbling words I would never say out loud. Chains rattle against their legs—on all four of them. "What about my cousin?" Liam asks with a gnarly grin. "You gonna rat her out, too, old man?"

"I'll make sure Miss Melody gets back to the school. But as for the four of you? I'd hightail it back to class, blending in with the students after the fire drill, before you all catch hell. If you run, you'll meet up with the last class going back in," Hank the janitor states, like he knows something no one else knows. But all four of them, including my cousin, leave in a hurry with their backpacks slung over their shoulders. Liam is the only one still grumbling his favorite F-bomb.

I look at Hank. He looks at Hammer. Then they both look at me. "I found your new schedule in the hallway. I put it on the principal's desk," Hank says and shakes his head. "Good old Eugenia Babcock. Damn, she's a nasty old biddy if I ever saw one."

"Clue me in," Hammer says as he comes closer.

"Looks like Babcock took the opportunity to change Miss Melody's schedule. Took her out of that special choir and changed all her classes to basic skills," Hank informs, still shaking his head.

I can't believe a ghost, that apparently everyone can see, is intervening on my behalf. I can't believe I'm listening to this conversation between ghosts and not saying a word.

"Damn it," Hammer says. He runs his fingers through his long brown hair as his gorgeous face twists. "Jeff will do something about it. He has to, once he sees all the changes."

Jeff? Hammer is on a first-name basis with the principal, with my mother's college friend?

"We ain't gonna let this change happen, Hammer," Hank replies in a calm voice.

"Hell no, man," Hammer agrees.

Yeah. Now I find my voice. "Hold on. Both of you. I mean, thanks for putting my schedule change on his desk, Hank, but that placement test—"

"Means absolutely nothing, Mel," Hammer says. "You aced the language arts section. All right, not so much the math. She has no right to put you in basic skills. No right at all."

"I…I have a…a history," I confess.

"A history," Hammer repeats like a question.

All the fight has gone out of me. I need to explain. "I talk to ghosts. *They* think I talk to myself. I get feelings and I sense things, so I get mad and, before I know it, I'm angry at others—even before they go after someone like a bully. The guidance counselor at my old school labeled me with aggressive anxiety." It hurts to say the words, but I have to be honest. My shoulders slump as I hug my backpack.

"Miss Melody," Hank says in a soothing voice, "We know ya'll ain't aggressive. And we know why they think you talk to yourself. It's all good. Sensitive souls like you are always easy targets. Nobody has to know anything, right, Hammer?"

"We protect our own," Hammer says. "Well, most of us do."

"Okay. This is freaky." I stand and brush off the seat of my jeans. My backpack comes over my shoulder and I blow out a breath as I fix my blouse, which isn't purple or teal today, just plain old white. "It's easy to label me a weirdo. I get it. I mean, I've lived it since the first time I talked to a ghost."

"How old were you?" Hank asks.

"Ten," I reply.

He scratches his chin. "That's pretty young."

"My father died," I whisper.

"Oh, shoot, Miss Melody, that must have been so hard on you," Hank answers.

"I guess," I mumble, thinking, *yeah...gut-wrenching hard*. "But how is it that everyone can see you but not Hammer or the others?"

Hank looks away with a friendly smile on his face. "I serve a purpose."

"And what would that be?" I have to ask.

"Miss Melody, let's get you to the principal's office. I'm sure Jeff saw your schedule by now. He's had enough time to understand what the old biddy did."

Sensations race through me. Does the principal know that Hank is different? Does he know his school has ghosts? Odd, how the timing of the alarm worked to my advantage. "Wait. The fire drill?"

Hank smiles. "You can thank Hammer for that one."

My eyes go wide. "*You?* Why?"

Hammer shrugs. His green eyes meet mine. "We wouldn't want you unhappy being here. It's been years since anyone other than Hank sees or talks to us. And your schedule, as well as your emotions, shouldn't have been manipulated by that nasty old Babcock bitch. Man, she's just as bad as crazy Cutlets."

I laugh at that one. "You mean Miss Cutter?"

"Whatever. I see her and I think about fried pork cutlets," Hammer answers.

"Hammer, that's about enough," Hank says in a reprimand. "It's time to go back in."

We take a different way back down to the school building, one that doesn't include scrunching through bushes. Hank walks me into the principal's office, right past the secretary, who doesn't try and stop him.

"Jeffrey, you need to fix this," Hank said as Principal Moore looks up from his laptop.

"Melody," he says throwing his hands up, "Oh thank the good Lord above, honey. I was just about to call your mother. Where was she, Hank?"

"She got caught in a class leaving for the fire drill and got herself right plum turned around. But I found her."

Genuine concern coming from both solid ghost and man vibrates through me.

"Oh my. Are you okay, Melody?" the principal asks.

"Yes, sir," I say. "Hank helped me find my way back, um, after the fire drill."

Principal Moore frowns. "Someone pulled the alarm right down the hall." He nods to Hank, who leaves us, and then he points to my revised schedule on his desk. My stomach does a quick flip-flop and I bite my lip, forcing my eyes not to tear. "This is…an outrage. I've already told Mrs. Babcock that you will follow the schedule I prepared for you, not this piece of…crap."

I let myself breathe again and swipe the corner of my eye. "Thank you."

"Mrs. Montgomery says you have a beautiful voice, and you're a welcomed new member of the motet choir. Miss Woodson feels your ELA records support that you are perfectly placed in her class. I took your student folder from guidance, and I'll speak with our Child Study Team personally."

He hands me a clean copy of my original schedule.

I offer another, "Thanks."

"No worries. Changing schools is hard enough for a junior. You don't need the added stress of a placement test that is out-of-date, and you certainly don't belong in basic skills classes, not with grades like yours. Listen. My door is always open. Not just because your mother and I go way back. Everyone deserves a fresh start. I'm sorry your first full day of classes at Pinedale started off so badly. It won't happen again any time soon. You have my word." He stands and comes around the desk. "Do you know where your locker is?"

I nod with an easy, "Yes, sir."

"Great. Miss Marciano," he says as we approach the secretary's desk, "Kindly write Mel a hall pass and have her excused from first period. Then have Mrs. Babcock come to my office"—he glances up at the wall clock—"at 9:45. Call the CST office and get a member to attend at that time as well." He smiles at me and waits until his secretary hands me the hall pass. "Will you circle back before Mom picks you up and let me know how the rest of the day went for you?"

"Sure," I say before I leave.

Hank's in the hall mopping in front of the trophy case. I smile at him. He smiles back. Hammer meets me by the stairwell up to the second floor, where my locker is. He falls into step beside me. "Thanks," I whisper.

"Like I said, we take care of our own," he answers.

How am I one of their own? Is it just an offhanded expression he uses? Or am I accepted by ghosts who like to talk to a living person? *Each to his own*, as Mom would say.

After a very tumultuous start, all is, once again, right in my world. I doubt that nasty old Mrs. Nosy Red

Lips will try something like this again. Principal Moore has her number. So do I.

Chapter 10

Justin

I only missed one period of American History, and when I see the Federalist Papers projected on the white board in the front of the classroom, I breathe a sigh of relief. We had already covered them in Willow Valley High so I have a good grasp of where things are going. Funny. It seems like the Junior Curriculum in the south is exactly opposite the one in the northern states. It really is to my advantage, right? I guess I have another thing to give thanks for.

Biology Lab is a double period, and I notice that Justin, not Liam, Cam, or Blaze, is in class with me again. Which means that either he failed it in junior year and had to take it over again, *or* it's extra science credits because he had taken a different science last year. But I sense that he really does have more brainpower in his head than he lets on. I triple up with Merva and Bev at their request—like another thanks be to God. My backpack is now as heavy as ever, with a biology and history textbook, after the beeps signal the change of classes.

Together, the three of us head to the end of the wing for the walk-across talking about classes and homework. Once we make it through the security doors, our conversation stops and we slow our steps. As we approach the music room for motet choir, what smells like something close to pizza, along with the distinct smell of fruit and bacon, fills the hall.

Principal Moore has a teary-eyed Mrs. Montgomery and my cousin Liam out in the hallway. A school security guard dressed in gray stands behind Liam. We slip by and into the music room as my cousin side-eyes me. Ten square boxes of pizza pies sit piled up high on the music teacher's desk. Hammer and his two ghost BFFs are high fiving each other. All five purple ladies are dancing the jitterbug to three Elvis look-alikes singing *Jailhouse Rock* in unison as if this were an American Bandstand party. I can't believe what I'm seeing!

Instead of taking my place on the second tier, I stand by the open door, fiddling and rummaging through my backpack, listening to the conversation as it heats up in the hall.

"He took the phone right off my desk during general chorus and then must have placed the order," Mrs. Montgomery is saying, all flustered and very upset.

"I was friggin' hungry on my way to fuckin' hangry," Liam answers with a stifled laugh in his voice. "How was I to know you had a credit card on file?"

Ohmygod! What a horrible thing to do to her, I think. And all ten ghosts are juiced up on happy vibes? Are their exuberant mood and Liam's actions somehow connected?

"Enough out of you, Liam," Principal Moore orders in a voice I personally would *not* challenge. "Do you really want another suspension on your record? Can you get it through your thick skull that Mrs.

Montgomery could press charges for theft? That'll go on your permanent record. Where would something like that land your father again, Liam? Huh?"

"He has no regard for anyone." Mrs. Montgomery sniffles as she talks with a tissue dabbing her eyes. "I gave you a second chance and took you back into chorus when every other teacher in this school said I shouldn't. I put up with your silly little disruptions and now, as we approach serious concert rehearsal time, you do something like this."

"You'll spend the rest of the year in ISS instead of chorus, is that understood? And you're banned from the music room. Fail him for the semester," Principal Moore states. "Let's go."

"Get your fuckin' hands off me, asshole," Liam shouts to the security guard, who barely touches his arm.

"Watch your mouth, son," the principal says slow and calm. "You can cuss all you want on the street, but not in my school."

Justin rushes in, glances my way before sprinting into the bass section. I make it to the risers and step up onto the second tier to stand with Merva and Bev. I want to do something kind. "Hey Bev, why don't I stand next to you on the other side so you can be by Merva? Do you think Mrs. Montgomery would mind?"

"No. I don't think so. That's so nice of you, Mel," she whispers, almost coos.

"No worries," I reply. I *really* need to score a few points in the please-still-be-my-friend category. I sense genuine sweetness in Bev. Merva too. And that is that. Maybe it will keep them both happy and I'd get to learn another soprano's name in the process.

The ghostly dance party stops when Mrs. Montgomery puts the tissue in her pocket after another sniffle. They immediately disappear through the walls when Hank comes in and takes the ten smelly pizza boxes away. Mrs. Montgomery takes attendance on her electronic tablet. And then she still looks upset, sitting at the piano to play a major chord. We all snap to attention and vocal exercises start.

All I can think about is Liam's latest mischief, not the ten ghosts who immediately disappear when they see Hank. *Ten pizzas that smell like bacon and...pineapples? Oh, yuck!* What a horrible stunt to pull on any teacher, not to mention putting that kind of money on her credit card. Everything is over-the-top expensive these days, right?

Now I understand more about my Uncle Tim and Aunt Sarah. I feel bad for them, especially knowing that my kind uncle already had a heart attack. I'd give anything to have my father back, while Liam doesn't seem to care about his, or his mother, either.

When warm-ups end, we start with the Thompson *Alleluia*. It's *a cappella*, so all Mrs. Montgomery gives us is one soft pitch. We begin *sotto voce,* and I rarely glance down at my folder. I concentrate on my pitch and my breathing and her conducting. About twelve measures in, Bev turns to me with a thumbs up and a friendly smile. It is a start. I'm already on my way to fitting in.

****

I decline to sit with Merva and Bev at the crowded table during lunch. It would mean that someone has to give up a seat, and I do *not* want to make waves in the budding friendship department. I'm also fully aware that Justin sits all alone by the window many tables away, as if he's been exiled. I know where my cousin is now, that's for sure. But where are Cam and Blaze? Maybe in some kind of lunch detention for cutting first period? That makes sense. Had Justin been smart enough to cover his tracks and dodge punishment? Yeah. Because he has more brain cells than the other Goth boys.

After deciding on the chicken wrap again, and as my stomach rumbles, I pay the lunch lady and grab a bottle of water before walking over to Justin. I put my tray down across from him. He looks up with guarded eyes, one of which is bruised. I hadn't noticed it this morning, but I don't mention it now—at least, not yet.

I have to say something, right? I choose a cheerful, "Care for some company?"

He lifts his chin off his palm and takes his plastic spoon out of a bowl of red gelatin. "Where you sit is your business."

Ouch. That hurts, but I persist and sit across from him. Hammer suddenly appears wearing a scowl, standing right behind him. I don't flinch. I don't meet those green eyes.

"Where are your friends, you know, Cam and Blaze?" I ask.

"In ISS because they didn't show up for second period, either," he mumbles before he takes another spoonful of red goop.

"Oh wow. I was in social studies…uh…American History, you know, the Federalist Papers, another junior class." So I am running off at the mouth, embracing anxiety again.

"I took that last year."

"So you're a senior...uh, but in English Lit and Biology lab with juniors?"

"Yeah. I aced Chemistry last year, so I took Bio to boost my credits and English Lit to help a friend instead of sitting in another study hall or friggin' ceramics class."

"So that's why I didn't see you in American History."

Justin shrugs as he mumbles, "I was in Principal Moore's office...with my father."

I sense his anger while Hammer smirks, running his hands through his long hair. Curious, I ask, "Why?"

"Babcock called him and said that I cut first period again."

I zero in on his bruising right eye. "Did your dad do that to you?"

"Yep. Clocked me a good one as soon as we left Moore's office, like in the hall so no one saw him do it."

A little chink loosens in my heart. "I'm sorry, Justin."

"Why are you sorry? It's not about you. Shit," he mumbles.

"He deserved it," Hammer says.

"Shush," I blurt out and Justin eyeballs me before turning around. Of course, no one alive stands behind him. Then Hammer reaches down. Justin's hand jerks and the plastic bowl of red gelatin goop on his tray shoots across the table and hits me square in the chest. I gasp and stand up as splotches appear on my white top, as it quickly soaks the cotton fabric and turns into fruit juice.

Justin's mouth forms a perfect "O" as his eyebrows

shoot up. He puts the bowl back on his tray. "What the hell! I didn't...I mean I wouldn't...how did it...oh shit," he exclaims.

I am speechless, knowing who the real culprit is—a ghost with a mean streak and some kind of grudge against the boy sitting across the table from me.

"Wait. Stay right here, okay? Don't move," Justin says as he stands. "I mean, like wipe it off, but...hey. I'll be right back. I promise. And I'll make it all better, okay?"

I didn't think a person could move that fast. I sink down to the round stool and huddle low. Hammer snickers as I seethe. "You're a real cool character, aren't you," I mutter with my hand in front of my face, slinking as low as I can go at the cafeteria table. "You did that! You swatted his hand like a jerk! I saw it. Thanks a lot! Most of my clothes are still in boxes being stored somewhere, you know."

"Wow. It looks like pop art," he chuckles.

"Pop art, shmop art," I mutter in anger. "It's not going to come out, which means it's ruined. And I get to walk around like this all afternoon. All because of you. I don't get it. This morning you made him cough like he was choking, and now you make him feel even worse? What's wrong with you, Hammer?"

Thankfully, I hear Justin's belted chains jingling and shut my mouth. "Here," he says, out of breath, holding a folded purple Pinedale High T-shirt out to me.

I sense his worry and see this as an act of kindness, but reply, "I'll be okay."

"No. I insist. Take it," Justin says really fast, "I keep one in my gym locker, just in case."

Boy, do I ever hesitate, knowing that unless it's an extra-large I'll look like I have sausage rolls around my middle. Are boys sizes the same as girl sizes? Do they cut T-shirts differently or are they unisex now? The look on his face is a good glimpse into his emotions. They are scattered all over the place and shimmer off him as if I could reach out and touch each one. Sad. Misunderstood. Scared. Angry. Sympathetic. Embarrassed. Anxious. *Welcome to my world*, I think. I take it from him with a "Thanks," as a flush creeps up my face and settles on my cheeks.

"Do you, um…want to go to the girl's room and change it or what, like, put it on right over this one, you know, so no one sees? Maybe? I swear I'll turn my back and hide you while you do it."

My heart is breaking for him in a strange sort of way. "Nope. No trip to the girl's room. I don't even know where it is. Here's just fine."

He turns his back in the empty cafeteria. Second-lunch students had to be fast eaters, or maybe they couldn't wait to get outside in the humid air for a few minutes before the next bell, because the cafeteria is suddenly empty except for us.

Praying like a bandit on the run, I crinkle it up and put it over my shaggy moussed hair that has no body, anyway. I unbutton and then worm my arms out of my ruined blouse and shrug it off. Thankfully, my arms punch through the armholes of the purple school shirt, confirming it has lots of room to spare, and I shimmy it around, making sure that my belly doesn't show. I breathe a sigh of relief as I stuff my ruined blouse into my backpack. Truth be told, I am no longer hungry for the chicken wrap on my plate.

I hear Justin breathe a sigh of relief. He sits next to me but faces the other way with his long legs stretched out.

"Now get away from him, Melody," Hammer quips like he expects me to listen to him.

"Do you want the rest of my chicken wrap?" I ask Justin.

"Melody Marie," Hammer says as his hands fly into the air. "Oh, man. What do you have, like, some kind of selective hearing or something? Don't encourage him!"

"I could eat," Justin mumbles.

I use a plastic knife on my tray to cut past the bite marks and notice, at the same time, that there is only the little plastic bowl of gelatin on his plate. That isn't a full meal. He had to be hungry as a bear.

"Where's the rest of your lunch?" I ask.

"Don't eat lunch, usually," he says as he chews and then takes another big bite.

"I'm up for a piece of cake," I say to see his reaction. He uses his free hand to dig into his pocket as I add, "Nope. It's on me. It's the least I can do for being saved from walking around the rest of the day in a splattered shirt."

I pull a ten-dollar bill out of my pocket while walking back to the serving area before he can say anything. I grab another chicken wrap, two bottles of water, and two pieces of chocolate cake, pay the lunch lady, and come back to the table.

Justin's head is down with his elbows behind him on the table holding him up.

"Here. Eat. It's my thank you," I say in a soft voice.

Hammer scowls. Runs his hands through his hair again with a tense, "Oh, man. Now you're being *nice* to him?"

I give him narrow eyes before Justin turns around to face the right way. My new friend devours the chicken wrap. It makes me happy to see him eat. I don't know why, except for the weird feeling that he doesn't get the chance to have lunch with dessert all too often.

"You don't owe me anything," he finally says after the last bite of cake.

"You bet your bippy she don't," Hammer grumbles in an angry tone.

"Do you ever get the feeling someone's watching you?" Justin says.

I freeze. "Yeah. Sometimes," I answer.

"If I didn't know any better, I'd think someone was staring at me right now."

Oh. Boy. No. Way. "I don't see any lunch ladies looking over here," I reply, as innocent as ever.

"Yeah. No. I guess not." He shrugs his wide shoulders. Takes another big bite and swallows before saying, "I don't know. It's just a feeling. I think this whole school is weird. You know, a lot of kids died here."

Oooh. More info. I want it. "Really? Like recently?"

"No. There was a school fire in the 1950s. My grandma told me about that. Then, three kids died right outside the front door of the school. They were hit by a black pickup truck in the 1970s and they never found the driver."

"Wow. No kidding? Really?" Okay, that comes out surprised enough.

"Yeah. My grandpa's uncle was one of them. John Hammersmith."

"Really. So what…that makes him your great-great uncle?" I ask with interest.

"Yeah. Something like that. My dad doesn't talk about him too much. They say he deserved it, what with acting like he was something special and all that talk of peace and love while he rode a motorcycle like some maniac."

The beeps sounds an end to lunch. Justin forks the second piece of chocolate cake down until the plate is clean. He cracks open the bottle of water and chugs it down.

I put my bottle of water in my backpack. I'm so nervous, I could never have eaten that slice of chocolate cake and I am glad that he had. My mind churns with new information, putting it together and trying to fill in the blanks.

I glance up at Hammer once again. His arms are crossed and he looks ready to murder someone. That would probably be Justin for telling me—or me for asking. Either way, it doesn't matter. I like Justin. Maybe even more than I like Hammer.

We leave the cafeteria and make it to English Lit on time. Miss Woodson looks at both of us as we hurry in. "And the last two coming into class get to be Romeo and Juliet today."

I stop short, wanting to turn around and do another escape like I had this morning.

Funny how you think everyone's going to fall on the floor laughing at you. Yeah. There are some serious stares, but no laughs or giggles. Hammer stands in the front corner of the room by the bulletin board glaring at me.

Justin seems to take having to read Romeo in stride. We both sit in the back. Harold hands Justin a script, but I pull mine out of my backpack. After Miss Woodson takes attendance, she gives us twenty minutes to look over our parts and to silently read the last two acts of the play. I look up at the essay questions written on the white board and my jaw drops. How could they be in the last acts already?

But I know almost every line by heart. Especially Juliet's. My love of the dramatic is right up there with my love of singing. I'll tone my reading down, though, being the new kid in class and all. Yeah, I'll really have to reel in my acting flair for the infamous death scene of these two star-crossed lovers.

Justin slumps back in his desk chair and extends his long legs, crossing them at the ankles as he reads his part flawlessly and with just enough emotion to keep everyone's interest. He glances over at me, and I grin like oh-well-we'll-make-the-best-of-this. *Awkward much, Mel*, I think. His eyes are such an incredible deep blue, his mop of hair such a deep dark-brown. I wonder what he would look like in this purple T-shirt of his and regular blue jeans and sneakers.

But, just like Liam, he seems at ease in the monotone drabness of all black. Sort of cool, too. I know this boy has a brain. So why is he hanging out with Liam and acting like a no-brain flunky?

Miss Woodson signals us to start the next scene. I do my thing, pretty much in charge of my inner-actress. Justin speaks his lines fluidly with just a hint of more emotion, which surprises me. *He really keeps his smarts hidden, like he doesn't want anyone to know, doesn't he*, I think.

Hammer moves to the other corner by the window—walking right through Miss Woodson. She kind of gasps and shivers before she clears her throat and puts her hand over her heart. Hammer smirks, then scrubs his face. That scowl appears again. Directed at me. Miss Woodson sits at the desk listening to us with a smile on her face. Suddenly, Hammer reaches up and some of the essays pinned on the bulletin board flutter to the ground.

Some students shuffle but none of them stand up and scream at the odd occurrence. I glance at Justin. "No worries," he whispers, "This kind of shit happens a lot. So do other strange things sometimes. In other classrooms, too. I told you this school is weird."

Nope, I think, *it's just chock full of dead teenagers who have nothing better to do than cause a little mischief when things don't go their way.*

I narrow my eyes and aim them at Hammer. He holds up his hands. "It's just a little innocent fun, Melody Marie. If you don't want it to happen again, then don't sit anywhere near Justin next time."

Jeez, I wish he could read my mind. I have a whole hell of a lot to say to him. Not only about this, but also about the way he treats his great-nephew. When will I get the chance?

Chapter 11

Research

The phone on the classroom wall buzzes just as we are getting ready to leave for the day. Miss Woodson had complimented both of us on our reading, and some students even clapped. I blushed with embarrassment and a little bit of pride, not anxiety. Just as I sling my backpack over my shoulder, Miss Woodson approaches me at the back of the room.

"That was the principal's office," she says.

"Oh. Yeah. He told me to stop there before I leave campus," I reply.

She grins, saying, "I think it's a change of plans. Your mother will be at least an hour late picking you up and Principal Moore has been called to a meeting. He asks that you wait in the library." She glances at Justin. "Would you walk her there when the bell rings, please?"

"Yes, ma'am," he answers, and it isn't a mumble.

That blush deepens. Here I am wearing his shirt, reading Juliet to his Romeo, and earlier, we had even shared a lunch table before he came to my rescue. "Thanks," I whisper.

"No problem," he replies as he one-shoulders his backpack and waits for the three short beeps as well.

At the front of the room, Hammer glares. His two

ghostly biker buddies join him, walking right through the wall of the classroom. Suzette and Carmen stand by the door. Why do I get the feeling that they are getting ready to put on a show? I can't shout out a warning, right? But I'll follow along and join in whatever reaction looks normal, for sure.

All the whiteboard markers slide off the metal ledge and roll around the floor. Students lift their feet as if the little round rods were mice. Windows unlock themselves and fly open before crashing down again—a perfectly produced bit of mayhem that has students gathering their things and ready to run.

"You know the drill," Miss Woodson shouts over the students' accelerating reactions. "Everyone out into the hall."

Some are pushed through by Suzette and Carmen. Ohmygod! Some are tripped, landing outside the room. Justin grabs my hand. Yeah. I am totally stunned by this blatant show of ghostly forces, but not scared. "I'll get you out safely," he says, pulling me through the door with a fierce mumble of, "Out of my way, bitches."

The beeps sound and chaos continues in the hall. Locker doors have ghostly fists pounding on them. Some fly open. I see too many ghosts, all dressed like Suzette and Elvis look-alikes, to count. Students scream and run for the stairs. Justin walks fearlessly, with determination, dodging the screaming mob and keeping me tight behind him, holding both of my hands. "Keep them clamped at my waist, okay?" he hollers through the screams and shrieks.

I feel turned around. I have no idea where the stairwells are as books clutter the floor after landing like torpedoes. He steps aside and turns until my back hits a wall, letting the criers and screechers, mostly girls, pass us up and head to the stairs.

"I'm not afraid," I yell over the many scared shouts.

"I'm not either," he yells back.

Seeing an opening, he unlocks my hands, takes one of them, and heads for the closest staircase. We are running now as the mayhem continues behind us. A book slams into the back of my knee and I feel myself going down.

Justin turns, grabs my fleshy upper arm, and rights me. We make it to the security door. It slams shut as a rumbling beneath my feet begins. "No way, no frickin' way," he shouts. "Ya'll let us out, damn it, do you hear me?"

The anger sharpens his voice. He bangs on the door and jiggles the bar, but it doesn't budge. More smacks to the door. More howls of laughter echo down the corridor aimed our way.

I spin around and face a horde of ghosts with mischief written all over them. Girls and boys, not an adult among them. "Stop! Just stop," I mutter through gritted teeth. "Back off. Every single one of you!"

They glare with smirks and sneers. Justin hits the bar on the door again, and it springs open. I feel him grab my hand tighter and we run down the stairs, do not stop until we come to the library door in the other wing on the first floor of the building.

He is breathing hard, still holding my hand so tight that it hurts. "Aren't you going to ask me what that was back up there?"

Still trying to breathe normally, I don't know what to say. I don't know how to answer. *Too many lost souls who won't move on to a peaceful afterlife?* "Was that like, uh…an earthquake?" I whisper.

He takes a slower breath and looks me right in the eye. "They say the school was built on a fault line that extends all the way to the Blue Ridge Mountains. I don't believe that shit. I swear this school is haunted by students that died here and just don't want to move on."

Down the hall, Hank is mopping the floor, humming a tune.

"And that one over there," Justin whispers, jerking his head toward the janitor, "He knows what all this really is. Maybe he's like one of them, too, only different."

A shiver runs through me. How can I say that I agree and not give away my ability to see and hear them? "Oh wow," I answer, and say nothing more.

Justin seems to shake himself out of that protective mood. "You'll be okay in the library. Nothing much happens in there but reading and research."

I smile. "Thanks for getting me here safe. And thanks for the school shirt. I'll wash it and get it back to you."

He shrugs. "Nope. It's a swap for buying me lunch. Keep it. It looks nice on you." He keeps his gaze off to the side and doesn't look over and down at me. "I gotta go."

"Where? To meet Liam?" I ask, very nosy and, for some reason, somewhat concerned.

"Nope. Gotta go straight to my father's and work. He was pissed to hell that he had to come to school this morning."

"He won't hit you again, will he?" I really have to know.

"Depends on his mood and how much he's had to drink already. Anyway. I gotta run. See you tomorrow." He pulls his back off the wall and leaves me standing at the door to the library.

I blow out a breath and settle myself. Maybe the library is off limits to the ghosts at Pinedale High. I am definitely not in the mood to talk to Hammer, or any of the others. But I'm ready to do some research of my own. There has to be a history of the fire that happened in the 1950s, as well as the accident that occurred in the 1970s with Hammer and his two ghost buddies. If I have an extra hour before pick-up by Mom, then I'm more than ready to dig up the truth.

****

Located in the back corner of the school, you could tell the library had been updated when the new wings were added. But it didn't have a contemporary flare, well, none except for a computer station with twelve all-in-ones that formed a hub. Although it would be great to google Hammer's name with a couple of keywords like motorcycle accident or Hammersmith, leaving a digital footprint isn't smart. I roamed the stacks and it took a while before I found the Pinedale yearbooks, all the hard copies neatly organized by decade.

I let my senses do the walking and choose the 1972 yearbook, leafing through student pictures by class starting with the freshmen. No Hammersmith there, so I thumb the thick pages until I get to the sophomores. Hadden, Hamm, and bingo…John Hammersmith with a mop of dark hair and a small smile. But why start in the middle, right? I pick up the previous yearbook and find his freshman picture. His hair isn't as long, but the face looks pretty much the same, only fuller.

"Likes girls and rock n' roll" is under Hammer's name. Football, Chess Club, and Chorus were his activities. I search the activities sections and see him in a choral performance, in a chess club picture, but I have a hard time finding him on the football team. Which only makes sense. Most yearbooks focus on upperclassmen, not the newbies.

The next yearbook for 1973 had Hammer in the same activities. Not much change there, but his hair is longer and his face more mature. Once again, I find him in the chorus photo in the tenor section and at a tournament for chess. And there he is on the football team, standing in the third row.

I take the next one down. It has a flower-power theme, and long-haired boys ruled in the junior year student picture section. Hammer was a featured player on the football team. He was also pictured in the Junior Honor Society this time. There he was, now in the bass section of the chorus again, I don't see him in Chess Club.

The 1974 yearbook has an In Memoriam section that pops out at you as soon as you turn the first page. The photos are all in black and white. My eyes glaze over, looking at three boys who had obviously sat for senior pictures months before their lives were cut short. Hammer's senior photo is in the center of the page. His dark-brown hair is like it is now, past his broad shoulders, and he has on a dark graduation gown that shows a white shirt and dark tie while holding the mortarboard against his chest. He has a serious look on his face, not a grin or a smile. His eyes are intense, like they just jump out at you and demand that you to look into them.

The other two students, Terrance Collins and Andrew MacDonald, are centered together under Hammer's picture. They have the same pose, but both wear proud smiles. Maybe they are the first in their families to finish high school. Maybe they had put their goofiness aside and took the photo session seriously. Maybe all three of them are headed to college. I couldn't know.

"What are you doing back here?" I hear and spin around, coming face to face with who? A librarian. It has to be, because she pulls the yearbook out of my hands, slams it shut, and reshelves it with pursed lips, a quick click of her tongue, and narrow eyes.

"I'm sorry. I'm new—" I sputter.

"No one comes back here, and we don't need archived books all fingered up. We don't need tragedies drooled over, either," she adds in a purposeful scold.

Trying again, I admit, "I just wanted to know—"

"It was a tragedy. A cryin' shame that happened some fifty years ago and, to this day, no one ever served time for their murders."

The hostility in her voice, the pain in her heart radiates like a glowing lamp. It also seems over-the-top. Had she a personal connection to one of them? She doesn't look very old. I place her in her forties and younger than my mother.

"Murder," I whisper. "I...I didn't know. I'm so sorry. I'm new to Pinedale."

"And you just happened to zoom right over to the yearbooks and look up three students who died? Do I look like I was born yesterday, little miss nosy pants?" She clicks her tongue again and blows out an exasperated breath, continuing to glare at me.

Okay. Time to lie. "I'm really sorry. I don't know why I picked that particular volume. I just wanted to learn more about my new school."

She turns and walks away. Something makes me follow her, as if it's an invisible rope pulling me along. She sits behind the circulation desk scanning returned books under a device, slamming the covers and putting them in a pile on the other side. Then she looks up at me and stares again.

I have to say something, but I don't know what is appropriate. Most of all, I get the strong sensation that she knows more about the accident, or as she called it, murders?

"I overheard some students talking about what happened," I lie. "One of them said it was a…a blue pickup truck that was involved."

It looks as though she has suddenly deflated and slumps back in her chair. She doesn't reach for another book to scan. "It was green, the newspapers said," she whispers, "And don't think the cops didn't know it." She looks aside. "Why are you so interested, anyway?"

Another lie is about to roll off my lips, but I have to keep her talking. "My new friend, Justin, told me about the accident, and I got curious." Okay. It was just a little lie, right?

"Justin? Justin Hammersmith?" she asks.

"Yeah. That's his name. We have a couple of classes together…and…we, um, sat together at lunch. And then, leaving at the end of the day? Well, we were in the hall and all of a sudden lockers started slamming and books went flying. Justin made sure none of them hit me. I'm Mel, by the way."

Chapter 12

The Librarian

She looks around the library. Seeing no students other than me, I sense her stress level at some type of inner conflict dip. Coming around the circulation desk, she points to the table where I left my backpack. We both sit, and her shoulders relax. "I'm Beth Collins," she says in a soft voice. "You know this school is haunted, don't you?"

How much can I let on without giving my abilities away? "I'm kind of sensing that."

"Well it is, you know. Forget about that lie that it's built on a fault line. There's no such thing. It's a cover up. Just in case anyone gets the heebie-jeebies when strange things happen… like books flying through the halls for no reason. Or windows opening all by themselves."

Had I found a kindred spirit…no pun intended. "I'm thinking these three students weren't the only students who died on school property."

She rubs her palms together before interlocking her fingers on the wooden library table. "Some say the school was built on an old Cherokee Indian burial ground. Back when the high school site was proposed, many townsfolk fought it, including some direct descendants of the Cherokee Nation. I've lived in

Pinedale all my life, but my parents sent me to a private school some towns away. They told me never to step foot inside this building."

I grin. "You didn't listen to them, did you?"

"Nope. And I married into the Collins family. All the boys went here."

"So...your husband is somehow related to Terrance."

She nods. "I think that's what made me take the job here as librarian when I was fresh out of college and looking to settle in someplace with good benefits and most of the summer off. My husband graduated from here. His family never got over the fact that the police dropped the investigation and chalked up Terry's death to just some hoodlums riding motorcycles on the school campus in the middle of the night. Everyone in that family mourned that boy as if he were a saint. He should have been the first one going to college. He had a bright future. My husband and so many others in the Collins family were named after Terry."

"Oh, I'm so sorry. How do you think the accident really happened?" I ask.

"It wasn't an accident. It was murder," she replies. "I did my research once my future husband and I got serious. He said Terry's mom died of a broken heart and left four younger boys motherless with her grief and the righteous feeling that because they were dirt poor, no one cared how he really died. Others say it was Johnny's fault it happened."

"Johnny?"

"Everyone called him Hammer. He was the first one to get a motorcycle. They said Terry and Andy looked up to him like their leader. Johnny's family owned a garage. That's how they got into motorcycles in the first place. Terry's parents objected something fierce. And alcohol and gambling ran rampant in the Hammersmith clan. Johnny's father gambled a lot. Almost lost the garage a couple of times. Folks said he wasn't right in the head. But those damned motorcycles. The three of them were like rebels. Even rode them to school, which made the principal really angry. Then they'd come back and hang out right in the front of the school for everyone to see. The cops were called almost every night."

"They were all seniors?"

"Yep. And just around the end of April, Terry's family believes that one of the farmers had had enough. Said his cows started to dry up and give less and less milk, all because of the noise from the bikes."

"Only one farmer?"

"Not really. You know, there's always a hothead who steps to the forefront and twists smaller minds so he comes off righteous enough. Terry's family says that Andy's father was furious that his son hooked up with Johnny. It was the seventies. Boys were being shipped off to Vietnam and coming home in pine boxes. Too many farmers lost their sons. All three boys had turned eighteen already and had numbers in the top twenty, which meant they'd probably end up in those rice paddies half a world away. When Nixon ended the draft in seventy-three, they say the three of them went hog-wild. They kept their hair long, dressed in those leather jackets and bell-bottom blue jeans to spout peace and love. Folks thought them a menace."

"But this accident happened in seventy-four," I interject.

"By that time, nothing could stop Hammer's little gang of three. People started saying they stole things and caused havoc with livestock. They smelled funny from what they smoked. And they drank wine instead of beer. They made themselves easy targets in a place that didn't take kindly to the changing times. They looked different, talked different, and acted different."

I feel her mind wandering, but I have a better picture of their hometown ways and the climate for tolerance in Pinedale. "That's why you think they were murdered," I whisper.

"One hundred percent. Like they were some type of demons that deserved to die. That pickup truck mowed all three of them down on purpose. Right in front of the school. Three beat-up and bloody bodies right there on the front lawn of the school. All three motorcycles heaped on top of each other like a mangled mess. Those boys knew how to ride. They weren't stupid or reckless. They were targeted."

"And they never found the pickup truck?" I ask, as if I wasn't getting the whole story.

"No. Some family friends of the three boys visited every farmer in a ten-mile radius. No green ones had any sign of damage that didn't make sense. No blue ones, either. The vehicle simply disappeared. Andy's father only had him. He sold his huge farm to land developers within weeks of his son's death. Packed up and moved away, never to be heard of again. As for the investigation, with nothing more to go on, the cops dropped it like a hot potato. Some folks turned the other way and said good riddance to bad garbage. Three families suffered an incredible loss. Their kin, innocent kids with the same last name, were shunned. And somewhere out there, some nasty SOB got away with murder."

I sit back. I'm at a loss for words, finally deciding on, "Thanks, Mrs. Collins. I promise I'll keep what you said a secret."

She gives a weary smile. "No one cares anymore. It's just another tragedy attached to Pinedale High, like that fire that took all those innocent kids' lives in the 1950s."

"At least the three of them died together. Maybe they're still friends, you know, in the afterlife." Okay. Lame comment, but I have to say it.

"I imagine they still walk these halls," she whispers, "along with all those students who died in the fire. Maybe some others. More young lives lost." She shakes her head and stands. "Nice to meet you, Mel. I'm sorry for the way I spoke to you before when I caught you snooping through those yearbooks. I was out of line."

"No worries," I reply. "And thank you for all the information. It's appreciated."

"That Justin runs with a horrible group of boys. It's a shame. He's too smart to ruin his life getting into all kinds of trouble."

"I get the feeling his father—"

"Jeb Hammersmith is an alcoholic just like his daddy before him, my husband says. They should have taken that boy away from Jeb when his wife died. That boy's probably in some kind of living Hell in that run down shack behind the gas station."

"He…he lives in a shack?" *Couldn't be, not in the twenty-first century!*

"Folks say Jeb drinks his profits, instead of keeping

it fixed up for him and his son. And that boy is bright. I know the types of books he reads. Why he just runs through the classics. It's religious, like clockwork, every Monday morning he returns a book and takes out another one. I heard that in the fall, when Justin applied to colleges, his father beat him something awful. The principal even called the police."

Shocked, but easily seeing how it could be true, I ask, "What happened? Did they arrest his dad?"

Mrs. Collins scoffs and starts to scan returned books again. "He does oil changes on all the police cars for free. What do *you* think? Money is the root of all evil. Right up there with cruelty."

"Thanks, Mrs. Collins. You filled in a lot of blanks."

She smiles. "Don't be a stranger. Make the library a habit. I think you like to read."

I smile back. "I like to help out, too. My mom should be picking me up soon, but how about I come back after school when I can, and help you shelve some books or like, whatever you need done?"

"Why, Mel, thank you for the offer. That would be fine, but you can just come on back to talk a while, too, maybe take out a new novel, you know. And welcome to Pinedale High."

"Thanks, Mrs. Collins," I reply.

I take my backpack and decide to sit outside in the yucky humidity and wait for my mother. After all, an hour has already passed, and I have found another place in the school where I fit in. And now, I have a whole bunch of new information to mull over, like names and dates to google. My imagination spins wild as I fill in the blanks with tons of what-ifs.

The halls are empty, except for Hank who mops the floor right in front of the trophy case. I wave and smile.

"So I gather you met Marybeth Collins," he says, leaning on the mop's wooden handle.

"Yeah. She's really nice. I looked at some of the yearbooks, too."

He chuckles. "Yep. I can see you doing that. Specifically, the ones from the early seventies," he adds as his eyes narrow.

"And then Mrs. Collins told me all about the motorcycle accident."

He has a faraway look as he glances above my eye-level. "It shouldn't have happened. Not to those three boys. But people are superstitious and prejudiced with no rhyme or reason, especially back then, when the town was reeling from the toll of the war and what it took on them and their boys. Civil rights activists, hippies touting love and peace, wild music with driving drums and electric guitars…it was a hard time for many who didn't want change."

"They were murdered, weren't they? Hammer, Terry and Andy," I state.

He gives a slow, sad nod. "Mowed down like rabid wolves."

I take a chance. "Did you see the driver of the green pickup truck?"

He pauses for way too many seconds. "Not my business. Not yours, either. But those innocent boys didn't ask to die." Just about to question him further, he shakes his head. "No, Melody Marie. It's not your place or anyone else's to know what I know. I see what I see. It's not my place to interfere. Not yours to nose around, either. Let sleeping dogs lie, I always say. You can't change what happened, and pointing a finger don't make you judge and jury." He nods once. "Now skedaddle. Your mamma's been waiting a full minute at the curb and she's starting to worry about her little girl."

I open my mouth and my eyes go wide. "How do you know?'

"Like I said. I know what I know and I see what I see. Until the morrow, young Juliet," he says, tipping his baseball cap with a flourish and a bow.

Chapter 13

General Warkowski

I run out the front door and down the front steps of the school. Hammer is at the curb with his arms crossed and a glare in his green eyes. I ignore him asking where I have been, get in the front seat, and latch my seatbelt.

"I was getting worried," my mother says.

"Sorry," I answer. "How did the in-person interview go?"

"Great. I signed the agreement and I start on Monday. How was your day?"

Oh, where oh where to start... The schedule fiasco, the fire drill, the hiding spot full of graffiti, the reason I have on Justin's T-shirt? Making a new friend who hangs out with my lame-ass cousin, the ten smelly pizza pies fiasco, lunch, English Lit, or the storm of ghosts at the end of the day... Nope. No way. And I am not telling her about the library visit, either.

"Nothing special," I answer with a shrug.

"How's your new schedule working out? How were your other classes?"

"Really good."

"That's all? Just really good."

"I made two friends today. Merva and Bev. I'm going to be their third-wheel in biology lab."

"Oh. Terrific. Are they in your other classes, too?"

"Only biology lab and motet choir."

"Did you buy a school shirt?" she asks with enthusiasm. "How much was it? Did you have enough for lunch?"

"It's cool, Mom. Yeah… I had enough left over for lunch." Okay. Add another lie to the list for today. I do not want to explain about Justin.

"I'll give you twenty dollars as soon as we get to the new place."

Oh no…I can't deal with the possibility of another ghost wanting to talk to me today. "Why do we have to go there?"

"I want to keep measuring so I know where all the furniture will fit. The movers are taking everything out of the storage unit tomorrow. Well, I think I'll leave Christmas decorations and other things from the basement there for a while. Then I'll meet them at the new house and begin setting it up while you're at school."

"Ohmygod! Why are you in such a hurry to move in there?"

Just my luck, we are at a light. She glares over at me. "Honestly, Melody, don't you want to settle into your own room in your own house? I want everything to be in place so that when I start on Monday, I know where I'm coming home to and what's in the fridge so I can cook us dinner."

"We've only been here two days, Mom. What if the closing doesn't happen and something goes wrong?"

She looks straight ahead. The light changes and she continues through the intersection at a cautious speed. This time of day in Willow Valley would be a nightmare to maneuver through. Not in Pinedale. If this is their idea of afternoon traffic, then I can't even imagine what their idea of a crowd is...maybe three or four people?

"Stop thinking like that. I don't need your brand of negativity, okay? Sure. There are a million things that could go wrong. I need to stay positive and pray that everything fits into place without a hitch. I'll lose my head if everything glitches on us. We have to make it all happen. Think it and make it be so. That's my new motto, Melody."

I shut my mouth and roll my eyes while looking out the side window. "I need my laptop from Uncle Tim's if you're going to make me stay in that house with you for like hours."

"I'm not stopping at my brother's house first."

"Okay. Then I'll walk there and get it myself," I remark.

"There's no Internet service yet. It's on my to-do list for tomorrow. But you can get a jumpstart on your homework by hand and then type it in when we get back there."

Great. Two-step homework. I think about the essays for Romeo and Juliet. I could type it on my phone, maybe. I unzip my backpack and pull out my schedule. A double period of math tomorrow instead of American History.

Maybe I can organize my five-section notebook. Maybe I'll just sit outside in the humidity on the front steps and mull over everything I've been through today. Then I wouldn't have to deal with the ghost of an old man staring at me from the living room. Hopefully, he is bound *inside* the one room. I frown. *What are the chances? Nil. Nada. None.*

When we reach the house, Mom gets out quick and slams the blue-box's door. I move like a snail on purpose and mosey on up the path to the front door. "I'll just sit out here," I say.

"You what! With everything that has to be done? I'll give you a choice of bedrooms. Pick one out and start deciding where you want your bed, dresser, and desk, bookshelves…you know, everything. I have index cards on the kitchen counter and sharpies. Take some and get to work so I know where you want the movers to put things tomorrow. *Now*, Melody," she says in that General Warkowski tone.

I want to click my heels, stand at attention, and salute, but I also don't want another argument so soon after the last one. I eye old mister who-knows-what in the corner of the living room and pray that he'll stand there silent, as far away from me as possible.

Too much has happened to me already today. I don't have the energy for another argument with Mom, or another sob story from a ghost bound to the mortal plane. Jeez. Can't a girl catch a break? I moved away from the hectic rat-race up north, where every which way you turn there is always another issue. The south is supposed to be slower paced, easy going.

Not for me. Today had been an entire month of emotional see-saws packed into seven hours of school. Plus, the day isn't even close to over!

With index cards and a purple sharpie in hand, I walk both bedrooms on this side of the house. I pick the bigger one that has windows on two sides, even if it is farther from the bathroom. The room in between could be a study or a den with my own television. Like a private get-away when I didn't want to watch old movies with Mom or I just want to read, curled up in a comfy chair, not my bed. I take the plunge and write 'bookshelves' in bold capital letters on two of the cards and place them along one wall in the smaller room. Maybe this task has merit.

This leaves more space in my bedroom. I corner my bed in between two walls on a slant. I put the desk under the window that looks out at the backyard. I put my dresser along the inner wall next to a closet. I place my mother's old cedar chest at the foot of my bed. Then I go back into the other room and add a card that reads "new comfy chair" and one that reads, "Mel's very own big screen television."

But wait. If I put my bookshelves out here, then I have nothing to put my stuffed animals on. Some of them have been with me since before Dad died. Many of them hold precious memories of him. I mean, I know when every single one had come into my possession.

I sit on the floor missing him. And Jonathan, too. Somehow, in my heart, the two of them are linked. It's like one had left me and the other had found me. I don't want that creepy old ghost man in my room. Somehow I sense he never comes in here, either. Is it too painful a memory? Not my problem. Not my business. I turn my thoughts back to Jonathan.

That first night I saw him, I had found comfort in his arms like he was a big brother. He didn't take Dad's place in my heart. That was a special spot that would never mend. Jonathan had created his own special spot. I could cry, or just stay against his chest. I could tell him anything. Especially things I couldn't tell my mother. He understood the anxiety that came from keeping secrets. I think he knew his heart had an early expiration date stamped on it by God. I think he knew he was going to die young and kept it from his parents. Maybe it was that guilt that kept him bound to my room. Maybe he wasn't ready to move on. Maybe now that he didn't have me to take care of anymore, he would. No one had these answers. Least of all, little old anxious me.

"That's it? You're done?" My mother stands there with her hands on her hips.

I shrug. "I don't have a whole house to set up, Mom," I answer in a snarky tone.

"What's with the Mel's very own big screen television and a new comfy chair I saw in the other room?"

"I'm sixteen. I need my own television."

"You have a laptop. You can get the app. And I'm not planning to buy any new comfy chairs until I see how this teaching position goes. Lord knows the salary isn't even close to what I made in New Jersey."

Money problems? Really? Both of my hands shoot up in surrender. "Okay, Mom. I get the message. Nix the big screen and chair."

"It will be a spare bedroom. My brother may need a break from Liam every once in a while."

I wince and look at her. "Uncle Tim's separating from Aunt Sarah?"

"Now why would you think that?" As if it dawns on her, she adds, "No. The spare bedroom is for Liam."

Oh crap! No way! "You're going to take him in? Liam's going to live here?"

"Not live here, Mel. When I see my brother, or his wife, for that matter, getting too stressed out, I'll have

Liam sleep over for a day or two. Maybe on the weekends."

"Mom, you have no idea how *wrong* that is."

"Why?"

"He's like a nightmare waiting to happen. He has a reputation at school. I mean just today, he…" my voice trails off. I know the look on her face.

"What happened in school today?" she asks.

"Nothing," I answer.

"What happened in school today, Melody Marie, and don't give me nothing."

"I don't care if he's your nephew," shoots out of my big mouth, "I don't want him in my house. It's bad enough I have to see him at school." I haul myself up off the floor and walk out of my room, giving her a wide berth. She reaches out to grab my arm, but I have a wide enough side-step.

Chapter 14

Unexpected Visitor

In the living room, the old man ghost reaches out with a hand. I block him out and go straight for the front door. Sitting on the top step, I inhale through my nose and push both my anxiety and anger down deep into its hiding spot.

Being under the same roof as Liam, even for just a weekend, burns me. Without a doubt, my room would be snuck into and studied so he'd have some juicy ammunition to use on me in front of his misfit friends. I'd have to take inventory of everything that belongs to me every time he left to go back home.

My mother's kindness isn't the answer to his problems. He needs a therapist, not me. The psychobabble buzzwords, oppositional defiance disorder, are three perfect descriptions of what is wrong with Liam. Why hadn't *he* been classified years ago? Clearly, his behavior issues hadn't suddenly popped up when he found out relatives were coming to stay with him.

I sit on the step with my elbows on my knees and my palms holding my face, watching a lonely ant burrowing beneath a crack in the cement. No way is my mother going to be saddled with him. Not. Ever. His kind of weird needs professional help. I tell myself to pedal it back and be kind, but I can't. For all I know, Liam already has a dark soul. I sense it's a real possibility, and not because of the way he dresses or the piercings or the black eyeliner and nail polish. What makes my mother even think that she can turn him around?

"Hey. What the hell are you doing sitting here?"

I look up. Justin, my savior at school, is halfway up the walk staring at me. My heart skips a beat or maybe two. "I could ask you the same thing."

"I asked first."

"My…my mother bought the house and I…I—"

"Shit," he mutters, "of all the frickin' houses in Pinedale. You moved in already?'

"No. Tomorrow. Why?" I ask, not sure if he knows about the ghost inside. Does he?

"My great-grandfather built this house. His grandson lived with him, I think, you know, the one who died in that motorcycle accident in front of the school."

What! Hammer grew up here? Lived here? Oh God! Did I just take his room? "Hammer," I whisper.

"Yeah. That's what they called him. How do you know?"

Oh crap! What do I say now? "I don't know. Maybe just shortening your last name or something like that?"

His dark-blues flash like they're backlit. They narrow as he pushes his hair off of them. I quickly scooch over. He takes the hint and sits next to me, stretching his long legs out, crossing them at the ankles of his work boots. Crossing his arms at chest-level, too. He smells of gasoline and motor oil. Do I care? Hell, no.

"So what are *you* doing here?" I chance to ask.

"Gonna see if Liam can come out and play," he answers.

I laugh at the way he says that. "Going to get the Goth boys together and terrorize some little kids? I saw what you did yesterday with that freshman's backpack."

He holds up his hands. "It wasn't my idea. I told Liam to pick on someone his own size."

"I gather he didn't take your advice."

"Never does," he mumbles.

I feel so proud that I led him away from discussing the house, so I add, "Someone better be able to talk sense into Liam and really soon. He's headed down a singular path."

"You sense that one, too? What are you, psychic or something?'

"No. Why?'

He shrugs. "Don't know. You're different, somehow, 'cause I don't talk to junior girls unless they're…"

Anxiety, here I come. "Go ahead. Say it. I don't mind. In fact, I'm used to it."

"I only meant—"

"Not a cheerleader here. No long blonde hair cascading over my skinny shoulders and a waistline like an hourglass." I don't want it to hurt, but it does. "I'm surprised you didn't write me off as a loser during lunch."

"I wouldn't do that, Mel."

His reply comes out strong and really fast. "Yeah. Right. So what's keeping you here now? Go on. Run down the block and be Liam's best flunky."

"Shit. You got a mean streak, girl."

"Yeah. We didn't move to North Carolina for the humid air and the heat," I reply with a scoff.

"Whoa. Rein it in, Mel. I'm not the enemy here."

I have another snarky comeback on the tip of my tongue, but I stop. I take a breath and blow it out. My shoulders sag. "Okay. So now you know."

"Know what?" he asks as clueless as ever.

Do I really have to spell this out? "I've got anxiety issues. Because I feel things. I've got aggression issues, too, because I feel things." I tell him about the placement test yesterday and today's schedule change. He curses under his breath, which makes my eyes start to tear. I sniffle them back and toss my head in a defiant way.

"Frickin' old lady Babcock," he mutters, sounding just like Hammer at that moment.

"It's all fixed, thanks to Hank. He put the schedule on Principal Moore's desk, and I got the impression that Moore put Mrs. Nosy Red Lips in her place."

He chuckles at my nickname for her. I do too, which stops the soppy, sappy expression I'm wearing.

"I liked your reading of Juliet in class today. It gave me something to work with."

"Was that your first play reading without a southern drawl?"

He fully laughs at that one. His teeth are even and white, even though I know he smokes. "Yes, ma'am. But seriously, I thought you brought some nice drama to Shakespeare's words. You had rhythm in your speech."

"We did the play reading before I left Willow Valley High…in north Jersey. Okay. I'll also admit I like the play and may have read it by myself doing all the different parts a couple of… um, hundred times since then. My mom says she read Shakespeare's plays like ages ago, with a boy from Ireland. He told her that back then, the Irish accent is closer to the original English accent, in the fifteen hundreds, than what we consider proper upscale British now."

"Wow. Cool," he replies with wide dark-blues. "I guess southern just doesn't cut it."

I shrug a shoulder. "You sounded pretty good yourself, like you enjoyed it, too."

"Don't go telling on me, now, Mel. I like my image," Justin replies.

"But that's just what it really is, Justin. Just an image. It's not the real you."

"And we're right back to psychic," he huffs.

I blush and look away. "Now you have a reason to leave for Liam's house down the block."

Before he can answer, my mother opens the door. "Who are you talking to…oh. Hi. I'm Melody's mom."

"I'm Justin Hammersmith, ma'am. Pleased to meet you," Justin replies in a pleasant, respectful voice. "I'm a friend of Mel's…from school."

"Hammersmith," she says with a curious look. "Are you related to the owners of this house?"

"Distant relations, ma'am. My grandfather's brother owned this here house. He outlived his wife, I think. Kept to himself a lot. Died right after he lost his grandson who lived with him here, my grandma said a long time ago." The look on Justin's face changes to serious and almost sad.

"I'm so sorry," my mother says. "Would you like to come in? All I can offer is some cookies and iced tea from the cooler." She holds open the screen door.

I look at Justin. Just about to tell my mother that he has somewhere else to be, he answers, "Thank you kindly, ma'am."

"Call me Mrs. Warkowski," she says with a smile.

"Yes, ma'am, I mean, Mrs. Warkowski. I just got off work and I could use something cool."

We follow my mother into the kitchen. She opens the cooler and adds some ice to a plastic cup before handing it to Justin. She opens the jug of iced tea and fills his glass. "So you work after school? And you consider yourself already a friend of my daughter's? Do you have classes together?"

And here comes a list of probing questions. General Warkowski would get every single answer out of him during the interrogation before making a judgement as to whether he was truly friend or perhaps, dangerous teenage foe. But then Justin answers every single one with enthusiasm. He is articulate and at ease speaking to her. I wonder if it is the latent actor in him that has suddenly taken over the Goth boy.

"I like your friend, Mel." My mother smiles her approval as if it is a two-thumbs up. "You mentioned Bev and Merva in the car. Why didn't you mention Justin?"

Now I'm on the spot. *Because I don't tell you everything* wouldn't cut it. "I…I just…I just… forgot," I end the stammer with the wrong word. I should have said that it slipped my mind. Nope. That wouldn't work, either.

"Hummm… Forgot," she says with a raised eyebrow.

Justin chuckles. "I guess I didn't make a very good

first impression on Mel, ma'am."

"Mrs. Warkowski," she corrects, like the neat and orderly freak she is.

"Yes. Sorry. Mrs. Warkowski," he answers in a sheepish tone.

"So you know this house. Any quirks I should know about?" Mom asks in a pleasant way.

The old man ghost is in the doorway. My eyes slide to his. Justin sniffs and sort of jerks. "My grandma used to talk about the garden out back. Said it was always full of jasmine at night and roses bloomed like for months on end. Other than that, I can't say that I know anything else."

He leaves out the part about his great-grandfather dying in the living room. Maybe he doesn't know. Maybe he doesn't want to spook her. I don't, either. I wonder but say nothing.

"What a lovely thing to know about our new home. I'll have to brush up on my gardening skills. It looks quite overgrown," she says with a warm smile.

"No worries, Mrs. Warkowski. I can come over on the weekend and get some of the vines and weeds out of there for you," Justin offers.

"Really? I'll pay you, but…don't you have to work?"

"It's my dad's business. I can give you all day Sunday."

"I pay ten dollars an hour," she replies.

His dark-blues shoot wide. "Naw…that's too much."

"Sorry. I'm a Jersey girl. I paid our neighbor's son ten dollars an hour for yardwork. For shoveling snow it was ten dollars an inch. Do we have a deal?" She sticks out her hand. Justin puts down his tea and wipes his right hand on his black jeans before he shakes it. "I'm so glad you just happened by today, Justin."

Time to put an end to all the sweet syrupy goodness. "He's a friend of Liam's, Mom." Now that changes the look on her face. A lesser amount of friendly smile remains.

"Oh. You know Liam," she says and clears her throat.

"Sometimes I try and keep him focused, like I do in English Lit, together with Mel," he says and glances at me. "Kids are saying that Mel has a really fine voice."

Good move at changing subjects, Justin, done like a pro. "I do. That's why they let me into motet choir," I say.

"Oh…so you know my nephew, just in classes," Mom says, as if she sniffs out just a little lie.

"Yes, ma'am." He rolls those dark-blues and meets her gaze again. "Mrs. Warkowski. Sorry. It's just hard not to add the ma'am. It's a southern thing," he says in a charming way.

Mom looks aside. "Well, I want to wash out the cabinets before we leave tonight."

"I could help with that," Justin suddenly says. "I mean, why should you or Mel have to climb on the counter? I can do it easy like. I'm good at cleaning."

Oh great. Now we get the rest of the charm. Why doesn't he just take the opportunity to leave General Warkowski to her cleaning? I start to feel anxious again.

"Isn't that sweet of you? It's a deal." Mom has to be under some kind of spell.

As the two of them start to talk cleaning cabinet

strategy, I go out into the living room and look out the front window. "Thank God for central air," I whisper. After all, this is an older house with curved wooden arches and a fireplace. Does it ever get cold enough to use?

"He's a good boy, my brother's grandson," I hear behind me.

I don't turn around. "Please don't talk to me. It's been a rough day."

"I've never been seen before. I had to wonder if you'd hear me, as well, little lady."

"I'm not a little anything. I'm Mel. Period. End of story," I reply in a whisper just in case the cleaning crew happens to leave the kitchen.

"Pleased to make your acquaintance, Mel. I'm John Hammersmith. Named for my daddy and his daddy before him. My grandson, well, he—"

"Died in a motorcycle accident right in front of Pinedale High. But it wasn't an accident, was it? That's a rhetorical, so don't answer."

"You know an awful lot for someone who just moved into town," he says in a soft voice. There is a kindness within him I sense, a truckload of sadness as well.

I keep my words at low volume. "I've met Hammer already. Terry and Andy, too."

"Oh no. Good Lord. You mean my grandson and those two boys never moved on?"

"No. He hasn't. Neither have they. I'm so very sorry." That is all I can say.

"You tell him I love him, and I never believed any of those stories. He was a bright boy, accepted to three colleges and not on no football scholarship. It was all academic scholarships. He was a straight A student and then some, my Johnny was. You tell him I love him."

My eyes well and I bite my lower lip. "I will. I promise. Tomorrow morning. As soon as I see him, Mister Hammersmith."

"Well, very good, then. And you tell him something else for me. You tell him that Andy's father was behind the wheel of that green pickup. That's what I was gonna tell them police, but I came home, sat on the couch, and…"

I spin around so fast that I get dizzy. I grab the windowsill behind me. I feel flushed and sweaty. It's too humid and hot to go outside. I make my way to my empty room. I sit in the corner of the room by the air vent. I take one deep breath after the other.

Oh God. Hammer's grandfather died of a broken heart! And how on earth could a father kill his own son? There has to be more. I am just too stressed out to go back out there and hear the rest. I close my eyes and hold my empty stomach. The nausea will pass, if I can only calm down.

Sometime later, my mother comes in with her rubber gloves still dripping wet. "Justin called down the hall before he left. Why didn't you answer him? Why didn't you tell me about him?"

Usually there were three questions all in a row. Before she could get out a third, I say, "I really had a long day and I've got homework. Can we go back to Uncle Tim's now? Please?"

I guess I don't look too good. She strips off her gloves, nods once. "You should have had a couple of cookies to tide you over before dinner. It's almost eight o'clock. I'm sure there will be something at Uncle

Tim's. I'll just turn down the air. Ready? And don't forget your backpack."

I pull myself up. Lean against the wall for a second before grabbing my backpack and throwing it over a shoulder. I meet Mom by the front door. I don't want to eat. I want to sleep. Like for a week.

On the short drive down the long block, I don't bother latching my seatbelt. Uncle Tim's house is like ten houses away or so. I can sense my mother is just as tired as I am. Maybe there won't be any more questions over dinner.

No way will I tell her anything else about my day or what I found out in the library. And definitely not the old man ghost in our new home. I want to get up to our room, take a shower, change into sweats, and research the hell out of John Hammersmith, aka Hammer, not his grandfather.

Chapter 15

Not So Fresh a Start

When my mother gets frustrated, she often grumbles *the best laid plans of mice and men, dot-dot-dot*, and that's what ran through my head last night. As soon as we got back to Uncle Tim's house, I ran upstairs, grabbed a pair of shorts and a fresh T-shirt because just the short walk down the driveway to the front door had me coated in hot, humid sweat. Then I took a shower. By the time I came down for dinner, it was, like, over?

I had grabbed the plate off the table and scooped some mac, cheese, and peas out of the pot on the stove and took a fried chicken leg before sitting by my lonesome in the quiet kitchen. The smells of good southern cooking filled my nose, the hum of the air-conditioning cranked up high again sounded like soft, soothing white noise.

Then I heard muffled voices through the closed door of the living room. They were like French doors, paned with small glass panels and sheer curtains, and yeah, I was curious. Uncle Tim can be seen pacing in front of my mother and Aunt Sarah who sat on the couch. Mom had her arm around Aunt Sarah, and I could make out tissues in her hand that kept dabbing at the corner of an eye. I had no idea what was being discussed.

Then I went upstairs. By the time I finished transferring my homework to the school assigned laptop, I couldn't stare at the screen anymore. And after the long, bumpy day full of a palette of emotions, well, I stretched out on the trundle bed and fell asleep. I mean, could you blame me? And I had no idea what time my mother came up.

****

Mom is already dressed in shorts and a summer blouse when she wakes me, holding up my stained white shirt from yesterday. "Hurry and get dressed. You're going to be late if you dawdle. Do you want to explain this?"

I rub sleep out of my eyes and blink a few times. *Oh that? Well, you see, a ghost had some issues with me at lunch* wouldn't cut it, so I say, "I spilled some red gelatin on it."

"Is that why you bought a Pinedale shirt yesterday?" she asks after a tongue click.

"Um…yeah." So, what's the harm in a little fib, right?

"You should have told me last night. I don't think this will come out in the wash, Mel. Funny. You haven't worn your food since you were little." A ripe pause. "Is it the move, sweetie?" Cue the glistening eyes and a sudden sniffle. "I know it's a lot."

"No. Mom. I just…spilled some food on me," I answer with my eyes wide.

I get out of bed and rummage through my suitcase for some clean underwear and a bra, and blue jeans. I eye Justin's shirt, and decide, what the heck…I'd blend in better with it on again today. "Sorry, Mom," I mumble. She grabs my hand before I can make a clean getaway.

"Mel. I'm the one who's sorry. I know this is happening too fast. New school. New house, and new…new everything. Maybe you want to stay home with me today? You know, get settled in your new room and put things where you want to when the movers arrive?"

I yank my hand back. "No. Mom. I like school. I want a whole day of new-normal, okay?" And I want a long conversation with Hammer about his antics, which include spilling Justin's gelatin on me and that terrifying tornado of flying books in the corridor at the end of the school day. Plus, I have an important message for him. From his grandfather.

Her hand has recoiled and now rests over her heart. She seems to shiver before she blows out a slow breath. I hurry to the bathroom, and once the door is closed, I lean against it and shut my eyes. Back in Jersey it had just been Jonathan. Here? My ability to see what I see and feel what I feel is already on overload!

I cannot tell her. Nope. First, she'll think I'm having some kind of breakdown. Second, that would have *her* having some kind of breakdown, too. Third? Was there a third? This thing with seeing ghosts is something I didn't ask for, something too out of the ordinary, like finding out the hard way that vampires really exist and so do things that go bump in the night. I am not normal. And I am alone, negotiating through something that has already labeled me with aggressive anxiety issues.

I do what I have to do in the bathroom, fix my hair so it doesn't stick out every which way once I take a step outside and into humidity, and then grab my backpack, my school assigned laptop, and head down the stairs, already hungry like any other nervous eater.

Although it is another southern breakfast feast, which I happily dig into to taste everything, the mood is eerily too quiet. And I wonder where Liam is. Has he left already to get into all kinds of trouble before the first three tones sound? Or is he up by the rocks behind the school polluting his lungs and smoking with his Goth buds? And…why should I care? My cousin is bad news with all capital letters. I take another waffle and smother it in butter and syrup.

****

Mom doesn't say much on the drive to Pinedale High. She looks lost in thought, probably worried about what our furniture and what our things will look like when they are delivered or something. And I make it into the school building with minutes to spare and do the whole locker thing, ready for my first normal day without ending up in Mrs. Nosy Red Lips' office, and definitely no drama. And what do you know? Justin is in my Biology Lab double period class as well. I glance his way and take a lab stool at Bev's side. Okay. He glances my way a couple of times, but I don't talk to him. I find it odd that Hammer hadn't made an appearance at my locker. Nor did any other ghost, for that matter.

Merva and Bev are nice enough to let me be their third-wheel lab partner. They are great with catching me up and I feel wonderful. Ten minutes into the class, Mr. Morrow, the teacher, assigns me to Justin because his lab partner transferred out of the school at the end of the day yesterday. Was that the same student who had been absent in English Lit yesterday? Doesn't matter.

My heart doesn't know whether to sink at leaving my two new friends or to quicken that I am assigned to Justin. He is smart, not a slacker like Liam. Maybe it is fate. Maybe I could convince him to make new friends and, unlike the song, forget about the old. Maybe he'll have a chance to change the reputation that had to come from hanging out with someone like my cousin. I'd be a positive influence who just might save him from another black eye or beating from his father.

I settle next to him at the lab table and put my backpack on the floor. "Hey," I say with a hesitant grin.

"Morning, Mel," he replies. He eyes his Pinedale shirt.

"I thought I'd fit in better…maybe," I mutter opening my laptop to take lecture notes.

Okay. He is already logging on and not too talkative. I swallow and duck my eyes around the room. Maybe it is too early in the day to talk to him. Once in the notes section, I enter the day and date, ready to start.

Then the lights flicker and the power goes out. That tingling feeling begins. I hear hoots and hollers, but not from any living students in the room. Nope. The living students just sit there like they are all holding their breath. Strange sounds echo through the air duct right above us, reverberating off its metal walls.

I jump off the lab stool and look up, too. But no one else does. They stare…at me. That wormy feeling hits my stomach. Breakfast does a quick shuffle as if it is deciding whether or not to stay down. *Oh. Just great.* If I hurl, I'll be the gross object of attention. Someone to ridicule. The smell alone will label me outcast with a capital O like for forever! I cough once and sink back down on the tall stool. Everyone's eyes are still on me. I shift my look down and swipe my short hair behind my ears as tears threaten to spill.

Mr. Morrow announces we'll switch to handwritten notes since the Internet isn't available. But I feel paralyzed. I know what I hear. I know this power outage is on purpose. The teacher turns to write an outline on the whiteboard. Everyone scurries to get their notebooks and pens out, muttering how this hasn't happened in a long time or something. Various conversations can be heard as the teacher continues putting the outline for chapter thirty about blood cells on the whiteboard. I still feel paralyzed amidst the ghostly hoots and hollers.

Justin rips two sheets of paper out of his notebook. "No worries," he whispers. "Mel? You okay?"

Afraid I will burst out with the truth, I nod *really* slowly. He slides the paper in front of me and closes my laptop, moving it aside. My hands feel perma-glued to the table while listening to the cacophony of laughter coming from an uninhabitable space above. A pen appears before me. Justin's hand comes over mine.

"You're good. Just breathe," he whispers so no one can hear.

But *I* hear him and I sense his concern. I pick up the pen with my left hand and slant the paper so I can easily write the outline in a comfortable position that doesn't make my penmanship look like chicken scratch. I try to listen to the teacher's voice over the ghostly antics that are right above me. Feelings flush my face. Students take quick glances at me. I feel their decisions to stay away and leave the new girl sitting next to the Goth freak alone. Merva and Bev keep looking at each other. I feel its meaning. It is what I hoped *not* to see or feel. Some students are curious. Some are praying. But the majority are judgy.

I am suddenly thrown back in time to Willow Valley High. My spine stiffens. My heart beats like a war drum. Anxiety meets up with aggression, and they slither through me. *You don't know what I know! You got this all wrong. You don't see what I see!* I try to step out of myself and get a grip. I don't want the same reputation here. I want to be normal like the rest of them!

I drop the pen and put my fingers in my ears. It can't be disguised and it doesn't look subtle, just weird. My hair isn't long enough to cover the action. And I know what happens next. *Just run out of the room and go hide in a bathroom stall. Let the teacher call security just like in Willow Valley.* Take the detention and get sent to Mrs. Nosy Red Lips for an I-told-you-so.

Justin shoots off the high stool. "What the frig is wrong with you people? Got nothing better to look at?"

"Justin, sit down," the teacher orders.

"No, man. You're all staring at me. Look at you! Why? Take the friggin' notes and learn something for Christ's sake." He picks up his backpack and struts out of the room with the teacher calling his name.

That snaps me back to reality like a rubber band snapping against my wrist. I sit up and blink. The students go wild, talking to each other and shouting. The teacher keeps telling them to calm down. I sit there almost afraid to breathe. Something makes me reach over and pull Justin's notebook to my side of the table. I glance down and bite my lips, no longer worried about anyone else but him. "*I know it's not you! You heard something and felt something. This place is haunted. Meet me by the rocks during lunch period. I'm out of here!*"

Oh. My. God.

The students calm down some. The teacher is talking again and explaining white blood cells. The lights flicker and then stay on. The air conditioning hums after a quick burst of freezing air. Not one ghost makes another sound.

Then Hank the janitor walks into the room. "Everything's back on, Mr. Morrow. Just a tripped switch. I need to check the air vent in the back, though."

As Hank comes closer, I know what this is really about. "You okay, little lady?" he asks for the entire class to hear. "Did that fast burst of icy cold air startle you? This particular vent is a main feed. And you were just lucky enough to be right smack dab under it today. Don't that beat all? Why I jumped up like a jack-in-the-box the time it happened to me one night when I was in here, mopping the floor right under it."

Everyone turns to me. Some of the girls have their hands on their necks, their mouths perfect "Ohs" and their eyes wide...including Merva and Bev. There came a chorus of "Are you okay?" and "Thank the good Lord above it never happened to me." Then the teacher says, "Melody? Are you okay? Do you need a pass to the nurse?" His tone is full of concern.

Hank glances at me with a knowing grin. I know I have to answer, and I have to play along. "I'm...I'm fine, Mr. Morrow. Thanks. It just...just startled me, I mean the icy-cold blast and all. Uh...we didn't have air-conditioning vents in my old school. Just…uh…window units."

As Hank walks away, Merva and Bev come over. "Oh my, girl, that must have scared you out of your wits!" Merva takes my hand.

"You come sit with us, Mel," Bev adds with her eyebrows tight. "Justin's a freak, bolting out like that. He'll probably end up suspended for cutting class again." She picks up my backpack and my laptop. But I quickly slide my two loose papers over Justin's notebook and hug it to my chest.

Hank the janitor walks out of the biology lab. Someone brings a stool over to Merva and Bev's table. I whisper a quick "Thanks," and sit down.

"Nothing like a power outage to start the day," Mr. Morrow announces with a chuckle. "Let's save some Internet energy and stick with hand-written notes today. You know…the old-fashioned way."

There are some grumbles and some giggles. I turn to a clean page in Justin's notebook and start to copy the outline off the whiteboard. It's the least I can do for him saving my butt, not to mention deflecting attention so I don't look like the oddball I truly am.

Chapter 16

Act One Scene Two

As Merva, Bev, and I make our way over the glass enclosed walk-across, several students who had been in biology lab stop and ask me if I am okay. Loads of "Thanks" and "Sures" come with a personal sense of gratitude for Hank, the janitor's quick thinking cover-up.

Approaching the vocal music room, Mrs. Montgomery stands outside. Her hand brushes her forehead, and you can see her eyes, red-rimmed and glistening, even behind her glasses. Students from both ends of the corridor stop and encircle her, very concerned.

"I have some bad news and some good news," she starts with. "The vocal music room was vandalized yesterday sometime after school." There is a collective gasp. "The police are still investigating and we can't use it today. That's the bad news. The good news is that we will begin to hold motet choir class in the auditorium, so we'll have an earlier prep on the end-of-year concert. In fact, all choral classes will meet there until the end of the school year, I think."

"What about jazz band, Mrs. Montgomery?" Bev asks with concern. "I mean their set up on stage is like all over the space."

"I've talked to the principal as well as Mr. Gordon, the band director. We will rehearse in front of the curtain so as not to interfere with their set up."

"But the risers," Bev adds with more genuine worry in her voice.

"We'll angle the baby grand so that all of you will be in auditorium seats…for the time being. Let's just be thankful that there are no band schedule conflicts with chorus classes. That would be a nightmare. Now. Enough. I need two volunteers to get our choir folders out of the music room cabinet." She resettles her tote over a shoulder and hugs her laptop to her chest.

My hand shoots up immediately. So do many others. "Okay…Harrison and Melody. Come in with me."

And then the classroom door opens. All I can do is gasp. Written across the white board in glossy purple paint is "Go away!" in drippy, ugly letters. The upright piano is turned on its side. Mrs. Montgomery's desk is turned on its side, too, with papers strewn everywhere. Across the pretty bulletin boards and that wonderful saying about music being the heart, the soul, the rhythm of life, well, the hairs on my arms stand on end. "You don't belong! You never will!" is painted in bold black letters. These drips are huge, all the way down the wall to the floor. Some file cabinets are open. Octavos litter everywhere.

Harrison and I step around them. Yellow police tape crisscrosses the room. Luckily, the motet choir cabinet is just a few feet inside and to our left. Harrison hands me a bunch, holds the rest in the crook of his arm, and gives me a soft, "Come on. Let's get out of here. This place gives me the creeps."

I am in total shock. "Who…who would do something like this?"

"Liam and his goth gang of assholes," he murmurs.

What! My cousin along with his motley crew of Cam and Blaze? I realize I hadn't seen Liam last night. *Ohmygod! Is that what they were talking about in the living room while I ate a chicken leg? Is that why Aunt Sarah was crying?*

"How can you be sure?" I ask as we head into the hallway and begin to follow the class, led by poor Mrs. Montgomery, to the stairwell at the other side.

"I heard they arrested him and two others. The principal grabbed Justin before because I heard a detective was waiting to question him in the office."

"But he was nowhere *near* the school after the bell rang," I offer in his defense.

"That don't account for the rest of the night. And how would you know that anyway?" Harrison states with a shake of his head.

I shrug. "I…I don't, but he's not like the others." Again. Said in his defense.

"You don't never know somebody, Melody," he says with a thick drawl in a low voice.

"Call me Mel, okay?"

"Yup," he says with a slow nod.

"What if Justin has an alibi…until like eight o'clock or so. I mean, forensics can determine exactly how long it takes paint to dry, right?"

"You got a point, I guess," he offers.

I most certainly do have a point! But what will I be able to do about it? Just as I think that, Hammer appears at my other side. I jerk, just a little.

"I told you to stay away from him. What more has

to happen until you listen, Melody Marie?"

"Don't call me that," eked out.

Harrison turns to me on the stairwell landing to the first floor. "You say something?"

"Oh…I…I prefer Mel. My bad if that came out rude. I didn't really mean it to."

"Nope. Just kinda strange. I swear I'll only call you Mel from now on," he replies.

Thank God he seems clueless, harmless in a way. I get the intense feeling that all Harrison has going for him is his voice and his love of music. Hammer walks through the security door before Harrison opens it. I keep the frown off my face and thank him for the gentlemanly gesture as I walk through. I make some lame excuse about my backpack cutting into my shoulder. Harrison, once again full of southern manners, takes the chorus folders from me and races ahead to catch up with the others.

I hang back. Since the halls are clear, I turn around as I slowly reposition my backpack over both shoulders like a dork. "Listen. You have no say in me staying or leaving this school. You're not only rude, but dangerous by the looks of what you and your ghost friends are doing. Having fun yet? Blaming that horrible destruction of school property on my cousin?"

"Yeah, man. It was fun. He turned over the teacher's desk with his two friends after school. We did the rest after he left. Found the paint in the art room and went to town. Just because of you being here. I told you to stay away from Justin. Learn your lesson, and maybe, just maybe, we'll be cool and dial it back some."

"We need to talk," I say, knowing I have to turn

around and start moving again.

"Maybe. After school," he says, all full of himself.

"Meet me in the library," I mutter with my hand hiding my mouth.

"No can do. It's off limits to us. Think of someplace else," he says.

"By the rocks behind the school," I add, scratching my nose with my mouth hidden again.

"Right after school, Melody Marie. If you're not there when I am, all bets are off as to what happens next."

Is that a threat? Hell yeah, and before I can say it out loud, just like that he walks through the wall and disappears. Harrison is waiting at the auditorium door, holding it open for me.

"You're a peach," I say to him with a smile.

"Yes ma'am, uh…Mel," he answers with a puffed-out chest and a goofy grin. I even think I see him blush.

****

The auditorium is really beautiful, not to mention ice-cold. The huge stage has ruby-red curtains already closed. The stage is pretty big, but not nearly as big as the one in Willow Valley High. The seats are cushioned in material that matches the curtains. Between the audience and the stage sits a beautiful baby grand.

We hand out folders as Mrs. Montgomery takes attendance on her laptop, and we settle in the reverse way to our sections. A student comes in and hands the teacher a note. She reads it and her head shakes as she swipes a tear off the corner of her eye. She does a quick inhale and blows out a breath in a sad way as Justin strides down the aisle, many minutes late for motet choir class. He takes an aisle seat at the end of the bass section.

Vocal exercises begin. All is right with my world. I am standing next to Bev, doing my best to control my breathing and participate. In spite of Hammer and the disaster of the music room, I relax as tight harmonies of a major chord fill my starving soul. The intensity of four different notes moving up the scale has me in some altered state of joy I can't put into words. Soothing is not strong enough. Ethereal may be a better choice. In any case, it sends a sense of peace through me. Anticipation as well. Bringing little black dots with stems on a page to life is a thrill like none other.

Then, all that peace within me shatters as two police officers are suddenly pulling Justin out of his auditorium seat. Mrs. Montgomery stops playing and actually starts to cry with her hands covering her nose and her mouth. Students scream and all hell breaks loose for the second time today.

Justin fights the two cops off until one grabs him by the back of the neck and slams him down on the floor. The click of handcuffs is something I have never heard before! He keeps screaming, "Let me up! I didn't do anything! I swear I didn't do anything!"

They don't seem to care. They don't seem to listen. They just hustle him up and practically carry him as he kicks and shouts—all the way down the aisle and out the auditorium doors.

Like many of the other girls, I have my hand over my mouth, staring in horror at what I have just witnessed. But I am the only one shaking from head to toe. Just like Mrs. Montgomery, my eyes fill and I bite back a sob. Everyone around me sinks down to their seats. I do as well.

Mrs. Montgomery swipes the corners of her eyes and walks around the piano to address the class. She sniffles before saying, "I'm so sorry ya'll had to witness this. It hurts my heart to think that anyone could do what they did to our music room."

Why isn't anyone coming to Justin's defense? Why can I not say I know where he was after school yesterday?

"Let's all sit here a moment, shall we," Mrs. Montgomery says in a kind, soft voice. "I have to believe that Justin Hammersmith isn't capable of doing something like this. You have to remember that until something is proven beyond a doubt, that person is innocent. No matter how much you want to judge a person by the company he or she keeps, you cannot pass judgement."

"But, Mrs. Montgomery," someone says breaking the silence.

"Nope. Now ya'll listen to me, everyone. Fingerprints were taken this morning. I'm sure other DNA will also tell us who did this. Three students are already in custody, I understand. I will not give you their names, although I'm sure there is already talk around the school. Humph. Loose lips love to gossip." She turns aside and blows her nose before facing a group of stunned students again.

I feel her sadness. I feel her search her heart against deceit, not knowing for sure if Justin is capable of this kind of duplicity or not. She is a good soul with morals and values. I know that whether or not it is allowed in public school, many students join her in silent prayer for a boy they know much better than I do. I also know that every single student in the auditorium sees my cousin as the real perpetrator of this vile act of vandalism.

I let my senses fully open to a group of students I really want to belong to. Many of them have scenes swirling through their minds…Books slapped out of their hands. Mocking words on the walk home or during change of classes. Lunches taken away and thrown in the trash bins making him or her go hungry. Bully me this and bully me that. Liam's face is in every memory, for years it seems.

In some memories he is younger, not tough like he is now. In others, he is as I met him a few days ago, a mean Goth-boy with a huge chip on his shoulder. It makes no difference when he started down this path, but I'll bet that once he walked into Pinedale High as a freshman, his mischievous spirit seemed to bond with the ghosts that were pranksters in life and pranksters in their afterlife. Did he feed off their malice or did they feed off of his?

My worry for Justin deepens. My concern for Liam does not. I will have lots to say to Hammer when we meet behind the school at the rocks this afternoon.

I get the feeling that we won't be doing any singing during the rest of this period. Maybe it is a blessing that Mrs. Montgomery let students talk among themselves. Some ask questions about what they had just witnessed. She answers them with care and concern.

I just sit here taking it all in. I have no desire to talk to Bev or the other student sitting next to me. I guess I give off that kind of vibe because no one turns to talk to me. So I go deep into myself to worry about Justin. He isn't like Liam or those other two clowns. He is a sensitive soul, just like me, only *my* parent loves me and shows it. *His* parent uses fists. I don't even want to imagine what will happen to him now. But I keep hearing the click of those handcuffs in my head. I keep hearing his screams.

Chapter 17

Confronting the Ghost

Everyone is talking about it. The look on Justin's face and the way he fought the police. Him being hustled out of the school and again fighting the cops before being thrown into a police car. The damage in the music room. At lunch, the gossip is on overload. So are conversations about the school being cursed, happening at just about every table.

I shut down my feelings and push everyone else's far away. Because I know Justin is innocent and, although Liam is not, he had some other-worldly help in all that vandalism after school yesterday. I watch the gleeful ghosts from the 1950s circle the wagons and move like a subtle wind as they eavesdrop in the cafeteria. I see Andy and Terry, aka Hammer's biker boys, do the same, but they walk through tables, and look pretty damned pleased with themselves.

Nothing says I-know-what-you-did like their ghost snickers and meaningless high fives. But without Hammer, they look kinda lost. Like they have no one to show off their bravado. And they keep their distance from me, which is a smart thing to do.

I sit with Merva and Bev. We talk about the books flying at the end of the day yesterday, the incident in biology lab, and then, of course, our chorus room. I smatter a few comments here or there, very aware of Hank, the janitor, watching both sets of ghost students, and also eyeing me. He knows I see them. He knows they are staying as far away from me as they possibly can without ending up in a wall or outside on Pinedale's sprawling lawn.

I text my mother to see how the move is going. I also ask her to pick me up after four instead of three o'clock. I receive two thumbs up as a response and then turn off my phone and put it back in my backpack.

I buy a chicken wrap and eat very slowly, in a way too upset to keep on chewing. I think it is because of seeing Justin arrested. But these forty lunch minutes fly by. So does the double period of English Lit—with no ghosts in the room, thank you very much.

Miss Woodson gives us the first period to review Romeo and Juliet and the second half of the class to answer essay questions. For the most part, students are silent, mostly still in shock over the sight and sounds of Justin's arrest. I don't have a problem burying my head and writing like a fiend to answer in depth every single question. Words come easy and writing is a favorite outlet for me. In fact, I am still writing when the end-of-day three beeps sound. I hurry to get the rest of my thoughts down, send my responses to the English Lit Google docs cache, and catch a breath before leaving the school for the day. I use the back door, not the front one.

I have somewhere to be. And I have a heck of a lot to say.

****

I hike past students getting ready for field hockey practice as quick as I can. I only have Justin's notebook and my school laptop in my backpack, but it feels as heavy as a barbell or two. I have thoughts swirling through my head about what to say and how to say it.

The conversation with Hammer's grandfather comes to mind. I haven't had the time to do any more research into the fact that Andy's father was behind the wheel of that green pickup truck. I haven't looked up Hammer's obituary, either. Seeing Justin arrested keeps pulling my attention away from thinking through the conversation that will soon take place.

I pass the thinner bush line and take what seems a pretty well-worn path that snakes through the tall pine trees. When I get to the rock, Hammer is leaning against it. With his two sycophants. Like true Neanderthals, Andy and Terry think they will surround me. *Can someone please tell you that you aren't solid?*

"I thought you'd blow me off," Hammer says with his leathered arms crossed tight and a sideways glance before he stares into nothing but air. Talk about arrogance!

"I said I'd be here and I am." Turning, I add, "I really don't think you two standing behind me is going to do any good. Why don't you join your leader so I can look all three of you in the eyes."

Then I have three ghosts leaning like they are the cat's meow against the graffiti on the rocks, all with their leathered arms locked to their chests. Arrogance triples, just like that!

I bite the corner of my lip before saying, "You all have some nerve."

"It's ya'll, girl," Terry says like some brain-trust with a drawl.

"I'm a Jersey girl. I value every vowel," is my

reply.

"Well what do you know," Andy chimes in. "You're just one fascinating chick, Melody. All sassy and brave."

I let out a scoff and add a pfft. "You think you're the first ghosts I've seen? The first I've talked to? Why don't you and your sidekick ghost out. I want to speak to Hammer alone."

"No way," and "Nuh-huh," rival each other for indignation.

"She can't talk to us that way, right, Hammer?" the over eager Terry states.

"You heard the girl," Hammer replies. "Go get in a few trips with the field hockey team and leave us alone for a few."

Yeah. They leave. Just disappear into thin air. I suddenly feel sorry for the field hockey players. I hope there are no broken ankles and pray a quick prayer. Then I look at Hammer and I feel my right eyebrow rise.

"So what's your beef with me?" he asks as if he couldn't care less.

"This isn't the John Hammersmith that died in the 1970s. He may have looked tough but he was super-smart, not mean and menacing."

"You looked at the yearbooks," he says.

"Yeah. And I spoke to a nice librarian who married into Terry's family. So cut the crap. Look at me, too."

He rolls his green eyes which also seem to flutter. His jaw juts as if his tongue is working his teeth, but his arms appear to flex—his fists, as well.

"What's gotten into you?" I ask as if we are friends.

"I told you to stay away from Justin. You didn't listen. I told you I'd help you with the math section. You didn't listen. Then I warned you to stay away from that no-good kid again. And that was strike three, so you're out. Now I do what I do when I want to do it, and screw anyone who gets hit by a book or scared out of their wits. You brought it on yourself."

My jaw drops and my eyes widen. "I can't believe this is all because I talk to your great-nephew."

"The kid's trash. So is his father. So was my uncle."

"That's not true. You have your facts all wrong, I'm sure," I offer in defense of a friend.

"How would you know? Just because you see ghosts doesn't mean you know what happened."

"Well then why don't you tell me. Tell me all of it, and then I'll tell you what I know."

Hammer shakes his head. "Man, you got this all wrong. I mean, get in the groove and just admit you're in way over your head."

"I won't do that. I can't do that. Maybe I know something you don't. Maybe, just maybe, that something will stop your endless haunting of Pinedale High and you'll be able to cool it with the book throwing and air-conditioning episodes."

He comes off the wall and gets right in my face. Oh boy! He is *really* eye-candy with a twist of supernatural thrown in for good measure. "I died, okay? The three of us died, and why? Because we rode motorcycles. We dressed different. In blue bell-bottom jeans and muscle shirts. Yeah. And leather jackets. We were cool. We were in with chicks."

"You were an honor student with all straight A's.

Andy and Terry weren't, though. So you were their leader."

"Yeah. The 'Leader of the Pack.' I really grooved to that song."

"He died going around a curve in the road."

He steps back. "You know that song?"

I shrug. "My mother likes songs from the 60s and 70s. Classic vinyl too."

"I love 'Dark Side of the Moon,' " he whispers.

"Yeah. My favorite off that album is 'Great Gig in the Sky.' "

Hammer just stares at me. "Mine, too," he whispers as if suddenly far away.

"So be real with me." I swallow my hesitance, saying, "How did you die?"

"We were just having fun." Hammer slides down the rock and sits cross-legged on the ground. He plays with the small pebbles in the dirt. I take off my backpack and join him a good three feet away where the grassy patch starts. I sit the same way and wait.

"It was just a few weeks until graduation. I was going to go to college. So was Terry. Man, Andy's dad was a hard-ass. I heard rumors that he was deep in debt. I worked for my uncle at the gas station and had learned to fix cars. When an old motorcycle came in, I went for it with gusto and, man, I could fix that thing up and make it purr. My father told me not to ride the bike. I didn't agree. In fact, I got one fixed up for Terry and then Andy as well. His father, Andy's father, went ballistic. He actually came to the garage and told my uncle I was a bad influence on his son."

Hammer stops and shakes his head. I take in everything about the gorgeous senior who lost his life fifty years ago. The way his long brown hair frames such a perfect face. The way he sweeps it aside with a sure hand. The way emotion claims his face. I read it all. In life, the frustration at being misunderstood and the way he really did have it all together. The way he got a thrill to push having fun to its limits.

"We'd sneak out at night and meet at Pinedale. Play some touch football on the front lawn and then sit on the steps to the school talking about girls and life and shit. Andy got there late. Had a fight with his dad, which happened a lot that last year of high school. Terry and I had smoked a joint." Hammer looks aside and runs both hands through his hair.

I don't want to come off judgy, but I ask, "Did you get high a lot?'

"Nope. Just to relax every now and then. It wasn't like a habit or something." He laughs. "Andy didn't smoke, but he liked wine. Maybe too much. I smelled it on his breath that night. But there was always drama going on between Andy and his dad, going all the way back to when we were kids and his mamma died. We—"

I jump as my phone chimes, and then Hank is standing just a few feet away where the bushes are. "Um… I gotta go," I say.

Hammer didn't wait for an explanation. He just eyeballs the janitor and ghosts out. That leaves me and Hank. I stand up and brush off the seat of my shorts. Then I grip both straps of my backpack. Crap. I really want to know more. "Uh…thanks for this morning," I say to Hank.

"Ain't no reason to thank me, Miss Melody. When that kind of ruckus starts, even though the kids can't hear it, they get kinda mean, like the vibrations of the pranksters runs right through them. Plus, with the power outage, well, heck, we had ourselves a doozy in that classroom."

"Yeah, but you covered for me. So did Justin."

"That boy's one step away from seeing what you see. That's what I think," Hank says as we walk back to the school the other way, which is a bit more intense, but at least we wouldn't disturb the field hockey practice.

I am careful with my footing. The path that leads to the bleachers by the football field is a bit steeper. I end up behind Hank instead of next to him when it narrows. "You know they arrested Justin. Handcuffed him right in front of everyone in the auditorium," I say.

"Yep. I saw it all," Hank answers in a weary way.

"He had nothing to do with what happened in the music room."

"I know," Hank replies.

Jeez. I want more information. "Where did they take him?'

"He's at the county juvenile facility with your cousin and the other two."

My heart does a hard thump-thump in my chest. "He's innocent! How could they do that?"

Hank lets out a groan. "In these parts, you're guilty until proven innocent. They ain't lettin' any of them out into the custody of their parents. Not for this amount of damage."

"Liam's there, too?"

"Like I said. All four," Hank tells me as we start across the football field. "Maybe Justin's better off in juvey instead of at home. His daddy is quick with his fists. Always was."

Again, my heart flutters. "It can't be that bad."

"Old Jeb's a nasty one. And Justin goes off like a firecracker. He has some mouth on him."

"That's no reason to be abused," I answer. Why do I want to keep defending Justin? Maybe what I sense in him is totally off.

"Nope. Beating on a kid like that ain't right. The state almost took him away from Jeb a year ago. They should have followed through. Listen, Mel," he says as we stop walking and approach the school. "Don't get yourself too attached to that boy. He keeps tailing your cousin the way he does, well, he won't be graduating, but he'll be joining Hammer and the others walking Pinedale."

I literally shiver. Say nothing. I mean, what is the comeback to something like that? And why would Hank tell me this? Hank goes toward the side security door while I walk to the front of the school. The high-pitched beep of the blue box-on-wheels startles me. I hurry my steps across the lawn and get in.

"I said four o'clock, not four-fifteen, Melody. And with so much to do," my mother states. As I give a quick "Sorry," and click my seatbelt, she shoots off the curb and seems to forget that there's a speed limit in a school zone, even down south.

Her mood reads so stressed that I shiver again, as if sensing someone's inner-dragon just got poked enough to open an eye or maybe begin to breathe out a stream of fire. At the stop sign, Mom should have made a left, but she makes a hard right turn and the tires shriek. I watch out the window, taking in another part of Pinedale, North Carolina. Then the streets turn busier with more cars than I have seen up to this point, but not like in Willow Valley where after school traffic collided with end-of-workday traffic to create a slow crawl of cars and way too many waiting for lights to change.

The houses are closer together in this part of town. Less lawns and not too much curb appeal. We pass Tully's Guns and Ammo written in bright red block letters, and I definitely know I'm not in north Jersey anymore. Then I see a green sign with the gold letters welcoming us to downtown Pinedale, NC. The main street is lined with stores, including a quaint coffee shop with three tables outside. But it feels as if I've stepped back in time.

All the store fronts are forest-green as if there had been a sale on the paint color at…Zeke's Hardware and Feed Store? I take it all in, including the sea of pickup trucks, all makes and models.

Then Mom turns into an old-fashioned gas station and brakes hard. My eyebrows shoot up and I grip the door as I read Hammersmith and Son Car Repairs. Mom pulls up to the pumps and unclicks her seatbelt. When she gets out, I scream, almost in a panic, "Where are you going?"

"There's no such thing as gas station attendants outside of New Jersey. I have to pump my own." She grabs her wallet from the center console and slams the door.

I sit there watching a wiry man, with what my mother calls a crew cut, stand up from under the hood of a car and stare her way. He has on greasy gray overalls. Funny. Even at this distance I can tell that his eyes are blue and his face resembles wrinkled leather. He immediately gives me the creeps. He approaches our vehicle while wiping his hands on a dull blue rag stained with car gunk. I see him glance down at the license plate and frown with narrowed eyes.

I hear gas flowing from the pump into the car. I smell it through the open window. Something tenses inside of me as I stare at his hands. Those are what he used to fix cars and beat his son. Old Jeb, as Hank called him, doesn't look like someone you want to tangle with. I grow more anxious as the smell fills the car. Anger grows within me, not fear. I want to jump out and say, *"How could you do what you do to your son?"* but I don't. I just sit there and take in another glimpse into Justin's life. Between the rust stains and the worn wood around the garage and the business area, it all looks in dire need of repair.

The pump clicks. Mom replaces it. Old Jeb grumbles an amount. Mom pays him cash and says, "Thanks." He doesn't say "You're welcome" or anything in return. He just pockets the bills and watches her get back in and close the door. I blow out a slow sigh of relief.

She clicks her seatbelt and looks over at me. "What's wrong with you? You look like you've seen a ghost."

"What? No. It's just…well, that's Justin's father," I tell her.

"The nice boy who helped me out last night? How do you know?" she asks, starting the engine and pulling away from the pump. And yeah…he is still staring at us. I feel it. "Melody? I asked you a question."

Waves of stress come off her and I know I have to answer her. "I…I heard someone say that his dad owned the only gas station in town. I just figured that's got to be him."

She makes a left onto the same main street of Pinedale and says nothing. I take in the sights across the street we travel down, now going the other way. Yeah. I really think I have stepped back in time. And my worry for Justin begins to soar.

Chapter 18

Home

What do you say to a kind, loving uncle who's helping his sister while his son is locked up in a juvenile detention center? That's what runs through my mind as we pull up to our new home. Uncle Tim's SUV is in the driveway. Mom pulls up next to it and cuts the engine.

"Mom, wait," I say as she grabs her wallet, and before she gets out.

Her shoulders slump as she sits back and closes her eyes. "I'm sorry for being short with you, Mel. It was only fifteen minutes, but I knew I had to fill the gas tank before I forgot again."

"No worries. That's not what I want to talk about," I say.

She looks over at me. "I'm stressed. It's all too much too fast. What was I thinking? I should have rented a furnished place for a month. Let us get more adjusted to the move. I should have thought this out better. I'm so sorry."

"Mommy, stop, okay," I whisper. "It's the stress talking. I know it. I feel it in you. You don't have to apologize about anything. And I really should have been watching the time instead of…uh…you know, looking around the school grounds." *Oh. What a lie!*

But I had to. "I…I know about Liam."

She looks away and shakes her head. "How?"

"Come on, Mom. It's high school. Kids know things and they talk." Then I tell her about what happened in the auditorium. She clicks her tongue so many times I stop counting.

"Oh, Mel, that must have been traumatic to see. And I thought he was such a nice boy."

"He is. I swear he is." I couldn't tell her about what happened in biology class and how he saved me from ridicule in a class full of peers who were overly excitable because ghosts were disruptive and guffawing and wreaking havoc on everyone's subconscious selves. But I have to defend him. "I know Justin wasn't involved with what Liam and his Goth-boys did. I swear, he wouldn't do something that horrible. Besides, he was right here with us until, I don't know, like maybe eight or so, right? I heard that what happened to the music room happened earlier than eight. Justin was working at his father's garage…you know, the one we gassed up at."

"Well, then his father should tell them. I'm sure they'll release him right away," she replies.

I turn to face her. "You don't get it, do you?"

"Get what?" she asks quickly shaking her head.

"You saw his bruised eye yesterday. How do you think it happened? He didn't walk into a doorknob. His father did that. He beats him! It's…it's all over school. And his father drinks, at least that's what some kids say."

Okay. Another lie. But I can't tell her about Hammer or about what Hank knows about old Jeb, *or* all the ghosts gone wild in Pinedale High. "Mom. I mean it. His father is just going to let him rot in there until all the DNA evidence comes back to prove him innocent. There has to be something we can do to…you know…help him, like maybe vouch for his whereabouts last night."

Her face is serious, freakin' lined with more worries than I have ever seen! My senses hum as I read tons of conflict in her head that settles in her heart. It's like I am inside her skin with her. My eyes fill. "Please. We have to do the right thing. Justin is innocent."

"Let's get inside, Mel," she says and leaves, slamming the driver-side door.

I sit there stunned and angry. I grab my backpack, open the passenger-side door, and slam it shut as well. I follow her in. I glimpse old John Hammersmith standing in the living room that is full of boxes, some empty, some not. I follow her down the hall. When I enter my new room, I stop short.

"Hey, Mel," Uncle Tim says with a smile. "I hope I got everything right."

Now my eyes *really* fill. I drop my backpack and run to him. I hug him so tight as I sniffle back tears. He hugs me back just as tight.

"Your mother wanted it ready for you, so I put your bed together and followed her instructions and your index cards to a T," he whispers.

I pull my stuff together and look up into his kind face. "You're my hero, Uncle Tim. It's… it's just perfect." I smile, swipe my eyes, and stare at my new room.

"Tim," my mother says. "We have to talk."

"Thank you so much," I say as he leaves with my mom.

Then I take it all in, looking at a carbon copy of what I left behind. One wall, the one my bed is on, is dark, rich purple. The other three are lilac and the ceiling a bright white. All four walls are glossy, the way my old room had been. My bed is made the same way it had been in Willow Valley. My desk is set up with my personal laptop on top, already charging. My shelves are filled with books and all of my stuffed animals that hold precious memories of my father. Even my curtains are the same!

I shrug off my backpack and put it in the corner where Jonathan always stood. Then I sit on my bed and let the tears come. This is love. All of this is caring and kindness and understanding and so very unexpected. My room is filled with all the things that make me Melody Marie Warkowski. The only thing missing is Jonathan. Yeah. I let myself cry.

But I have secrets that I can't share with a mother who loves me, and an uncle who puts his own serious worries aside to address mine. Guilt rumbles through me. I have lied to my mother. Not once, but many times. I come off moody and angry because I can't tell anyone the truth. Will this ever get easier?

****

I allow myself ten minutes of poor-me time, and then sit up and haul myself out of the comfort of my bed. My mind doesn't go in the direction of homework, but rather opening my laptop and adding to my diary. I don't like using pen and paper. Maybe because I'm left handed and I tend to slant the page so I can write neatly. Plus, with what I have to say, I would be horrified if someone, especially my mother, finds it.

No. I don't have a word document entitled *"My*

Diary," either. I use my old homework folder and label entries as book reviews. I use third person instead of first person as if I were writing answers to book questions that have been assigned. I am just about to open one of my "reviews" when my mother calls my name and asks me to come into the kitchen.

As much as I want to write down what has happened since leaving north Jersey, I bite my lip and close down my laptop.

Uncle Tim is staring out the kitchen window with his back to me. Mom looks super serious. I stand in the doorway and wait.

"I told Uncle Tim about Justin. You're right, and we both agree that if his father won't help him and we know where he was yesterday, then it's only right that we go and help him."

I open my mouth but nothing comes out.

"So. Here's the plan. We are going to lock up the house, get in Uncle Tim's SUV, and go pick up Aunt Sarah. Then we are going to the juvenile detention center to see Liam and Justin."

Turning to me, my uncle says, "I can't promise you anything, Mel, but if they hear you out, maybe we can clear his name and get him out before all this DNA evidence comes in."

"You'd really do that?" I ask, not sure if I heard what I heard.

He gives a grave nod. "I know the sheriff. He's a fair man. If you're telling the truth, then yes. Your mother will vouch for him as well."

"But what if his father…I mean…"

"I know Jeb. I know he uses his fists. I'll talk to him," my uncle states.

"Maybe have him meet us there," my mother adds.

A little panic takes hold and I say, "No. Mom. He's not a nice man."

Her head tilts to the side. "Honestly, Mel, how do you know so much about all this? I swear, it's just not…not natural."

Oh crap. I have to lie again! "I told you, Mom, kids talk. So do teachers."

"Look, Zoey," my uncle says to her, "Let's just take things one at a time, okay? Sarah's waiting. I say we get on the road and get there. Some of the sheriff's officers over at juvenile hall know me because of Liam." He puts his hand on my mother's shoulder. She picks up her handbag and starts to turn off all the lights in the new place, except for the porch light. Then we leave.

Chapter 19

Emotional Highs

Wake Juvenile Detention Center is in Raleigh, North Carolina. I do my research on the web as Uncle Tim drives, keeping my phone in my left hand out of Mom's view in the back seat. It has twenty-four beds, and right now, I know who fills four of them. There is no lower age limit for those incarcerated, but seventeen is the maximum age. Uncle Tim confirms that Liam and the other boys are being held on trespassing, burglary, and vandalism. No weapons had been found on any one of them, thank God.

I put my phone away and marvel at the flatness of the land as we drive. It isn't hours in the car and, since traffic isn't an issue, we make good time and still have the sun. The building of light-red brick has very few windows and it is only one floor with a flat roof. It looks to be quiet enough, with well-kept grounds and lots of parking, but I have the strong sensation that all is *not* quiet and well-kept within.

Once inside, the veneer of caring is just that, is what I sense. And believe me, my special senses are in high-gear. The air feels warm and smells stale, and I stand to the side with my mother and Aunt Sarah as Uncle Tim talks to someone in uniform behind a desk.

Uncle Tim asks us to sit, and the three of us take

folding chairs as a heavyset man in a different uniform shakes his hand. "Sam," Uncle Tim says in a hushed voice, "thanks for meeting us here and doing this."

"No problem, Tim," whoever this Sam is replies. "Let's talk in the office."

As they leave us, the front door opens and I feel waves of anger coming at me even before I look at who has entered the juvenile facility. He still smells of gasoline and motor oil, still has on the same stained overalls. His icy expression meets my shocked one. Then he walks to the desk and announces, "Jeb Hammersmith, here to see Sheriff Sam Walker."

I know he recognizes all three of us, and when he walks over Aunt Sarah stands up. A look passes between them. I am sure of it. History, maybe? After all, Aunt Sarah grew up in Pinedale, a native North Carolinian, not Uncle Tim who relocated here long before I was even born.

"I'm so sorry, Jeb," my aunt whispers with a catch in her voice. Sadness and worry has her in an emotional tizzy. Not so with Justin's dad. He is all anger and irritation.

"Now Sarah, don't you go blaming yourself again. But this…why it's your boy's influence on them others. Always is," Justin's father mumbles, but the vein in his forehead is popping.

My aunt looks aside as if in shame. "I know. I'm sorry."

Jeb snorts. "You can say that until the cows come home, but it ain't making a difference. My boy's no good, neither. But yours got him outrun by a long mile. And this latest run-in with the law's gonna be the one that puts him in here for sure. Ain't gonna happen with my kid, Sarah. Nope. He don't need no record. I'll beat him down good, this time. Bringin' shame on my name again," he adds with a look of disgust.

And that does it for me. "Justin's innocent," I blurt out.

His ice-blue eyes snap to me in a squint. "And who the hell are you?"

My mother grabs my arm, but forget about being shushed.

"I'm Mel. Melody Marie Warkowski, and Justin was with me and my mom after he left work at your garage yesterday. He wasn't with Liam at all. He had nothing to do with what happened in the music room, and I'm here to vouch for him." Jeez, those sentences ran together like strands of spaghetti, but I had to say it.

Justin's father sizes me up first and then my mother. He runs a soiled hand across his mouth in a deliberate way. "What makes you think he didn't do this?"

"My daughter just said he was with us, helping us set up our new home, right down the block from my brother's house," my mother answers with an edge in her tone. "I don't appreciate you speaking to my daughter in that tone, Mister…Mister…"

"Hammersmith," I offer in a whisper as I lean into her.

Mom takes my hand. "Mister Hammersmith. Justin was a big help for a good three hours yesterday. He was polite. He even offered to clean up our backyard this coming Sunday. Look. I trust my daughter's take on people. Mel doesn't tolerate liars or bullies. Which means that Justin isn't in either category. And yes, I will vouch for your son's whereabouts when that vandalism occurred at the school. And as for your beating him down good, I will certainly tell the authorities what you plan to do to a child."

He takes a step closer with a mean look in his eyes. "Ain't none of your business what I do to my kid."

"Oh it most certainly is my business," my mother answers as she stands toe to toe with him, even though he is like six feet tall. "A child's welfare is everyone's business. And since you made this threat in front of an officer sitting right over there at the desk, you have more witnesses than needed to shut you down, for once and for all. I saw your son's black eye yesterday. I'll bet you were the one who gave it to him."

Way to go, Mom! You tell him, General! Take no prisoners!

I watch her sit back down when Justin's father takes more than a few steps back. He sinks into a folding chair across the room from us. He doesn't make eye contact with any of us. As for that anger within him, I'd like to say it has gone *poof* like a burst balloon losing all its air, but it hasn't. It sizzles like a frying egg in a hot skillet.

The door opens and Uncle Tim walks out with Sheriff Sam right behind. Justin's father all but leaps across the room and tackles my uncle. I can't believe what I am seeing! My aunt screams. My mother pulls me into her arms as Jeb Hammersmith punches my kind Uncle Tim. It seems forever before the sheriff pulls him off my uncle.

"Simmer down, Jeb," the sheriff states with authority in his voice. He has Justin's father up against the wall next to the office door. "Or I'll arrest you right here on the spot for assault, and this time, I'll make sure your victim presses charges against you."

Justin's father's face is as red as a stoplight. "You should've told me Tim was gonna be here, Sam. His boy's no good."

"His boy is his business. Your boy is yours. Now settle down," the sheriff orders. His hands come off the bully, but only right before the sheriff shoves him into the office. The door slams closed.

My aunt is sobbing as she helps Uncle Tim up. His lip is bleeding and you could see that his cheek and chin will bruise. Mom hands her a tissue. Aunt Sarah dabs at the blood as Uncle Tim pulls his face away. "I'm all right, Sarah," he says like he doesn't want to call attention to himself. "I'm sorry you had to witness this, Mel," he whispers.

"Ohmygod! Are you okay?" I huff with my hand over my racing heart.

"I'm fine," he quickly replies. "Don't you go worrying over me."

My mother takes the chair on the other side of me so he can sit next to Aunt Sarah. As he sighs and sits down, he says, "I told Sheriff Sam that Justin was with you, Zoey. It's confirmed, now, since they have Justin's fingerprints, that only Liam, Blaze, and Cam's fingerprints were on the overturned desk."

"Oh thank God," my mother whispers. "I'm so sorry, Tim. What happens now?'

"But Uncle Tim," I quickly say. "There was so much damage to the music room. I mean, file cabinets turned over, not to mention the piano on its side and graffiti all over the walls in purple and black paint."

Holding his chin, Uncle Tim shakes his head. "No fingerprints anywhere else in the room but on the desk.

They can't connect the rest of the damage to Liam and his friends, either. Without proof, it's still considered vandalism, but only the overturned desk. As for the rest of the damage, it can't be pinned on my son or anyone else."

"What happens to Justin, then?" my mother asks.

"He'll be released into the custody of his father tonight," my uncle states.

"His father will beat him," I say in a squeaky voice and a little panicked.

My uncle shakes his head again. "There's nothing we can do about that, Mel."

"There has to be!" I exclaim.

"He's a minor. He can only be released to kin."

"And what about Liam?" Aunt Sarah asks. "Can we see him?"

"Only you and me. Zoey and Mel will have to stay here."

Aunt Sarah sniffles. "Can we bring him home?"

"Sam wants to keep him and the others overnight. Maybe tomorrow after they go before the judge," my uncle answers.

As my aunt collapses against my uncle's chest, my eyes start to tear up. I can't imagine spending even one night in this place! Locked in a cell and all alone. Then another uniformed officer opens a different door and says, "Mr. and Mrs. Timothy Cooper?"

"That's us," my uncle states as they stand. They are told to follow him through that door. When it closes I look at my mother and bite my lower lip. Then the door on the other side of Sheriff Sam's office opens and Justin appears with another officer.

I shoot up out of the chair and stare at him. He is

paler than usual and his eyes look glassy with lots of little red veins running to his dark-blue pupils. The officer walks him over to the chairs across the room where his father had been. With a hand on Justin's shoulder, he says, "Take a seat, son."

Justin swipes his face. "Mel? What are *you* doing here?"

"We…my mom and I came to vouch for your whereabouts yesterday," I say.

"Is that why they're releasing me?"

"I think so. Your fingerprints weren't found in the music room, Justin," I reply.

He seems to shiver and looks away, shaking his head. "It doesn't matter. Everyone thinks I'm guilty," he mumbles.

"Don't look at it that way, Justin," my mother interjects. "The fact is, you aren't. People are going to say what they say and you can't control gossip. But what you *can* do is change your friends and steer clear of troublemakers like my nephew."

"Liam and the others said they had nothing to do with the painted graffiti or anything else. They said they turned over the desk and ran out."

"If that's the truth, then it will be proved," my mother answers. "I'd still change my friends, though. I think you have a good head on your shoulders. My daughter says you're pretty smart. Do you plan on going to college?"

He shrugs and runs an arm across his eyes. "Not in the cards for me."

"Why?" she asks, which I can't believe because Mom isn't the nosy type.

"I got the garage. I like working on cars, you know,

doing something with my hands."

"Then what about trade school? You can expand your father's business. I mean, with all the technical components in a car today, it couldn't hurt. Why don't you think on that and talk to the guidance counselor about it?"

We both snicker at the same time. Justin whispers, "You mean talk to Mrs. Nosy Red Lips? Like I'm worth something and like she'd actually help me?"

My mother looks at me, probably for an explanation. "She's not really with it, Mom," I offer. "That whole thing... Like caring for students? I don't think she has that gene."

She looks shocked. "You mean to tell me that there's only one guidance counselor at Pinedale?"

"Never seen any others, Mrs. Warkowski," Justin says with his elbows on his knees and his chin in his hands.

Before my mother has a comeback, Sheriff Sam's office door opens and Justin's father walks out. A much calmer version, for sure. Justin stands, but the officer pushes him back down into his chair. Held by the upper arm, the sheriff walks his father over to him. The sheriff looks even broader next to Mr. Hammersmith, who is thin and wiry, but they are the same height.

"The charges against you will be dropped in the morning at your court appearance, Justin. There is no corroborating evidence to support our holding you accountable for the vandalism at Pinedale High. We regret the arrest in front of your classmates, son, but you should not have resisted my officers. In light of all charges being dropped, you're released into your father's custody. Both of you will appear tomorrow morning at nine a.m. in juvenile court for the conclusion of this matter."

Justin continues to stare into his father's eyes. Maybe he is scared. Maybe he knows what will happen as soon as they get home. I feel a shiver run up my spine. I wish I had the power to make sure his father opens his eyes and really sees his son, and that he won't hurt Justin again.

As if Sheriff Sam reads my mind, he says, "I just had a heart to heart with your father. Right, Jeb?" His father nods in a slow fashion. "Should you show up tomorrow with anything other than your healing black eye, you will be taken away from your father and placed in foster care until the age of eighteen and he will be ordered by the court to remain no less than fifty feet away from you at all times. Should he break the perimeters of the restraining order, he will be arrested for child endangerment. With his history of abuse, he will serve time in jail, Justin. Get that, Jeb?" His father nods really slowly again. "You're free to go, son."

My jaw drops open, but my mother grabs my hand and squeezes. Following his father out of the juvenile detention center, Justin glances back at me with the hint of a smile. I give him a thumbs up and a tight smile in support.

The door to outside closes. I lean forward to watch him follow his father to a black pickup truck. Has that warning from Sheriff Sam been enough? I have no way of knowing for sure until I see him again. Will he be back in school after tomorrow morning's hearing? Will the whole school be talking about my friend? *Just let me hear one negative piece of gossip and that old aggressive anxiety will be put to good use.*

Chapter 20

Emotional Lows

I remain anxious as Uncle Tim drives us away from this ugly place. Aunt Sarah sniffles and blows her nose a number of times until we pull up to Lou's Diner near the center of town. Mom agrees with my uncle that she needs a strong cup of coffee, even though it's after eight o'clock at night.

I really want a comforting piece of chocolate cake, but I don't think my stomach can handle it. As they sip their coffees, I make my way through a single scoop of vanilla ice cream and a glass of ice-cold water. If God is listening, he will hear prayer after prayer for Justin's safety. I throw in a little, *"Please give his father some patience and open his eyes,"* as well. It can't hurt, right?

Uncle Tim puts down his coffee cup. "We should take Sam's suggestion, honey," he says to my aunt. "Take Liam out of Pinedale this time and put him into another high school to finish his senior year."

"They would do that?" my mother asks.

"Yep. It's been suggested before. There's a vocational high school not too far from Pinedale. He'll be bussed there and home. They'll help him try to get his grades up and maybe graduate. It's not out of the question that he'll have to repeat senior year, at this rate."

"Oh, Tim," my mother whispers.

"I think it will do him a world of good, getting a second chance to succeed," my aunt says. "We should have taken Sam up on the offer last year, Tim. Pinedale High has been nothing but troublesome since freshman year. There was a change in him, Zoey," my aunt adds with tears in her eyes. "We tried our best to see the boy who did well in school and tried hard to get good grades, but…I don't know what happened when he walked into that high school. It's like the Liam we loved just began to fade away. Like he was replaced by someone we didn't know." Aunt Sarah sighs. "Not in your regular rebellious way. Lord knows, David had his moments, too, but not like Liam. If I didn't know better, I'd think he was…possessed."

I perk up with *that* comment. "Maybe he is," I interject into an adult-only conversation.

"Melody Marie," my mother exclaims in a scolding tone, "How could you say such a thing?"

"Just hear me out. It's what I feel, Mom! I don't feel that aggressive anxiety at Pinedale…at least, not in the way I felt it at Willow Valley High. Sometimes there are strange vibes floating around Pinedale. Don't ask me to explain how I know. I just do. Maybe that's what happened to Liam when he entered the high school. I don't, like, mean, he was possessed…sorry, Aunt Sarah, but I think I know what she's saying, Mom." Now I'm on thin ice, and even the turn of a word the wrong way will give my secret abilities away. "I mean, don't you ever get feelings when you enter someplace?" *Nope. That doesn't cut it.* "What if Liam sensed something in Pinedale that changed him? I know about the fire in the school and that students died in that building. I also know about the three boys who died on school grounds in the seventies."

"That was a very long time ago," Aunt Sarah says.

"Yeah, but what if some people are susceptible to vibes that linger in a place where such tragic disasters happened? What if souls move on but spirits, maybe, don't?" *So far so good,* I'm thinking. "I don't know, Aunt Sarah, all I'm saying is that if someone is super sensitive, and those spirits are a little, maybe…angry about still hanging around where they died, maybe it makes a person do angry things without them knowing the real reason why."

"Melody, stop," my mother orders with her hand over her heart. "I'm…I'm sorry, Sarah. Melody has a very active imagination. Sometimes overactive. In any event, vibrations or not," she adds with a frown, "a new environment might be the best thing for Liam. If they offer summer school and he works very hard, he might still graduate on time."

"I never liked that guidance counselor," my aunt mutters with a sour look on her face. "She's a nosy busy-body who never had a kind word for our son."

"Sarah," Uncle Tim interrupts.

"You know I'm right, Tim," she remarks with more backbone than I've ever seen. "David was different. He was always focused and good grades came easy for him. Not Liam. He was our daydreamer. Always a curious little boy with a smile. He *did* change when he started at Pinedale, Tim. He *did* change."

My uncle's eyes slide up with a smile. "Hank. Good to see you. Having another late night?"

I turn to face Pinedale's janitor. So this is what

makes him different: He isn't bound to Pinedale High? "Yep, Tim. Evening, Miss Sarah," he adds with a dip of his chin. "It's a shame what happened with your boy. I know Liam fools around a lot, but I didn't think he had that type of malicious vandalism in him."

"He doesn't, Hank," Aunt Sarah says in Liam's defense. "And his fingerprints were found on the desk, but nowhere else."

Hank nods. "Now don't I know that already, Miss Sarah?"

"I know you watch out for him, Hank," she whispers. "Just the way you looked out for me all those years ago."

"I do. I remember you and your brother. Two well-raised, sweet kids that never knew a minute of trouble between them. David, too. I hear he's at law school now. Ya'll must be very proud of that one."

"We're thinking of moving Liam out of Pinedale High for the rest of the year," Aunt Sarah says with sad eyes. "Breaks my heart, in a way. I wanted to see him graduate from the same school we went to…all those years ago."

"Sarah," my uncle whispers in support of his sweet wife. "Sorry, Hank. She's a little raw right now."

"He's your boy, Tim. I'd feel the same." Then he says to me, "Well hello, Miss Melody. Is this fine lady your mom?"

"I'm Zoey Warkowski," my mother replies, but her eyes stay glued to Hank, not me. "You're at Pinedale High and you know my daughter's name already?"

"Yes, ma'am. You've raised a fine girl who's not only sensitive to others, but from what I hear, pretty smart. And she has a lovely voice too, according to

Mrs. Montgomery."

My mother continues to study him. "Do you know so many things about all the students at Pinedale?'

"Only the very special ones like Miss Melody here," Hank replies. "Well now, I got to get back to the school and continue cleaning up the music room. I'll be painting over that graffiti all night. Nice to meet you, Mrs. Warkowski. Tim. Sarah. Miss Melody." He tips his baseball cap before he goes to the counter, picks up his order, and leaves.

"He's a strange one, isn't he?" my mother says under her breath.

"Who? Old Hank? He's been at Pinedale High…well, like forever," Aunt Sarah says with a dreamy smile. "He looks out for students, doesn't he, Mel?"

"He sure does, Aunt Sarah." *Okay. I have to give them more.* Putting down my spoon, I add with enthusiasm, "Just this morning, the air vent right above where I sit in biology lab went wonky. Hank fixed it lickety-split so it didn't keep roaring ice cold air on me anymore."

"It just seems strange that a janitor would already know a new student's name," my mother grumbles.

"Welcome to small town America, sis." Uncle Tim puts down his coffee cup. "I know it takes getting used to. You liked Raleigh when you were in college. Living outside the city is a totally different reality. It'll grow on you."

Mom scoffs. "I hope I made the right decision."

"You did," I say to help Uncle Tim out, not to mention lead her away from sensing something more about Hank the janitor. "I like Pinedale High. I've already made friends."

"Ya see, Zoey? No worries from Mel," Uncle Tim states as he looks at the check on the table.

"Maybe I moved too fast buying that house," she says looking down as her fingers rim the empty coffee cup. "What was I thinking?'

Aunt Sarah's eyes are moist again. "You just saved a boy's reputation tonight, Zoey. If you weren't here, if Melody hadn't had Justin over, why, he'd have no alibi. How is that not a good thing?"

My mother shrugs and doesn't answer. As we slide out of the booth at Lou's Diner, I can't help wondering if that vandalism would even have happened if I hadn't been scheduled into motet choir. I read the writing on the wall, the same as everybody else. I know it is directed at me. I know that my own cousin, Liam, brings out the dark side in the prankster ghosts. This just adds to my guilt.

Oh boy, do I have loads to think about tonight.

Chapter 21

When Worlds Collide

I didn't sleep well last night. As soon as we got back to our new house, the ghost of old John Hammersmith kept following me down the hall, talking non-stop. "I know what you want to ask me to do," I had said as I held up a hand outside my bedroom door. "My room is off limits to you. And no. I didn't get to give Hammer any message yet."

In the morning, I go into the bathroom and, when I come out, he is no longer there. Ugh! In my room, I change into loose shorts and a T-shirt, sit at my desk, and whizz through my homework. I am still worried about Justin and go to bed with him on my mind. Will he have two black eyes and welts all over this morning? Or has his father finally gotten the message? Only time would tell.

Then, feeling like I had pulled an all-nighter, I shower and dress in black capris and the last clean purple blouse I own for school. I don't have anything teal and will have to rectify that situation soon. Maybe I'll buy my own school shirt from the school store today.

Forget about breakfast. I gulp down a half a cup of coffee with milk and sugar, tolerate a few bites of dry toast, not wanting to keep my mother waiting. Besides,

I can't wait to get to school. Plus, I have enough padding on me, anyway. Who cares if I skip a healthy breakfast, right? And maybe I'll get to the school store, buy and change into a new teal school shirt before first period.

We don't talk much on the ride to Pinedale High. I sense my mother is pretty much preoccupied with her own new life worries in our new home town. Then, as if she reads my mind, she hands me not one, but two twenty-dollar bills before the typical "Have a good day, Mel." As I open the door to get out, she adds at the last minute, "And stay away from that janitor." I roll my eyes thinking, *if you only know what I know and see what I see, Mom.*

During American History class, I listen with one ear and watch the minutes tick by on the wall clock. I keep up my silent prayer for Justin and add in a little *"oh please, let them release Liam to Uncle Tim."* I sense the new school idea, instead of continuing at Pinedale, is the right way to go. Hopefully, there are no ghosts walking *those* halls, specifically, no pranksters that his kindred sensitivities can feed off and get him into another mess.

****

The morning trudges on as if its feet are stuck in wet, grimy sand and, by the time I enter the auditorium for motet choir, my anxiety is reaching that danger level where only one sideways glance would start its eruption. I walk in with Merva and Bev and take my seat. I have heard not a negative word about my cousin or Justin, as if the gossip grapevine had a sudden power outage. As Harrison hands me my folder, Mrs. Montgomery's sightline raises high above our heads. I sense a wave of relief as she sees Justin and her eyes fill.

Justin takes his seat in the bass section. Harrison hands him a folder. Then the auditorium fills with hoots and hand claps of the happy, triumphant variety. I have goosebumps running up my arms and my cheeks, and not from the air-conditioning. Of course, I join in.

All through vocal warm-ups, I feel my cheeks tingle as I sing with gratitude in my heart. That forty-five minutes flies by. I join Merva and Bev to put my folder on the baby grand.

"Miss me" is whispered in my ear so close that I can feel his breath on my neck.

I jump. Just a little. "Ohmygod! How are you?"

"Not bruised, thanks to what your mother said to my father. Sheriff Sam told the judge how you and your mother stood up for me. Thanks."

"Hey, Mel, want to sit with us at lunch," Bev says.

"She's sitting with me," Justin replies.

"Well…uh…you can sit with us too, right, Merva?" Bev adds, a little unsure of herself.

"Yeah…nope. We have something to discuss," Justin says to Bev. "Maybe another time?"

Bev's eyes grow wide. "Oh. Sure. No worries." And then they are gone.

I wave a little "bye" and look at Justin. Nope. No new bruises! We walk side by side with other late-to-lunchers. For someone who always has something to say, I am tongue-tied. Nervous, not anxious. His hand grips my elbow when we enter the cafeteria, heading to an empty table by the windows. He leaves his backpack on it like staking a claim.

Knowing I have money to burn today, I blurt out,

"Lunch is on me." I know. Lame, right?

"No way. I pay for both of us," he says clear and full of...what is that...male pride?

"But—"

"You heard me, Mel," he says, taking my hand and leading me to lunch lady territory. My face is hot, and I know it has quickly colored to some shade of pink. And what a warm grip he has on my hand. It is steady, firm in a way that makes me want to smile like some goofy dork.

Are others looking at us? Will snickers and sneers follow? Oh, I am so unprepared. No boy has ever held my hand and led me anywhere. I am the oddball Melody-shmelody...a taller than average, overweight plain Jane who talks to herself and goes from zero to sixty in the aggression department in seconds.

I am the strange girl who cloaks self-consciousness with withdrawn quiet in uncomfortable situations. I am the new girl in Pinedale High who jumps like a baby goat at "blasts of cold air" that have to be explained by a ghost of a janitor. And speaking of ghosts, well...there's that, too, right? An ability I keep hidden from everyone. An ability that comes with sensing malice before it shows in a bully. And now, holding Justin's hand, I am spinning out of control with all the reasons he shouldn't be friendly with me.

"Chicken wrap," the lunch lady says.

I snap out of my latest internal rant. "Try something new," Justin whispers.

Everything looks good and smells even better, not like the pathetic lunches in north Jersey that also cost four times as much. My eyes dance over the fried chicken (messy finger food), mac and cheese (messy spilling food) and then they settle on something neat and simple. I can handle that.

"Grilled cheese?' I say.

"Is that a question or a choice?"

"A...a choice...please," I reply, feeling so awkward that I'm not sure I can eat.

"Me too, ma'am," Justin says to the lunch server. Then he puts two pieces of chocolate cake on our tray as well. At the register, my eyes pop. Six dollars? For all this food? He forks over a ten and waits for change. "Grab two bottles of water?" he asks, and I do, loving the cool, icy feel against my sweaty palm.

Although I look straight ahead on our walk back to the table, my peripheral vision takes over. No strange looks. No sneers, but quite a few small smiles. *Ohmygod! Is this what acceptance feels like?* Some of that anxiety melts away.

We sit across from each other. "Shit. I forgot the chips," Justin says as he shoots up. "I mean, what's a grilled cheese without potato chips, right?" Before I can answer, and I cannot think of *one* witty thing to say, he is gone.

And...leaning against the window is Hammer. His leather arms are crossed. His green eyes shine like polished emeralds. Boy, does he look angry. "Want another warning, Melody Marie?" he sneers.

"Don't call me that," I whisper with my hand in front of my face.

"What? The music room wasn't enough? Wanna see what we can do when we're pissed off to hell?"

"Stop it, Hammer."

"Why? Stop what? Maybe the English Lit room needs a little redecorating tonight."

That second bite of my sandwich sticks in my throat. "Go away."

"No friggin' way. I told you he's bad news. I told you to stay away from him. Maybe we don't want anyone else but Hank seeing and talking to us. Maybe you're not as friendly as you act. We got rid of Liam. Now, maybe you're next."

Is this another threat? Or is it really a warning? What if Hammer hurts Justin? Or would the next malicious prank push me over that line and lead to an angry outburst in front of classmates I want to call friends? Justin sits down, put a bag of chips in front of me. But the damage is done. "I'm…sorry. I…I can't. I can't do this," I say as I stand and clutch my backpack to my chest.

"Mel? You okay? What?" Justin says, looking behind himself and then back at me. I can sense his hurt. I can sense his anger, too.

"I…I have to go," comes out so fast that he is staring at me. Questioning me. Shouting my name. It doesn't matter. That old anxiety hits high-gear like never before! I run out of the cafeteria. Hammer is right beside me.

Chapter 22

Trapped

"Run, Melody, run," he says as if to mock me, to shove me over that cliff of anxiety once again. "What's the matter, girl, cat got your tongue?"

"Leave me alone," I shriek, stopping just long enough to get out the words. "Now is not the time so, oh God, just stop," I add like a fool. Suddenly, I am aware of all the students in the hall who are looking at me as if I'm a freak. I push them out of my way and run out the door.

"Yeah! Man, you are so easy to manipulate! Just look at you, huffing and puffing. Maybe shed a few of those extra pounds in the process."

"I said go away," comes out on the next exhale. I run around the building and through the field, heading for the rocks where I know I can hide. Where I can finally huff and puff away from everyone. But he is still at my side in a slow jog, with those long legs that move so much faster than mine. I make it to the path in the bushes. My empty stomach cramps and I want to puke. Hot humid air fills my lungs. Dots of sweat break out down my back, under my arms, and on my flushed face.

"Now you've gone and done it," he says.

"Done what?" I say as I slow to a walk in the heavy air. I really never like to run, anyway.

"They all saw you talking to yourself, Melody Marie. More than a dozen students. By the end of lunch, it will be spreading all over the school and, if kids had their phones out, all over these new social media sites. It'll get back to old lady Babcock and probably get embellished, too!"

I lean against a tall pine tree, bent over with my hands gripping my knees while eyeing my cousin's graffiti on the rock formation ahead—until I can stand up straight again. "You're a real piece of work, Hammer, you know that?"

"Wham, bam, thank you, ma'am," he chortles as he takes his favorite arrogant pose against the rocks.

"I'm not leaving Pinedale High. I'm not going to ignore Justin, either," I state with my hands on my hips. "You're a bully *now,* but you weren't in life. You act tough, but you're just as smart as your great-nephew. You died because Andy's father drove that green pickup, right up and onto the lawn. You jumped in front of your friend, didn't you?"

"I don't remember," he fires back.

And just like that, I recall last night, just before I fell asleep, listening to that sad old ghost's ramblings through my bedroom door as if he were whispering things in my ear. I'd shut Hammer down for good this time. Facts were adding up in my mind and coming together to see the whole picture. "Want to know a secret? My mother bought your grandfather's house. He's there, still worried about you because you don't know the truth."

The look of disbelief is shocking. "Shit. You're lying!"

"I see and hear ghosts, remember? Andy's father

was really mad that night. He didn't want his son hanging around with you."

"I know that. I'm not stupid," Hammer says with a shrug.

"What you don't know is that Andy's father followed his son after that last argument. He'd been drinking. At the end of his rope because he wanted to sell everything and get the hell out of Pinedale with his son. Only Andy didn't want to go. Like a misguided fool, he gets behind a wheel as drunk as a skunk. It was dark. He often drove with his headlights turned off. Terry was at the curb catching a football. He drove right into him. You yelled Andy's name. He was leaning against the brick post at the bottom of the steps going into the school. You were running to get Andy out of the way when the pickup hit you square in the chest. You flew into the air and landed at the top of the school's steps, but Andy's father kept going. Maybe in shock. Maybe too drunk to put his foot on the brake. The pickup slammed into Andy and crushed him."

Hammers hands are tangled in the thick hair at his temples. A look of pure agony claims his expression. "How do you know all this? How do I know you're telling the truth?"

"Your grandfather saw the whole thing," I yell back.

Hammer slides down the rock. His knees meet his chest. So does his chin. "No. It can't be true."

"Your grandfather often worried about you, didn't he? You lived with him, not with your parents. Am I saying something you don't already know?"

"My dad and my uncle worked long hours in the garage. Pops had no one in the house with him anymore. He was a World War II veteran. He was in the Battle of the Bulge, a pretty bloody battle. Didn't sleep much."

"After your grandmother died, he liked to walk, especially at night, all alone. And he often watched you and your friends act like idiots in front of the school."

"Pops was never right in the head, and, as he got older, he couldn't work anymore. I looked out for him, so yeah, I lived with him. He had an obsession with me getting good grades and going to college."

"And you *did* have good grades. Great grades, in fact," I state. "But let's get back to the story. He saw the whole tragedy unfold while standing across the street. He knew the color of the pickup and he knew it was Andy's father behind the wheel. He watched three boys die for no good reason. Everyone called him an addle-brained fool telling the cops on the phone that it was a green pickup and Andy's father was driving. Whoever investigated just accepted the excuse that Andy's father told them…that he had hit a buck. No one saw any reason to question a man who lost his only child in a tragic accident."

Hammer shakes his head and mumbles, "One hell of a small town with smaller minds. That's the way it was back then. And everyone saw us as wild, pot-smoking, hard-drinking assholes. They wouldn't give us the time of day."

"Hammer, the death of your friends wasn't your fault."

"Like hell it wasn't. We had to ride those bikes and aggravate the farmers with the loud sounds at night. We had to wear leather jackets and look the part, you know?"

"You were smart kids who loved to push the limits, taking it farther and farther. The same way kids do today."

"And that got us killed," he mutters.

"No. That got you noticed and made you a target. One man's blind rage, juiced up by false courage in his homemade whiskey got you killed. Murdered, in fact. Andy's father ruined three families and many, many lives."

"I didn't know," he whispers.

"Well now, you do. And as for Justin, he's just as smart as you were, like this high intelligence skipped a generation. His father beats him, you know. Your great-nephew has been abused since his mother died. His father drinks, just like Andy's father did. And *you* telling me to stay away from *him* isn't going to happen because…because he's my friend."

Some type of courage rears up in me, at this point, and I have more to say.

"So you and your friends can keep up the vandalism in the school. Hank knows it's you, Andy, and Terry. And you get some help from the other pranksters that lost their lives in the fire some twenty years before you set foot in Pinedale High. You and your ghost friends find the sensitive ones with imagination and make them your scapegoats, for what? Some type of thrill? What is it? A strong, stirring sensation, even though you're dead—or because you can't or *won't* walk into the light. Then do those high fives give you a release from frustration?"

"I don't know what you mean," he argues.

I will have none of it. "That's what happened to Liam. That's why the juvenile facility is full of so many misguided kids, right? They were impressionable. Maybe full of fear going into high school. Just ripe for the picking. Shame on you. Shame on all of you that are stuck here still looking for something you can never have. A frickin' life!"

He buries his head in his hands. "I'm sorry."

"You're sorry," I shriek. "You just ruined my life in a new school! You just *labeled* me for that nosy guidance counselor to poke me a few more times until my aggressive anxiety takes hold. Then my mom has to sell another house and move again!"

"They'll all think that Justin said something to you and made you crazy," he says and looks aside.

"Oh great. Just great. So Justin gets in trouble again for something he didn't do! You're not only a bully. You're cruel!"

"No. I'll make it better. I promise."

Was that honesty in his voice? "Why?"

"Because…because I like being able to talk to you. And I'll lay off Justin. I swear."

My eyes narrow. My jaw locks before I say, "You can't make this better, Hammer. What's done is done. You said it yourself. It will be all over the school, not to mention social media. You win. I lose." After settling my backpack, I turn and walk away. My eyes fill but I bite back the sob. The air is suddenly too heavy to breathe. My legs go wobbly and my mouth goes dry. I feel dizzy and sick to my stomach. Then my knees hit the dirt on the path through the bushes. *Oh God! No one knows where I am!* Everything starts to spin as if I am on a merry-go-round.

Chapter 23

Savior

"I've got you," Justin says with his arm wrapped around my totally squooshy excuse for a waist. "Jesus, Mel. Here. Drink this." A plastic water bottle comes to my lips. I reach with a shaky hand, but he adds, "No, ma'am. Just take a mouthful. I'll hold it for you."

Like some savior appearing out of nowhere, I let him take control. I lean against him and follow directions, too unsteady to do anything else.

"We'll take it slow and I'll get you to the nurse."

I shake my woozy head. Yeah. That only makes things spin faster. "No. No nurse," I whisper. "Just need to…to eat something."

"All I've got are some breath mints and a stale granola bar in my backpack," he replies.

"I'll take it," I say.

He moves with me into the clearing at the edge of the empty field, still far away from the back door of the school, and eases me down to the grass. I sit back on my knees as he digs through his backpack and then peels the paper off the granola bar before handing it to me. Not wanting to faint, I take a big bite and devour half the bar. Even though it tastes like paper, I chew and swallow. Justin hands me the water bottle to wash it down. Then I finish the sweet, brittle bar with another big bite. He says nothing but stares at me with concern and worry on his face. I cannot meet his eyes, feeling really embarrassed.

"Your blood sugar must have dropped. You should see the nurse," he whispers.

"I'll be okay," I lie. I really need to eat. I totally need another bottle of water.

"Yeah. Right," he mumbles, handing me a bunch of breath mints, which I take and swirl around in my mouth praying for enough energy to get back into the school on my own two legs. The sugar rush has to do its thing, like really fast. He ducks down trying to gaze into my eyes. "Who were you arguing with? I only heard your voice and…"

"I talk to myself, okay," I fire back to cut him off. "I'm weird, not crazy, and I like to say things out loud. So I totally understand if you want to head to class and leave me here."

He frowns and sighs a grunt. "I'm not leaving you here."

"You heard what I just said. I talk to myself."

"You're lying."

I huff, close my eyes and shake my head. "You don't want to know the truth."

"Try me."

I look him straight in the eye and say, "There are…things…in this school."

"What kind of things? Like ghosts? I know Pinedale is haunted. Sometimes when weird things happen, I get goosebumps up and down my arms. Maybe you hear them. Maybe you see them."

Oh. Wow. Why don't you go all the way and tell him the truth? My anxiety level hits new heights. "You don't know what you're saying."

"Yeah. I do. And it's happened before. We've had new students come in and then suddenly transfer out when weird shit happens…like what happened in bio lab yesterday, or like the type of malicious vandalism in the music room the night before. It's the ghosts feeding off strong emotions. Sometimes papers fly around the room or books fall off classroom shelves, just missing a kid. Or like what happened in the hall the other day. You can't tell me they aren't pranking students. I know what I see and it isn't the school settling over some fictitious fault line or anything that can be explained. You see them and hear them, don't you? So does the janitor. And don't lie to me," he states with conviction in his voice.

"This is not the place for this conversation, Justin. I…I have to get to class. So do you."

"Nope. You're going to the nurse and I'm taking you there," he states, standing tall and holding out his hands.

I am not sure if my legs will work and I am definitely not a ninety-pound cheerleader, which piles on more anxiousness. As if he's reached some limit of patience, Justin reaches down, grabs my wrists, and pulls me up off the ground as if I weigh twenty pounds less than I know I do. I crash into his chest and his arm comes around my shoulders. Full of embarrassment, my eyes water and I bite my lips. No boy has *ever* put an arm around me. I never let anyone this close, except for family or Jonathan. The hug feels so secure. And Justin doesn't pull away as if he has suddenly realized that I might get the wrong impression. No. He holds onto me.

"Now what are you two doing here? Cutting class

again, Justin, and getting Miss Melody in trouble along with you?"

Hearing the janitor's voice, I try to pull out of Justin's hug, but he won't let go. "I followed Mel out here. She started to faint and I gave her a granola bar and some water. She needs to see the nurse, like right now. That's where I'm taking her."

"Don't seem that way to me," Hank grumbles. Then he clicks his tongue. "Is he telling the truth, Miss Melody?"

I nod as Justin's arms loosen around me, but my legs still feel weak. "He…he got here just as I got really dizzy."

"Well, ain't that something. Maybe there's hope for you yet, kid. Come on. I'll walk the two of you back into the school, just in case there are any questions about the two of you cutting class," Hank says.

"Thanks," Justin replies. He takes my backpack off me and keeps a tight arm around my shoulders.

Funny how my anxiousness lessens in what seems like a protective hold. Maybe I can tell Justin what I see and what I hear. Maybe what I need is to confide in someone I can trust to not think me strange. We don't talk as we follow Hank into the building and to the nurse's office.

Chapter 24

Friendship

I eat the graham crackers and drink the orange juice. I let the nurse take my pulse and check me out. I listen to the school nurse call the principal's office to let them know what happened. "Both of you are officially excused from English Lit," she says as she hangs up the phone. "That was quick thinking on your part, Justin. Thank you for finding her."

"No problem, ma'am," he says as he sits in a chair by the closed office door. "I can go to class and then come back to get Mel afterwards. I'll get the homework assignment and bring it to her."

Don't leave me! Please stay!

"Why that would be fine. I'll write you a pass," the nurse says, and she does just that.

****

Minutes later, I watch Justin leave, wondering if it is just an excuse to finally get away from the weird new girl who talks to herself. I will not blame him, if he does. And once the social media posts have a freakin' field day on me, anyone would distance themselves, right?

I suddenly see myself in Willow Valley High again. Hearing my grumbled "get away from me" or "I don't want to hear you" that I had said out loud in the halls and classrooms of my old high school. Or getting worked up as soon as I sense the bullies starting their diatribes on the less fortunate nerdy kids, or me, for that matter. Or striking back at them with words meant to cut them down and a good shoulder-shove when the mood hit me. Then, being walked to the school psychologist for another useless therapy session that always ended with my mother being called and a suspension for aggressive anxiety.

The compassionate school nurse is busy with paperwork. I sit on the cot holding my stomach, wishing I could fade into the bland walls and disappear like Hammer and his ghost buddies can. I stare at the floor and let myself go to that dark place.

What would it feel like to be normal? To *not* sense someone else's feelings? To *not* see and hear the ghosts stuck where they died? Would I just be an overweight sixteen-year-old girl who fades into the walls and doesn't give off friendly vibes? Would I be just as miserable? Maybe less anxious because I wouldn't sense what other kids think about me and just go through high school pretty much clueless and invisible.

The nurse, whose name I can't read on her photo ID hanging from a purple Pinedale lanyard, comes over with another packet of graham crackers and a bottle of cold water from her small fridge behind her desk.

"Thanks," I whisper, taking them both and sitting up straight.

"Your mother is coming for you," she says in a gentle voice.

I look up at the wall clock. Classes will let out in fourteen minutes and that old saying, *thank God it's Friday,* echoes through my head. I eye the posters about dental hygiene and lists of dos and don'ts in a medical emergency like I've never seen them before.

"I'm Mrs. Faragalli. Come to my office anytime you get the feeling like you're going to faint, Melody. I always have crackers and juice on hand," she adds with a warm smile.

Just in case she thinks "starvation diet disorder," I say, "Thanks, Mrs. Faragalli, but this is a one-time thing, not a habit."

She sits on the cot next to me. I sense her understanding and smell the light fragrance she wears mix with an antiseptic cleanliness. "Starting a new school in junior year is stressful. Getting comfortable with new surroundings, especially for someone moving to a different climate down south. Making new friends is never easy, Melody. You feel free to come by anytime."

I give a grin and bob my head. She rips open a corner of the cracker packet and hands it back. After a caring pat on the shoulder, she goes back to her desk. I munch the cracker's corners first and then eat the rest. I do the same with the second one and then open the plastic water bottle to wash the gritty sweetness down.

There is a knock on the door and a bright, "Come in," from Mrs. Faragalli.

"I have Mel's English assignment, ma'am," Justin says as he enters.

My face flushes and I look down in an awkward way. *Just great!* What I really want to do is to take one last look at a totally good-looking someone who is sure to run the other way when he sees me in the halls on Monday morning.

"Justin, I like this side of your personality," Mrs.

Faragalli states with a bright smile. "I always knew it was there. You're a fine young man."

Did he just blush and smile in an "aw shucks, ma'am" kind of way? "Thanks, Mrs. Faragalli," he says as he walks over and sits close to me on the cot. He picks up my backpack and puts the paper and a new play inside before zippering it up. "We start *Taming of the Shrew* on Monday. Miss Woodson said for you to look at Kate's lines. I'm doing Petruchio."

I've never read this Shakespeare play, and I answer, "Oh. I'm…I'm sure she can get someone else to read Kate."

"Why?" he asks like he's putting me on the spot. "You don't want to read with me? Is that it?"

I clear my throat. "No. I just thought that maybe you wouldn't want to read opposite me."

"Yeah? Nope."

What kind of answer was that? "Thanks for before," I mumble, expecting him to race out the door.

"No worries." And…he is still sitting close to me when my mother walks in.

I say nothing as she introduces herself and talks to the nurse. It doesn't matter that Justin hears it all. After all, if he hadn't followed me, I'd probably still be unconscious somewhere in the bushes behind the hockey field.

"And thank you, Justin," my mother says as she saunters over.

"No problem, ma'am," he says and stands. Then he takes hold of my upper arm and helps me to my feet. I don't feel wonky anymore, but I'm not ready to run out the door as quick as a bunny, either. He has my backpack over a shoulder with his own. "I'll walk her out to your car, if that's okay," he says to my mother.

Her eyebrows shoot up. "Oh. Sure. Thank you. Of course," and after thanking Mrs. Faragalli again, we leave the nurse's office.

Just then, the three beeps sound. I'm not ready for my walk of shame. Left and right, classroom doors fly open. The hall fills with loud conversations coming from a tsunami of students. Justin pulls me closer, with my mother walking behind us. I wait for the side glances and "ew, that's the oddball who talks to herself" looks, but I guess everyone is too involved in celebrating the end of the week. We make it past the principal's office and almost down the front steps when I hear Merva call my name.

She runs over with Bev not two feet behind. "Ohmygod, girl! I heard you had some kind of low blood sugar episode and ran out of the cafeteria."

"It's all over the school," Bev adds in an excited tone.

"Are you okay? They said you were so out of it that you were rambling on, almost incoherent! Oh Mel, we were so worried until Justin came back to class and told us how you almost fainted. You gotta eat, girlfriend," Merva states with conviction. "Three meals a day and lots of water for hydration in this heat."

What? Justin said that? "Thanks, but I'm okay," I reply.

Merva scribbles something down and rips the page out of her notebook. "This here's our numbers. Put them in your phone. We both expect a call from you, okay? Harrison was really worried, too. We saw him at the lockers. Later, Mel," Merva says as she pulls Bev away while Merva's sidekick gives a little wave and a big smile.

I just stand there. *Did that just happen? And I got a "girlfriend" too!*

"Nice girls," my mother says as she moves in front of us.

"Those two are good people, ma'am. Harrison too," Justin says. He still hasn't let go of my fleshy arm, though, and we continue toward the blue box-on-wheels.

"You told them how you found me?" I whisper.

"Sure did. Everyone in class, including Miss Woodson, was concerned."

"You can let go of me now," I say.

"No way. Just walk to the car with me holding on, Mel," he whispers in my ear.

"I'm really okay now," I argue.

"And I'm really likin' holding you up," he argues back. "We need to talk."

I feel myself blush, and, in some type of dream state, I answer, "When?"

"I get off work at eight tonight. Is that too late to stop by your house?"

"I don't think so."

"Great." He opens the passenger-side door and I get in. "Ma'am, uh, Mrs. Warkowski? Do you mind if I stop by around eight tonight, you know, after I get off work? I want to explain our English Lit assignment to Mel."

"That's fine, Justin. And thank you for taking care of my daughter today," she says with an easy smile.

I click the seatbelt in place and take my backpack from his outstretched hand.

"Thanks. See ya'll later," Justin says as he closes

the door and taps it twice.

I glance over to see him standing at the curb with his hands in the pockets of his black jeans. I also see Hammer and his two biker buddies standing off to one side. A good twenty feet away are the 1950s gang. They are staring at me. I purse my lips and stare right back.

"So tell me what happened," my mother says as we pull away from the school.

"I...I didn't eat breakfast and then at lunch, I...I..."

"That's not wise, Mel. We've talked about this. You eat healthy and you are healthy."

"Mom," I draw out, doing it in three different tones.

"No. Friends accept you for who you are, not what you look like. I was never thin as a stick. Warkowski women aren't built that way. We're healthy, hardy stock."

"I don't need this lecture again."

"Well, too bad. I think you do. Going all loopy in school because you didn't eat," she grumbles. "And then walking out of the school and going off by yourself only who knows where and why! Thank God that Justin found you!"

"I'm really okay, Mom, I swear. The tuna salad had loads of mayo and it tasted off to me. I ran out of the cafeteria thinking I'd puke or something," I lie. "Then I just kept going out the door and through the hockey field. You know, Liam did some job on those rocks up there. They are full of graffiti!"

"Don't change the subject," she orders.

"What happened with him in court this morning?' I ask, *really* changing the subject now.

She blows out a breath, which seems to calm her down some. "Liam actually apologized to the court. The judge ordered a hundred hours of supervised community service. My brother asked that he be placed in a different school to finish his senior year and the court agreed to it. He'll be bussed and supervised there. And it was determined that he threw over the desk, but he didn't do the rest of the damage. His two friends are suspended next week and then they'll be back at Pinedale. It seems only Liam has an excess of suspensions that date all the way back to his freshman year, so I believe, as does my brother, that a different environment is the best thing for him to try and get him to fly straight again."

"Wow. You know, I think you're right."

"I know I'm right," my mother replies. "My brother is not going to have another heart attack because of Liam. And Aunt Sarah shouldn't have to worry herself into a nervous breakdown, either."

I have to know more. "What about Justin's father?"

"That man was given a stern warning by the judge. He won't be beating on his son again, not without having to face jail time. From what my brother says, that boy's been through too much already in his young life. Well. No more." She takes the next turn very slowly, as if lost in thought. "Now tell me what really happened today."

I stare out the side window. I am not ready to tell her the truth. So here I go with another lie.

Chapter 25

The Truth — Part One

When your mother makes the best tomato sauce in the world, there is no such thing as an eating disorder. The smell of frying garlic and onions wafts through the house. Then the scent of tomato paste and other things like oregano and fresh parsley join them. And two hours later, *voila*! Spaghetti and meatballs, my comfort food since forever. Mom bristles, complaining that it doesn't taste the same. I agree, but it is really close to what my olfactory nerve remembers from the kitchen in north Jersey. Since it is the first full meal in my stomach since yesterday, I feel like I can think straight again.

Of course, I have no idea what is being said about the new girl's "episode in the hall" on social media. After dinner, I have the chance to call both Merva and Bev. They are still genuinely concerned. We promise to keep on checking in with each other over texts. I don't let on that Justin is coming over tonight. I put away my laundry and make a short entry in my journal. I have to steer my head away from anxiety and think about what I will say to Justin when he gets here.

****

My mother feeds Justin as soon as he walks through the door. He had answered her invitation with a shrug and "I could eat, ma'am, uh…Mrs. Warkowski." I load the dishwasher and then dry the pots, very observant of the way he inhales a heaping plate of pasta and three meatballs.

I'm not about to suggest that we talk in my room, so I tell my mother we'll be on the front porch—with the door closed, thank you very much. Since not a window is even cracked open and the air outside is still hot and sticky, she will not hear a thing.

Anxiety rears its familiar head again, not knowing where or how to start. *Retie your sneaker, check out the overcast sky, and look up and down the block*…it works for just about a minute. I rub my calves and take the plunge. "So… Tell me what you heard."

Justin sits close at my side with his elbows on his knees. I see faded oil stains and smell the faint odor of gasoline on his hands. That garage stuff has to be really hard to get rid of, even though he has washed them. "Who's Hammer?"

A loaded question, right? Lies are nasty things. They come back to bite you. So I opt for the truth, come what may. "Your great uncle John Hammersmith."

He looks over at me, his dark-blue eyes narrow. "What the hell is that supposed to mean?"

"He's one of the ghosts at Pinedale High. He died there."

"I know. Along with two friends in like 1975."

I nod once and keep eye-contact. "It was May of 1974, just weeks shy of graduation. His friends were Terry Collins and Andy MacDonald."

"My dad doesn't talk about him. Says he was a troublemaker."

"He wasn't. He was very smart, and he died trying

to push Andy out of the way of Andy's father's pickup truck."

"No shit," he whispers in surprise.

"Terry was struck first. Andy's father was drunk, by the way. He hit Hammer, your great-uncle, who then flew in the air. He slammed into his son, pinning him against one of the brick posts at the side of the front steps of the school."

"How do you know all this?"

I take that step off the cliff. "Because I see and hear the ghosts at Pinedale High."

I expect Justin to pale, like I'll have to grab *his* arm and hold him up, but no. That isn't his reaction. "Okay… Go on," he whispers, full of calm and cool.

I'm already in free fall so I say, "Your great-great uncle, Hammer's grandfather, has been roaming the living room of this house for like almost fifty years because he wanted someone to know who really killed his grandson. Everyone else in the family simply wrote Hammer off because he rode a motorcycle and looked like a long-haired hippy. But that's the thing. It was only a look, not the person he really was. His grandfather knew he was smart and kind without a mean bone in his body."

He runs his hands through his hair pushing it off his face. "No way. The police had to have investigated. Hitting someone head on would leave blood on the truck, and dents."

"Andy's father said he hit a buck in the road. No one would ever guess that a father would mow down his own son, so they kept on looking for a red pickup truck instead of a green one. And when Andy's father suddenly sold his farm and moved away really fast, everyone thought it was out of grief…you know, to get away and not have a reminder of where his son died."

"And you know this because another ghost told it all to you? How did he know? Maybe he made the story up."

"No, Justin. He saw it happen from across the street. Hammer's grandfather, your great-great-uncle never had a full night's sleep after he came back from the war. After his wife died, he took night walks, maybe to try and slay his own demons. He ran home very, very upset, and he called the police to report the accident. Then he sat down on the couch and he…he…"

"He died," Justin whispers. "Oh my God. It all makes sense."

"And the whole town grieved three young men who should have had bright futures. The librarian's husband is related to Terry's family. She helped fill in some of the blanks because I…I looked through the yearbooks and she caught me. I never got around to researching the Internet. But I guess I didn't have to, with Hammer's grandfather giving me a play-by-play last night."

"So what? You mysteriously end up in our town and buy a house that was owned by someone related to all this ghost stuff, and then you find out you have the ability to talk to them?"

"It's not the first time," I offer, very hesitant about saying anything more. But telling the truth means just that, doesn't it? "Right after my father died, I met Jonathan."

"Who's Jonathan?"

"A teenager that died in my bedroom back in New

Jersey. I was ten years old the first time I saw him. I don't know. Maybe the trauma of my father dying brought this ability out in me. Jonathan would sit on my bed at night, sometimes cuddle me, and then I'd be able to fall asleep. He never left my bedroom. I'd close my door and talk to him." I am not about to go into the ghosts I see on the street or like everywhere I go.

"And your mother allowed this?"

I shake my head. "My mother doesn't know."

"No way," he scoffs.

"Yes, way," I say to convince him. "I'd only whispered to Jonathan even when my door was closed. And the few times she came into my room and caught me, well, I'd say I was talking to my dad. Then she would tear up and put her hand over her heart and leave the room."

"But you never spoke to your dad, right?" he asks.

"No. I...I never saw him. I think he went straight to Heaven," I reply as my vision clouds. I sniffle and rub my eyes, adding, "The world isn't full of ghosts. I think, or rather, I sense...that some of them just can't move on. Those are the ones who want to talk to me."

He looks all around. "Are they, like, all over?'

"There's none on this street. I think they stay where they died, like the students who died in that school fire in the fifties. I call it bound. They're still walking the halls trying to make sense of it all, along with Hammer and his biker buds."

"No way," he whispers again.

"They do stuff, like making books fly through the hall."

"Or papers fall off bulletin boards when no one's near them."

"Or cause electric panels to crap out and air-conditioning to stop along with the Internet."

His dark-blues get wide. "Like the other day in bio lab."

I nod twice. "There was no blast of cold air that made me jump up. They were in the air ducts laughing like hyenas."

"But the janitor said—"

"I can't go there, Justin. But Hank sees them, too. I think maybe he's like one of them but with some type of special powers or something. He saved me from being the weird new girl in bio lab, because he knew exactly what was going on."

"No shit," he whispers. "And he was the one who found us at the rocks." He scrubs his face like trying to accept the reality I live. "So you were arguing with Hammer by the rocks, right? Why?"

"He keeps telling me to stay away from you. He says you're not a good person, but I refuse to believe that. Hammer really uses Liam's penchant for mischief. I think he and his two ghost buddies saw Liam overturn the teacher's desk and then did all the damage to the music room because I was talking to you in English Lit that day. He gets pretty angry."

"I got a strange sensation when I messed up your white blouse with that red goop."

"You didn't do it. He nudged your arm. He can touch things and people too."

"Did he touch you?"

"Once or twice… He tried to help me fill in an answer on this stupid placement test Mrs. Nosy Red Lips made me take. He touched my hand."

"Shit. And he doesn't want me anywhere near

you," he mutters.

"If you had a sensation when he touched your arm and that gelatin flew at me, then you're sensitive to them. That's what I think happened with my cousin Liam, but on some subconscious level. My uncle says he was a super-sensitive kid in middle school. When he got here as a freshman, I think Hammer kind of attached himself to Liam, you know, like Hammer could feed off him and make him do things that were mischievous."

"Yeah. He started wearing all black at the beginning of sophomore year. Blaze and Cam and I started getting closer to him. Then he went with the Goth look, you know, chains, black nail polish, and eyeliner. I didn't go in for the eyeliner thing. Not the nail polish, either. My dad went nuts when I started hanging around with him."

"But your grades didn't take a nosedive," I state.

He squints, again, those dark-blue eyes pierce mine. "How do you know that?"

I shift, because I'm at the point of no return. "I sense things about people. And sometimes I react with…you know, like, aggression, but only with people who have mean thoughts. It happened a lot in my other school. That's why we moved. Not only to be closer to Uncle Tim. I kept getting suspended for my aggressive anxiety."

"So why didn't you just tell your mother the truth?"

"What? That I see and hear ghosts? That I had a teenage ghost in my bedroom with me? That I can read a person's feelings and can't stop the reaction when I sense the malice in them? Are you for real? She can't know this!"

"You've got that all wrong, Mel. She's a nice person. If you sense things, then can't you sense that she would worry about you? I mean, why put her through that?"

"I don't want to talk about that part anymore," I state. "Maybe someday, but not right now, okay?"

"Sure. It's your call," Justin replies. "I'm only saying—"

Getting off that merry-go-round, I cut him off with, "What's the social media scoop? Are the kids saying what a weirdo I am to be talking to myself in the hall?"

He pulls out his phone and scrolls through a social media app that is very popular with teens. "Have a look-see for yourself," he offers.

I take his phone and start to read the chit-chat. Nothing about me is popping. "Okay, so these are your friends. What about the others?"

"You heard Merva and Bev," he says with a shrug.

"You fixed that one for me," I reply.

"I didn't have to fix it. Good people don't say bad things about a friend. Not everyone's a bully, you know. Not everyone is staring at you, either."

"I wish I could believe you," I say.

"I don't lie. Not to you, anyway. You and your mom saved my ass from a night in that juvenile prison. You and your mom cleared my name."

"You were innocent, Justin."

"Innocent or guilty…it don't mean much. I did lots of stupid shit with Liam and the other two."

"But not anymore. Liam will be in another school, and you can ease off Blaze and Cam. They aren't real friends if all you have in common is getting in trouble together."

He chuckles. "I gave up all the good ones my sophomore year. Did some mean things to them along the way as well."

"Merva and Bev saw the good in you for helping me today. Why won't the others?"

"Because I have a reputation. You can't undo what you've done."

I smile. "I don't believe that. If I can adapt to a new school and new *everything,* including this yucky humidity, you can change and show people who you really are."

"Then there's my father," he mutters. "He's got a reputation, too."

"You aren't your dad, Justin. And maybe, after what the court said to him today, he'll turn a corner, too."

"Yeah…nope. Ain't gonna happen."

"He didn't hit you last night, did he?"

"Nope. There's that."

"Then give him a chance. Okay. Keep your guard up but show him you're not the kid he thinks you are. Let him see the good in you, Justin." I sense he still isn't convinced, and add, "Look. If Hammer had embraced his smart side, maybe what happened wouldn't have happened. They wouldn't have been at the school at midnight smoking pot and horsing around like they owned the place. Andy's father wouldn't have been so blind with rage that he got into that pickup drunk as a skunk to go hunting for his only child and Hammer."

"You think that's why he wants you to stay away from me? Like I'll do something stupid and drag your reputation down to my level? Is that what you think?" Justin asks.

"I can't really say. But I sense one thing for sure. He gets very angry around you and then takes it out on me. Is it to warn me? Maybe in some strange ghost way, it is. Embrace a little change, Justin. Start wearing a school shirt and regular blue jeans to school. Start using your brain, like on overdrive, and stay away from my cousin, Blaze, and Cam. If your father can't reach out, then you do the heavy lifting. Give it a week and let's see what happens."

He stands, brushes off his jeans. "That's a lot to think about, Mel."

"I know. I'm...sorry," I whisper.

"You shouldn't be sorry for saying something you feel," Justin replies. "I'm gonna go. Tell your mom I'll be here on Sunday, bright and early to start on the backyard."

"You mean you're willing to talk to me again, even after I told you about...um, things?"

I want to pull out my phone and capture that smile forever. He is eye-candy to me with all that dark hair, and such perfect features, not to mention his height and broad shoulders. I feel my heart flutter as I wait for his response. Especially if he is going to come out with some lame excuse like, "I promised your mom I'd do this, that's all."

The captivating smile doesn't fade. He leans down and kisses my cheek. Ohmygod! I can't move. I can't breathe! I just sit here like a big lump on a cement step wondering if I imagined it.

"Tell your mom I said thanks for the super spaghetti dinner."

My heart feels brittle enough to break into tiny pieces.

He puts a finger under my chin so I am staring up at him. "As for me being willing to talk to you again, now that's a load of crap. I like you, Mel. Being different doesn't make you weird. It makes you…you. And in my book, you're special. I don't want to let that go. See you Sunday."

He turns and walks away. I put my hand over my heart and take in a breath. He turns around at the curb, smiles again, and waves good-bye. I know I am waving back. I don't think I am smiling. I can't feel my face, and when he turns the corner at a jog, I touch my cheek.

Ohmygod! Ohmygod! He… He kissed me?

Chapter 26

True Confessions — Part Two

Okay. Friends kiss friends all the time, and friends can, you know, touch your chin so that you are eye to eye, I tell myself. I walk into the house and look at Hammer's grandfather standing by the mantel. I hear the dishwasher whirring really loud. Instead of going to find my mother, I walk over and catch the weary look in John Hammersmith Senior's eyes.

"I told your grandson," I whisper. "Hammer knows the truth."

That weary, weathered face turns serene. "Thank you, young lady," he says.

"Mel? Is that you," my mother calls out as she comes into the living room. "I thought I heard your voice."

I spin around and stare at her. "I was just…I was just…" I swivel my head back, but I don't see him. I examine the dining room. I don't see him. "Oh…nothing. I was just admiring the carved marble around the fireplace. It's nice," I reply.

"Well, I'll be in my room ironing some clothes. I start on Monday," Mom tells me.

"You're happy about being in the lower grades again?" I quickly ask.

"You know, yeah. I think it's going to be better

than middle school. It will be different, but it's a good place to start." She goes down the hall off the dining room and into her bedroom.

I check the kitchen, and even look out the window to see if he is standing in the overgrown weeds of the backyard. I don't see him. I check the bathroom, and even the laundry room next, and then my mom's room—just in case he is watching her ironing. No ghost of John Hammersmith Senior.

I go back through the dining room, pass the kitchen to check the empty bedroom that will be our den. Nope. No ghost. Then I approach my room, ready to hiss like a snake, "I told you my room is off limits!" *Nothing. No ghost.*

I sink down on my bed and look around. Something about the air has changed, and not because we have a central unit to cool the house. I do not sense another's presence anymore. That makes me shiver. So I get up and do the whole house again, this time opening cabinets, the washer and dryer in the laundry room, and every single clothes closet…until I stand in my mother's room. Her closet holds no hiding ghost, either.

"You look like you've seen a ghost," Mom says as she stands the iron up on the collapsible old ironing board that had belonged to her mother. It is made of wood and recovered with a printed pattern that screams of Mom's unique flower-power taste.

I manage to hide the look of surprise with a quick, "Ha-ha. Very funny."

"What did you and Justin talk about, or shouldn't I ask?"

"Just school stuff. That's all." Okay. I lie. I do that

with her a lot.

"Really? I guess there must be tons of stuff going on because that was some lengthy conversation between the two of you."

I narrow my eyes and cross my arms. "Were you looking at us through the window?" Well, I can't ask if she heard anything I said, right?

"Anything you want to tell me," she states, not asks.

"Why?"

She begins a sneaky grin. "Oh. I don't know. Maybe the way he said goodbye is a good place to start."

I put the laundry basket on the floor, sink into the winged chair in her room, and blow out a long, slow breath in resignation. "So he kissed me on the cheek."

"Uh-huh," she draws out.

"Friends do that."

"Uh-huh," she draws out again, only longer this time.

I smirk. "He said thanks for dinner and he'll see you on Sunday morning." Then I think about it again. "Unless, maybe because he did that, like, you don't want him near me anymore."

"Why do you always have to go into the dramatic, Mel?"

I didn't expect that question, so I shrug. "I'm not getting dramatic."

"Yeah, you are. A cute boy kissed you."

"Only on the cheek."

"Melody Marie! Let me try this one again. A cute boy who is very nice and has good manners likes you."

I roll my eyes, bite my lips together, but can't stop

the smile. "Ya think?"

"Yeah, I think. Ooh... His eyes are so blue," she says like she's telling me a secret.

"I know, really so dark and dreamy." That last word slips out.

She smiles, picking up the iron again. "He's a couple of inches over six feet and from the looks of his shoulders, he could be a football player."

"Mom! Stop," I huff.

As the steam bursts and she presses a blouse's collar, she says, "Good looks aside, Mel, Justin is a very nice boy. He's shown himself to be much more than just skin deep. Is he your first kiss?"

This time, I screech, "Mom! Stop!" But why am I not flying off the chair and out of her room with a look of sheer horror on my face?

"Well, you're sixteen and very pretty—"

"Ohmygod, will you stop! I'm taller than most girls. Wider than most, too!"

"With curves and a chest, and wide, brown doe-eyes that are so lovely to look at. So you're shapely and tall. I'm half Italian, you know. On my mother's side. Not too many girls your age can wear their hair short and shaggy like that and look the way you do. Then there's your heart, and your beautiful, sensitive soul. And that angelic voice that you got from both me and your father, God rest his soul. You're the perfect package, Melody Marie, and don't you ever feel otherwise."

"Seriously? Are you done?"

She is ironing the heck out of that blouse! I am not sure it will survive. But then she puts down the iron and stares right through me. "You think you're different."

She practically bites out those words.

"I know I'm different," I exclaim.

"How? How are you so different than anyone else? Are you going to say it or do I have to pull it out of you?"

"I'm aggressively anxious! You know what the therapists say."

"You're highly sensitive and you see…or…perceive things that other people can't."

I am shocked! My mouth drops open as my eyes bug out of their sockets. "What are you talking about?'

"You know what I'm talking about."

"No. I don't!"

"Don't try and kid a kidder, Melody Marie."

"What's that supposed to mean?"

"Who were you talking to in the living room?"

I stare at her. She stares right back. "No one."

"Try again. And I want the truth. Who did you see?"

My heart races as my skin prickles. My face pales as that spaghetti sits in my stomach. "Why?"

"Who did you see, Melody Marie? Was it a man or a woman? Young or old?"

"Why are you asking me this?"

"Oh come on. The truth, remember? You get the same look in your eyes that your father did, all those years ago."

"Why are you bringing up Dad?" I fire back. "I didn't see him after he died. I never do."

Uh-oh. Oh. Crap on a cracker. Did that just spew right out of my mouth? I had just gone through truth-time with Justin. Now, I have to go through it with my mother? She pulls the blouse off the ironing board and hangs it on a plastic hanger in the closet. Then she faces me again. "Well, talk, Melody Marie. Spill the beans, as we used to say." Then she sits on the bed to face me.

Something nudges at me. "Did you know about Jonathan?"

She nods once. "Your father told me. He died in your room of a heart condition. He never left that bedroom."

"Ohmygod!" I slap my forehead. My hand slides down to my cheek. "Why didn't you ever say anything?"

"Why didn't you ever come and tell me what you saw? Christ, you were only ten when Daddy died. It was only afterward that I'd hear you whispering to someone. I thought, at first, that you were talking to your father, maybe seeing him?"

"No. Mom. I swear I never saw him."

Her hand goes to her heart. "Oh, thank God, because if you were keeping something like that from me…" Her eyes begin to water. One tear makes it down her face. She swipes it away and clasps her hands as if she wants to wring them. "He saw them everywhere we went. Of course, I got the impression that he had something unique about him, even before we married. And right after he proposed, he came clean and told me what he could see and hear. He said if it was too much, then he'd end our engagement and never see me again."

I have goosebumps on my arms. "What did you do?"

"Well, not that, obviously," she replies with a flutter to her eyes and a tight smile. "Your father kept them at a distance from us. They never entered our personal space. Every once in a while, he'd see someone we knew that died a tragic death. He'd talk to them. Maybe help them along to unravel something that held them tied to here. He was always discreet. I mean, don't get the wrong impression. He wasn't some kind of ghost detective or anything like that. And he sensed Jonathan when we bought the house. It was only a two bedroom, and he swore to me that Jonathan had no bad intentions."

"He didn't. He stood in the corner of the room most of the time, but he was there for me until the day we packed up and left."

"Daddy said he was a gentle soul. That he died in his sleep."

"He was, Mom," I softly whisper.

"I could hear you talking to him sometimes." She pauses. "Mel, why didn't you ever come and tell me?"

"Why didn't you ever come and tell *me*?" I reply.

"No. This had to come from you. It wasn't the other way around. It is your gift. Your talent. Is that what happened in Willow Valley? Did you see ghosts there?"

"I did, but I didn't talk to them. I…I can sense things, Mom. I can sense meanness in people. Okay. Yeah…sometimes I told the ghosts to leave me alone. Kids thought I talked to myself."

"That's what the school psychologist told me…about you talking to yourself."

"Now couple that with the fact that I knew who was going to bully a sensitive kid. I'd get very nervous, very anxious, and then I'd strike out before they got to the let-me-rip-this-kid-apart stage."

"Aggressive anxiety…that's where the label came from. I didn't know, honey."

"How could you? Those girls went a step too far getting even with me. When they smashed Daddy's guitar and posted their last attack all over social media, I really lost it, Mom. I'm sorry. It's because of me that we had to move," I whisper. I cannot let myself feel anymore. I'll be crying my eyes out in another minute.

"That's one of the reasons we moved, but not the only one, honey. You weren't comfortable in that school. I wasn't comfortable being so far from my brother, anymore. I guess the timing was perfect. He was fully on the road to recovery from the heart attack and still needed some extra support with Liam. Sometimes, it's like the stars align."

"Like we were meant to be here?" I ask.

"Yeah. Maybe." She pauses again, studying me this time. "What's up with Pinedale High?"

I roll my eyes, relax back in the wing chair. "It's haunted by a slew of ghosts. You won't believe what I've been seeing there."

"How about we talk over some bowls of chocolate ice cream in the kitchen. Am I sensing your need, Mel?"

I chuckle. "You are," I lie. But it is a good lie because it makes her smile and it eases the worry right out of her. "I have a lot to tell you, so what do you think? Two scoops?"

"Maybe three. I won't tell if you don't tell."

"My lips are sealed, Mom," I reply. This talk is like years overdue. I am prepared to tell my mother everything.

Chapter 27

Perspective

Did you ever live the most perfect weekend? On Saturday, Mom and I spent the entire day shopping, not only in Pinedale, but in Raleigh where we had the most delicious dinner, too. We selected things for the house. New clothes for me, some of the tops are teal… It was heaven.

But I want to turn Sunday into my very own version of *Groundhog Day* and just live it over and over again. It starts out, though, with me very anxious because Justin doesn't get to my house until noon. But he arrives in something that looks like an old, royal-blue jeep that matches the color of his eyes and growls like a pumped-up beast. It has wide roll bars as a top frame and it sits really high off the ground on huge tires.

He jumps out, rings the doorbell and, after chowing down on a plate of leftover meatballs and spaghetti, he gets to work out back while my mother washes, irons, and puts up new curtains in the living room. Then, together, she and I hang up all of our family pictures. After Justin clears like six feet off the back deck, I go out to help him, with garden gloves on my hands and completely covered in bug spray.

It is heaven doing this clean-up with him, in spite

of the humid air and hot sun. Then, together with my mother, we dine on a huge salad and grilled burgers as the sunlight dims. Even though both of them know about me and my secret talents, we don't discuss any ghosts.

Justin talks about living in Pinedale and what he has learned working at his father's garage. Mom talks about her new job, starting tomorrow morning. I watch the easy conversation with my heart full of joy. Then, Justin and I sit on the back deck reading through *The Taming of the Shrew*. We laugh and sit closer to both be able to read the scenes we have together. I had no problem playing feisty. He had no problem channeling his inner alpha male to bring Petruchio to life. I smile a lot and my heart skips a beat when he puts my cell number in his phone. Then I walk him out the front door and he says good-bye. The soft kiss on my lips echoes through me like thunder. So does his easy smile that reaches his dreamy eyes. I am somewhere up there floating in the clouds when I walk back into the house.

Yeah. This must be heaven.

****

I shower off the stink of bug spray and float back down to reality so I could finish the rest of my homework for the next day at school. I text both Merva and Bev, say nothing about Justin, and then friend them on social media sites.

It is like a new beginning, looking forward to my new friends and classes for the first time in a long time. After I read Justin's last text before going to sleep, I hold the phone to my heart, reliving the kiss and tingling from head to toe. Words can't describe what I feel, and I wonder if Justin feels the same way, too. It is my first real kiss, much better than that little peck on the cheek. And it happened in such a natural way, as if it is meant to be.

Even though I am dead tired from all that physical activity cleaning up the yard, I can't fall asleep.

****

I wake up even before the alarm on my phone goes off. I shower again because I don't want the slightest stink of bug spray on me or my hair. New denim capris and Justin's gift of his Pinedale High shirt, that had been washed and ironed, seem the perfect outfit for this new day. I eat breakfast with Mom, sensing her nervousness and anticipation over starting a new life in our new home.

Before I leave the old blue box-on-wheels with Mom's favorite oldies playing on a cassette, I scooch over and kiss my mom on the cheek, wishing her a great first day in her new position at the elementary school. She takes my hand and squeezes it really hard. I think for the first time ever, I see her for the strong woman she truly is.

Firsts are really hard. Scary, too. And I sense that finally *"spilling the beans"* has somehow brought us closer. We Warkowski women are smart and tough. We are there for each other now, in every sense of the word.

I leave Mom with a goofy smile on my face, and I wave a genuine goodbye when she pulls off the curb in front of the school. Then I turn and my smile gets even goofier. Justin stands at the bottom of the steps to the main entrance—waiting for *me*! Yeah. He had texted me right after he got up and told me he'd be here waiting. I am walking into Pinedale High actually holding hands with a real looker of a senior boy! That strange tingle goes up my bones and settles in the blush on my face.

****

As we reach the junior-senior wing, I see Hammer, Andy, and Terry leaning against the wall. We walk past them, hand in hand. Justin kisses my cheek right in the crowded corridor in front of everyone. I leave him to go to my locker, which is at the other end of the corridor. I say hi to Merva and Bev, plus other kids I recognize from classes and choir. No strange looks. No side-eyed glances. Could this be real? Could this be happening? I blow out a breath as I swivel the lock to some random numbers.

"Melody Marie," Hammer says as I turn to head to class.

I dip my chin down and whisper, "Leave me alone, Hammer."

"Did you talk to Pops?" he asks, still next to me as if someone has spread paste all over our sides and stuck us together.

"Uh-huh," I say under my breath.

"Give him a message for me."

"No can do," I whisper without moving my lips.

"I'll leave you and your new boyfriend alone if you do. I saw that kiss," he says.

I stop walking. The halls have mostly cleared. I turn into the girl's room, hoping it is empty, and breathe a sigh of relief after checking all the stalls. Hammer suddenly walks through the closed door. I guess we do this here, right? "Look. I told your grandfather that I talked to you. He's gone, Hammer. I think he's moved on now that you know the truth. Now leave me alone."

His green eyes glisten like he's about to cry. His expression is full of emotion. "I…I can't. You have to tell Andy and Terry the truth about what happened to us."

I jerk my head back. "Not my place. Not my problem. You tell them."

"I just said… I can't. Every time I start to talk about the night we died, I end up outside the front of the school again." He runs his fingers through his thick hair at his temples. "That kind of thing never happened before. And I can't find Hank to talk about it. Man. I don't understand this shit."

"What exactly are you saying?" I ask him.

"You have to tell them. That's what I'm saying, Melody Marie. Because if you don't, this will be a day you come to regret. Lunch time. Under the bleachers. Be there." He walks through the closed door.

I just stand there. Talk about a way to deflate my happiness. For once, Hammer has come off aggressively anxious, not me. I run out of the girl's room and just make it to first period American History as the bell rings. I have to take a seat in the middle of the room because it is the only one available. Merva and Bev look at me with question marks in their eyes. I grin, pull out my school laptop, and prepare for another lecture on the Federalist Papers. But I cannot concentrate. Funny. When I came into the building, I saw Hank where he always is, mopping the floor in the hall by the trophy case. Why couldn't Hammer find him? Are there some kind of ghost rules I didn't know about?

It just doesn't make sense.

Chapter 28

Getting Even

I sit next to Justin in Biology Lab, and before I pull off my backpack I look up at the air-conditioning vent. I pray for no rinse and repeat recalling last week's ghost episode. The teacher informs us that we will begin final review before exam week. It suddenly dawns on me that classes aren't ending the last week in June anymore.

Cripes! I have like three weeks left of junior year! I pull out my laptop, prepared to listen to another lecture, this time with no shakes, rattles, or howling guffaws. Even though my grades have transferred over, I am not a whiz at biology and I need to concentrate.

Hammer walks through the wall and struts over to stand right in front of our lab table. His arms are crossed against his leather jacket and his look is as cold as ice. At least he isn't saying anything.

"What gives, Mel?" Justin whispers.

We both push our laptops to the edge of the table so we can lean forward and not be seen talking to each other as the teacher goes over the science material projected on the whiteboard.

"Hammer's standing right in front of me," I say.

"No shit. Why?" Justin replies.

"He wants me to talk to Andy and Terry, the boys

who died with him. During lunch. Under the bleachers," I say.

"Are you gonna do it?"

"I'm not sure," I reply, knowing that Hammer can hear every word.

Aaannndd…holy hell breaks loose! Both of our laptops are swept across the room. Justin ends up on the floor as his lab stool crashes into mine. I grab the edge of the table just in time and hold on for dear life so I don't end up on top of him. Screaming begins. Full. Blown. Chaos.

Two kids I don't know are bleeding from the impact of our laptops to their faces. The teacher is on the school phone asking for help. Students are jumping off their lab stools and taking cover under the tables. Some are crying. Some are too terrified to say anything.

Hammer, Andy, and Terry are having a grand old time watching all of this happen. I reach down, but Justin is already getting to his feet.

"What the hell just happened?" he says.

I can't answer as I look around the room.

"You're out of here," Mr. Morrow shouts as he approaches our lab table. "You never learn, do you, Justin?"

"I saw the whole thing," one kid says. "He did that on purpose."

Justin's brow crinkles, saying, "No…wait, I—"

"I'm calling security. You," Mr. Morrow bellows while pointing to Justin, "Come up to my desk right now."

Justin picks up his backpack and does as he is told without trying to defend himself.

That snaps me out of my silence. "Please, Mr.

Morrow, don't call security. He didn't do anything. I was sitting right next to him and—"

"No. Don't try and defend that boy," Mr. Morrow states with the school phone in hand again. "Send the nurse. And Security is needed in the Biology Lab," he says and then hangs up. He glares at me. "Kids like him, Melody, always get caught. This is all on him."

Tense minutes pass as my classmates line the walls and move farther away from the two victims on the floor. The nurse rushes into the room and goes directly to the two students whose heads are bleeding something awful. Merva hands me my laptop, whispering, "Come on. Stay by us, Mel."

"But he didn't do this," I tell her with my voice something like an octave higher.

"Mr. Morrow's right. Don't defend him," she whispers, taking my backpack from me. "Trust me when I say, this has been coming for a long time. He's been bad news for years, with or without Liam egging him on."

A school security officer enters and grabs Justin's upper arm. He pulls away. "I don't need you touching me, asshole," he says with a sneer. Where is that cute smile? Not anywhere to be seen. He hitches his backpack over one shoulder and walks out of the lab with the security officer right on his heels. The nurse leaves with two bleeding students in tow.

Merva places my laptop on her lab table. "Where is Justin's laptop?" I ask.

"I'm not touching it," she says. "Let the teacher pick that one up."

"No. No way." I push off the stool and find it. I close it and come back to their table, sliding it into my backpack.

"You're still going to defend him," Merva says with her hands on her hips.

"I'm not going to have someone take his laptop and then have him responsible for the loss." I narrow my eyes. "I'm telling you, Merva, Justin had nothing to do with both laptops flying across the room and hurting anyone. I didn't, either."

Bev leans in. "There are ghosts in this school, Merva. You know it. We all do. We just don't talk about it, Mel."

Ah. The moment of truth. Again. "I totally get what you're saying, Bev. I believe you're right. And when they get rattled, all hell breaks loose, doesn't it, Merva?'

Merva looks away. "I don't believe in ghosts. Or vampires. Or zombies, for that matter."

"I don't believe in vampires or zombies, either. But ghosts? That's a different story," I say. Bev keeps bobbing her head in agreement, as if I've said something out loud that everyone knows to be true. "Too many weird things have happened here, and I've only been in the school for a few days!"

"Oh. It gets terrible sometimes," Bev states.

"Like what happened to the music room terrible?" I ask.

"Oh…not that terrible…uh, usually. Just, you know, books falling off shelves, or like what happened at the end of the school day last week."

"Or two laptops suddenly flying across the room and aiming for students' heads?"

Both of them look at me. I see their eyes go wide as if they finally get it.

Then Bev says, "You know, I…I don't believe their story that the school's built on a fault or whatever."

"I don't either, Bev," I reply. "I'm telling you Justin had nothing to do with injuring those students." But I know who did. And boy, was I ever going to tell him off at lunchtime.

****

My mother has loads of quirky, sometimes old-fashioned sayings that she uses all the time. One of them, *how you could cut the tension with a knife*, comes to mind during motet choir rehearsal in the auditorium. Six students in choir had witnessed the mayhem in Bio Lab. Justin's name is as good as dirt. Someone says he is being held by security and because of what happened with the music room, the cops have been called to the school. Everybody has their own version of what they witnessed. Only I know the truth.

Not even ten minutes into class, right in the middle of another performance piece, the 1950s gaggle of ghosts sit across the stage staring at our rehearsal. I eye them. They eye me back. But not one of them says a word or joins in the singing. Then Hammer, Andy, and Terry walk out of the wings and stand on the stage. They look ready to rumble, as my mother would say.

I close my eyes and let myself absorb the tension, the fear, the worry in all the students around me. Funny. It is usually my *modus operandi*, another of Mom's phrases, to try and squash all those sensations like a flyswatter hitting a fly. After all, these aren't my personal feelings, so why get so involved? Not one, but now two people, know what I can see and hear and communicate with. One loves me unconditionally. The other, well, he has a good soul, a good heart, and he is my friend.

What I find truly odd is that there are no bullies with dark, nasty feelings sitting in the choir with me. The room is filled with good people who have no negative intentions. Well, not the ones that are breathing, anyway.

"Don't do it," I mouth to Hammer and friends.

His handsome face has that nasty expression on it again. He blows me a kiss and looks up at the stage lights. I look up at the stage lights, and, just like that, I know what's coming next.

I turn to Bev, whispering, "Scream like the place is on fire. Please. Just do it!"

A piercing screech filled the auditorium. Mrs. Montgomery's hands come off the keys and fly into the air. Now, it is my turn. I scream even louder than Bev and shoot up out of the auditorium seat jumping up and down. "A rat! A huge rat! Ohmygod! It was brown and huge! It just ran over my sneakers!"

And just like that, mayhem begins. I grab Bev's hand and climb over a petrified, screaming Merva. The rest of the choir students follow suit, running out all six auditorium doors. Mrs. Montgomery is right there with us. She calls out, "Everyone to the cafeteria!"

Some of us, already running in the other direction, change course. We race down the hall to the security doors, passing Hank the janitor at record speed. I give him a look. He nods once. Some students are still screaming as we race down the stairs. Once in the cafeteria, packed with freshmen and sophomores in first lunch, we wait for further instructions.

Mrs. Montgomery says, "Everyone gather by the

vending machines."

The amount of chatter continues among us. I lean against the wall to catch my breath. Bev is right beside me. "What just happened?" she whispers.

I swallow, wait, and wonder what the heck I will say. "I just got a feeling that something strange was going to happen again during rehearsal."

Merva joins us, paler than usual and holding her stomach. "I think I'm going to be sick."

"Just breathe with me, in and out, in and out," Bev says. Funny. I have never seen her take the lead. "You'll be okay. Just breathe."

I look at Bev. She gives a slight nod, sharing my secret. Ohmygod! I haven't given myself away, have I? Only time would tell.

Chapter 29

Hard Answers

The three sounds beep to signal the end of first lunch. The crowd of students has thinned the last ten minutes of their lunchtime, so our choir class takes up two tables near the vending machines. Everyone is engaged in hushed conversations, not one rowdy student among us. I sit quietly listening to Bev and Merva, relieved that Bev doesn't give me up as a prankster. Maybe she senses things too, but not as clearly or strongly as I do.

I begin to plan. I'm not going to meet with Hammer and friends on an empty stomach. I have to be practical. Realistic, as well. I manage to be third in line, leaving Bev and Merva somewhere at the end of it. I buy a warm grilled cheese sandwich and a bottle of water and marvel at another two-dollar lunch. I get the sandwich down quickly at a table in the back of the caf and shove the water bottle into my backpack before slipping out.

****

The humid, hot air hits me as soon as I leave the school building. *Maybe I should have bought two bottles of water,* I think as I head to the football field. *And where on earth is Justin?* Has he been arrested again for something he didn't do? Has he been suspended or sent to detention hall? What if his father goes off on him again? For something he didn't do…again!

Under the bleachers, I thank God I am not in the hot sun anymore. The air is only a degree or two cooler. Not much of a difference. The clammy kind of sweat starts to coat my skin. The heat on my face turns it flushed. Will I ever get used to this southern climate or will the Jersey girl in me forever crave northern seasons like fall and winter?

Seeing Hammer, Andy, and Terry appear under the bleachers irks me. A lot. I walk over to them, observe the serious faces as well as the crossed arms like they have somehow been wronged. Maybe they have. Maybe remaining in the place where you lost your life does that to a ghost. I know Hammer's anger can go from zero to sixty in seconds flat, just like mine. Is it the same for Andy and Terry?

Then it dawns on me. A feeling sends sweaty chills up my spine and then that feeling tingles in my brain. Is it real or just my imagination? I'll find out, and very soon, as the face-off begins. I stop short, just a foot away from three lost boys, and I am about to take a chance and truly trust what I feel.

"Why did you do that to Justin?" I ask Hammer, looking him straight in the eye and ignoring Andy and Terry.

"I told you to stay away from him."

"Why, Hammer?" I prod.

"None of your business," he grumbles.

"Well, then I'll make it my business. You're jealous."

"What the hell is wrong with you, man?" he says as

he tosses his hair and then pushes it all the way off his handsome face.

"Nothing's wrong with me. What's wrong with you?" I fire back. "Want me to say it out loud in front of your friends? You're jealous and spiteful like a ghostly bully because I like Justin more than I like you. Your great-nephew has a good heart, not a mean one. Just the way you had a good heart when you were alive. You dove in front of that pickup to save your friends. Justin would do the same, and you know it! Two peas in the same pod, my mother would say."

"Just tell them, Melody Marie."

"Stop calling me that like someone far superior to me and way too old for a sixteen-year-old girl. My name is simply Mel."

His hands fly up into the air. "Whatever. Just tell them."

"Why does it have to come from me? Huh? Because you can't say it. Because you're afraid of what will happen afterward. That's why you can't find Hank. He knows, doesn't he? You have the answer but you're afraid of what's next." I stop and see the fear on his face. I feel it, too, as if it can touch me. So I take a breath and face Andy. "Do you want to know?"

"Yeah," he softly says, but I hear the hesitance in his voice.

Is he ready? Will I break some ghost code doing this? Not my call. "You fought with your father and left to meet Hammer and Terry at the school. He was drunk already. You had nothing to do with that. He wanted to sell the farm and move away. You didn't."

"I had to finish out my senior year with my friends," Andy whispers. "That's all."

"But he didn't want to wait, Andy. He hated farming. You knew that."

"That's why he drank every single night, for as far back as I can remember."

"Right after your mother died."

He nods in a sad way. Kicks at the dirt, and then swipes his eyes. "Yeah. I knew."

"He drove to the school to make you come back home. To take you away from your friends. Only he was very, very drunk and very, very angry." I turn to Terry. He keeps nodding at me. "Do you want to know?" I ask. But Terry's eyes are already full of tears, and I hesitate.

"Terry, man," Andy whispers. "You have to want to know."

"Okay. Yeah," Terry says. Andy puts his arm around Terry's shoulders. In a show of support? I sense the answer to that one.

"You simply got stuck in the crossfire," I say as gently as I can. My heart is so heavy for this boy. "You were collateral damage, simply there to play touch football on the front lawn of the school. And it happened so fast. You ran wide to catch the ball and landed flat on the grass. Andy's father didn't see you. He ran right over you and kept going. You died instantly."

Terry sobs. Andy pulls him into a hug. Hammer folds more into himself, touches his forehead, and turns away. But I have to continue.

"Hammer saw it happen. Andy, you not so much. I see your head turned like you're looking away from the action. All three of you had smoked a joint. No. Two. So your reaction time was, maybe like, slower.

Hammer's wasn't though. Andy's father had hit you, Terry, as soon as his pickup jumped the curb. Hammer ran in front of the pickup truck. He yelled for Andy's father to stop. Shouted really loud, like midway to the steps of the school where Andy stood. The force of the impact threw his body up into the air. Hammer slammed into the front doors of the school. And Andy?" I look at him again. I see the tears streaming down his face as he holds onto Terry. "Your dad didn't, maybe couldn't, stop. The truck pinned you against the brick column at the bottom of the school's steps. Like Hammer and Terry, you died instantly. And he drove away."

I rummage through my backpack on my shoulder and pull out the bottle of water. I unscrew that cap off fast and drink half the bottle in seconds flat. Something forces me to look at all three of them. There is not a dry eye among three boys who *should* have led long, happy lives. Three boys who would have remained friends all of their lives. No. My eyes aren't dry, either.

Hammer comes over and stands right in front of me. "Thank you, Melody Marie."

"You're welcome, John. Rest in peace, all three of you together forever," I whisper.

He nods and walks back to Andy and Terry. I watch the group hug, their heads touching, their hitched sobs so very sad. In the blink of an eye, they are gone.

I am alone under the bleachers of Pinedale High. I sense calm settling over my own heart. I finish the rest of the water, put the plastic bottle back in my backpack while biting down on my lips. Tears run down my hot cheeks, and I swipe them away with the tips of my fingers.

"Those three boys have been waiting for someone like you since May 5, 1974."

I turn with a sniffle to pull myself together. Hank is smiling at me. He tips his baseball cap. "I don't know what you mean, Hank. *Waiting*? For *me*?"

"It's a rare gift you have, Miss Melody. To see us and hear us. To be able to tell us how and even maybe why we died."

"You saved so many the night of the fire," I say, because I know it is true.

"But I didn't save them all. No ma'am, I didn't. Don't know why."

I have to ask. "Is that why you're still here?"

Hank shrugs as his eyebrows rise. "There's no tellin' if that's the reason. I just am. Caught between two worlds, able to be seen in both. But I can't do what you do. Send them on through to peace and final rest. It's a gift from above, I reckon."

"I didn't know I could do that, I mean, help Hammer, Andy, and Terry like that. What if it's a one-time-only deal, Hank?'

He takes off his baseball cap and scratches his head. "Could be. Could be not. But you walk both worlds, just like me, only in a different way. A unique way that ain't got too many others on that righteous path. I guess only time will tell."

"My mom knows I have this ability to talk to ghosts. So does Justin. And she told me that my father had the same ability."

"Like an inherited trait?"

I shrug. "I guess."

"Well, don't that beat all," he says with a chuckle. "And somehow, someway, you managed to find

Pinedale High. Yessiree, Miss Melody, I guess it was meant to be."

I feel that way, too. Three beeps sound. I turn away to look at the school. Then I turn back. Hank has disappeared, but not like Hammer, Andy, and Terry. I sense him back in the school getting ready to mop the cafeteria floor.

I hurry back to the building, and I can't tell you about the plethora of feelings touching my heart. Calm. At peace with myself that I have done a good thing. Excitement…about my new life in North Carolina. Happiness that my mother knows about my abilities. Normal, in a way, and hopeful I will make true friends in my new school. Then there's Justin. I can't describe the feelings I have for him. But I sense he will be a big part of my life. More than just a friend. How do I know? Only time will tell.

Chapter 30

The New Normal

I jump into the old royal-blue bomb that sits high off the ground and kiss my boyfriend on the lips. We arrive at school after loads of laughs and conversation about what we are going to do this summer. I am wearing a new black dress my mother bought me at the mall in Raleigh. Justin has on a black suit complete with pressed white shirt and a purple tie. His unruly hair is tied back and he isn't wearing hoop earrings anymore, just small diamond studs. I have bright purple highlights in my shaggy, short caramel-brown hair.

The air is hot and humid as he drives to Pinedale High and parks in the student parking lot at the side of the school. He kisses my lips as soon as we stand together on the pavement, and we walk hand in hand into the school.

Principal Moore looks very handsome in his tuxedo. In fact, all the teachers are dressed like this is prom night. It isn't. This is the end-of-the-year concert, and we students are the stars.

The Motet Choir is the opening act. Mrs. Montgomery looks stunning in a soft, flowy black gown. The auditorium air is void of humidity and chilly. Backstage with the curtains closed, I hug Merva and Bev, even Harrison who looks awkward in his suit, constantly running a finger under his shirt collar. Every girl looks gorgeous. Every boy looks handsome. We do our vocal warmups as the auditorium fills.

I take a chance and peek out of the ruby-red curtain at the side of the stage. My uncle and aunt are out there with Liam. He looks good in a white polo shirt and blue jeans. He has really turned himself around in his new school. Blaze and Cam are sitting with them. There is no trace of black eyeliner on either of them. Uncle Tim's heart is doing just fine, and Aunt Sarah finally found a little peace in her heart. My mother is sitting next to Aunt Sarah, just as proud as a person could be. She enjoys teaching the little ones, maybe more than she lets on. Justin's father has stopped drinking all together. He and his son have fixed up and painted the little office attached to the garage. There are no more black eyes or beatings. Thank God.

Justin and I walk together to take our places on the risers behind the thick red curtains. "See any of them?" he whispers in my ear.

"The entire 1950s crew are standing in the wings on the other side of the stage," I whisper back.

"Are we going to have the air suddenly turn off or concert folders flying out of our hands?"

I grin and chuckle. "Nope. We're going to have a wonderful concert without incident."

"Well, that will be a first for Pinedale. It seems every year—"

"Not anymore. Now they have someone to talk to. I think all that pranking is in the past, at least while I'm around."

"No graduation mishaps, either, Mel? That'll be another first."

"Not a one. You are going to walk that field and take your diploma with a smile on your face, for sure."

He kisses my cheek. Takes his place on the top riser. I walk across the stage and take mine next to Merva and Bev.

"He's like *real* eye-candy, Mel," Bev whispers.

"And he cleans up real nice," Merva adds.

I grin. Okay. Smile wide… So very proud that my boyfriend has been cleared of every wrongdoing that got pinned on him. There are no more strange episodes of laptops or books flying. No spooky blackouts or Internet issues. Two worlds no longer collide at Pinedale High. Hank is still mopping the floor and greeting students and faculty members in the morning. Everyone says that the fault-line has finally settled. Yeah. Right.

The curtains open to raging applause with some hoots thrown in for good measure. You get used to hoots, along with the scalding humid heat outside. I know I have. So has my mom.

Mrs. Montgomery hits one key on the piano. The motet choir begins Randal Thompson's *Alleluia* sotto voce and at just the right tempo. The intermingled melodies swell in my heart, and I let it carry me away.

Melody Marie Warkowski has easily waved bye-bye to the tag of aggressive anxiety. For good this time.

I let joy fill my heart. I sense I am finally accepted by good people who are truly my friends. My tribe. I know I am home. Like my mom always says, I fit in at Pinedale High like a worn leather glove fits an old familiar hand.

Discussion Questions

1. *Haunting Melody* is told in first person point of view. What experiences can you relate to seeing through Melody's eyes?

2. Melody is about to be classified with Aggressive Anxiety. How do you think this makes Melody feel?

3. What is Melody's perspective of self?

4. What would you tell Melody to help her feel better about herself?

5. Have you ever been labeled? What did it do to your self-image?

6. Are you sympathetic to what Melody is going through?

7. Melody keeps her abilities a secret. Should she have told her mother sooner? If so, why?

8. Hammer is immediately drawn to Melody. What does this foreshadow?

9. Is Melody justified in her feelings about the guidance counselor?

10. Is Melody's take on Liam correct or is she too harsh in judging him?

11. Why is the saying, looks are often deceptive, relevant in *Haunting Melody*?

12. Would you befriend someone labeled a troublemaker and if so, why?

13. Does Melody grow throughout her new experiences at Pinedale High? Does Justin?

14. What do you think it feels like to have Melody's abilities? How would you handle them?

15. Melody makes a choice to help both Justin and Hammer. Would you?

16. Going forward, how do you think Melody will handle her unique abilities?

17. Which character(s) can you most relate to in *Haunting Melody*?

A word about the author...

M. Flagg's imaginative world is full of mystical warriors, witches, the not-so-normal vampires, and now teenage ghosts. With five novels in the paranormal genre, spinning tales about the paradox of love is a passion, and there is always a twist of fate involved. Mickey is a contributor in a book on urban music education and has published a piece in Still Standing, a web-magazine about loss and healing. She is a life-long New Jersey resident, a member of Liberty States Fiction Writers, NJ Author Network and NJRW.

Thank you for purchasing
this publication of The Wild Rose Press, Inc.

For questions or more information
contact us at
info@thewildrosepress.com.

The Wild Rose Press, Inc.
www.thewildrosepress.com